SHADOWED MEMORIES

Cathy Richard Dodson

ISBN: 978-1-60215-083-6

Published by **BooksForABuck**.com

Printed in the United States of America

If you have built castles in the air, your work need not be lost; that is where they should be. Now put the foundations under them.

Henry David Thoreau

Author's Note

This novel, written just before the computer age took off, was researched the old-fashioned way, with long hours spent in a library, pouring over ancient maps and books about this locale. Several years ago I had the pleasure of visiting Countisbury, England, where I traced the steps of my heroine along craggy cliffs high above the sea from Valley of the Rocks to the lush green paths that followed the River Lyn to Watersmeet. Details of that story, along with photos of many of the locations presented herewith, can be found by visiting my web site at www.crdodson.com.

Prologue

The night was filled with the still silence of moonlight as the tall severely clad man made his way across the churchyard. The square granite building in the distance was the one place he could always go for peace from the often harsh realities of his world. Tonight he felt his excitement rising as he contemplated his time of solitude, locked away from the never-ending complaints of poverty-stricken villagers, illness and death, even the chatter of his well-meaning companions. These were his few moments of relief, and he cherished them at the end of each day.

As he pulled open the heavy oak door, he breathed deep, savoring once more the musty odor of the old place, enjoying the damp chill which never quite seemed to dissipate, regardless of the season. His church! How hard he'd worked for it, and how he loved these cold walls etched with the presence of God! Now-to seek out his favorite place, the ancient bench with its swan-chained carving, where he would at last commence his prayers and meditations.

Then he heard it. A slight movement. A sound-almost as if someone were in pain. Moaning. . .

He moved toward the noise. *It's coming from the bench*, he thought, becoming more than a little anxious. What troubles had invaded his private spot?

Feeling his way along the pews, little by little his eyes adjusted to the darkened sanctuary. As he neared the bench, where the sounds seemed to originate, the noises grew louder, the breathing harsher and faster. *My God*, he thought, knowledge dawning as he peered into the shadows. Two people, not one, and not pain he heard, but rather the throes of passion. Fornicators! In the house of God, no less!

Anger unlike any he'd experienced rose in him like a phantom moon. He reached forward into the darkness and pulled one of the bodies up, away from its sinful embrace. Yanking it up like a madman, he shook the startled form until its teeth seemed to rattle aloud in the quiet, and then, without a second thought, he cast the figure aside like dirty laundry.

Next he turned to the unmoving form lying upon the bench. *His* bench. The girl, with still spread legs and full breasts tumbling from a half-open bodice, looked young, perhaps no more than fifteen, and even in the shadows, he could see fear outlined on her face. Yet she made no sound, no scream, merely stared at him, waiting, he supposed, for her own punishment.

Without warning he felt an unexpected emotion. She must pay for disrupting his place of piety. And he would make sure she did-in a way only she could understand. A hardness rose in his groin; he reached down and unfastened the buttons of his trousers. He took her quickly, before a second thought had any chance to dissuade him, ravishing, hurting, yet entertaining within his depths a satisfaction beyond his wildest fantasies. When at last he lifted his drained body from hers, he thought he caught a glimpse of triumph in her eyes; but no, surely not. He knew he'd caused her pain--still, she hadn't cried out, had merely lain there, taking his assault.

Abruptly, he remembered the other, the body of the boy he'd so carelessly cast aside. Had he slipped out unnoticed during the interlude or was he lying there yet, unconscious and needing attention? Guilt began to creep in.

The girl seemed suddenly to remember as well, for she pulled herself up and, holding her tattered clothes together, moved slowly toward the form, now lying still on the hard stone floor. She bent down and touched the fellow's head, slowly bringing her face close to his in the dark. She backed away from the body slightly, then without a word turned to face the wooden bench and he who sat there with shame in his heart.

Never would he forget the honeyed words that came next, in a voice as sensual and compelling as harem silk. Even in the shadows, he could see the faint trace of a smile playing at the corners of her mouth, and somehow he knew he'd been led into a drama from which he could never return. The girl held out her hand almost enticingly, and he drew back from both the words and the blood on her fingertips.

"Reverend Jaspar, I do believe you've killed him."

Chapter 1

As I went out a ragged child,
With wasted cheeks and ringlets wild...
Emily Brontë

Again, voices woke me, but this time they were real. Pushing aside thoughts of the whispery, nightmarish *others* that had haunted me from childhood, I listened with mounting curiosity to a heated confrontation occurring in the room downstairs. Due to the sultry August heat, my bedchamber door stood open, and the sounds floated in clearly through the still night air. That angry exchange frightened me long before I understood it was merely a precursor to events which would change my life forever; a forewarning of the choices soon to be made--choices affecting not only my future, but my past as well.

Lying silently in the large feather bed, I quickly noted the strange voice, and wondered with dismay who my guardian could be talking with at such a late hour--he rarely entertained, much less in the middle of the night. I became aware at once of anger in Rev. Jaspar's tone, whereas the other man seemed quite calm and collected. Then abruptly I realized *I* was the topic of their conservation, thus my attention drew away from the harshness of the voices toward the words themselves.

"I will not allow you to take Anne away!" the Rev. cried out, "she is young, and still impressionable. God only knows what would happen to her in those surroundings!"

"I really don't think you have a choice in the matter." The stranger's tone belied nothing but assured composure, as if he were merely playing a part for which he already knew the ending. "She's needed now, and in a few days I'll be back here to take her away. There's nothing to discuss."

"Needed, you say? Needed?" My guardian's outrage resounded in full sermon-like force. "And what about sixteen years ago when she wasn't needed? What about the day she was brought here to me because no one else wanted the little bastard? Did I need her then? Did I?" and even more violently, "Did she?"

His words roared out loud enough to wake the dead sleeping in the cemetery next door.

I could almost picture a twisted smile on the face of the other man as he gazed on at the tirade. After a long pause, the anger burst forth again. "What have I got to show for all these years of providing for a child I didn't need or want?"

This brought a low mocking spurt of laughter from the stranger, followed by a sardonic, "You have the satisfaction of knowing you're a holy man. Isn't that enough, considering the circumstances?"

Another short laugh followed, and I imagined the fury burning in Rev. Jaspar's face. He had a short temper and must surely be near the limit of his patience by now, but oddly enough, the room remained silent, as if he had indeed met his match and there was nothing more to say.

Echoing my thoughts, the stranger spoke again. "We've said all there is to say on this matter. As I told you, I'll return for the girl in three days. Have her things ready to go by then." With that I heard a loud slam, and the room fell strangely silent.

With the door's closing, the corridors of my mind flew open. Memories I'd thought forever locked out flooded the depths of my being. Suddenly a child once more, I sank deeper into the four-poster bed, wide-eyed, wanting desperately to put the pieces of my life into one complete picture. The conversation had reminded me that I didn't belong, for although I'd never really forgotten the fact, time had helped to dim the knowledge. Fresh pain confronted me with the remembrance. I was a person who had no beginnings. Alone, abandoned, without love, I had started this life, and certainly my time with Rev. Jaspar had done little to change that.

My guardian didn't enjoy telling the story, but I managed to get a rough idea of it from him; the rest I ascertained from bits and pieces of overheard conversations in the village, as well as our housekeeper's busybody prattle.

"Found you at the church, 'e did. Wrapped in a woolen blanket of some quality, mind you? Your folks weren't poor, whoever they were." Mrs. Rickett would cluck her tongue in disapproval at this, then continue in her austere tone, "Probably scared the poor man to death, finding you lying in that basket and crying your lungs out, but 'es a God-fearing soul. Took you in, and 'as brought you up in the Lord's way. And you should thank your lucky stars, little miss."

According to her story, Rev. Jaspar had been on his way to evening vespers when he spied me near the heavy wooden door of the building. Evidently I'd been placed there with the hope of certain discovery, but that is of little consolation to a child who wants only to be loved.

Love was reserved for God alone in the Rev. Jaspar Cowper's household. It wasn't something to be wasted on innocent, abandoned orphans. I knew very little about the man himself, except for the fact that he had gone into the ministry as a very young man, and that he valued his calling above all things. As I grew older, I often wondered if ever in his life had he felt love for another human being.

What I never understood was why he kept me at all when he could easily have shipped me off to some family who wanted a child. But keep me he did, and as soon as I was old enough, promptly proceeded to instruct me in the ways of righteousness.

"You were placed in my life by God," he often told me, "to be shaped and molded in the Christian faith. We must strive to carry out His will." And so would begin our morning Bible lesson, during which I spent hours kneeling on the cold, flagstone floor of the church thinking more about my aching knees than about God's holiness.

Besides our on-going study of the scriptures, Rev.

Jaspar taught me grammar, history, geography, as well as French and Latin; so I was certainly not lacking in a formal education. Attending the village school with other children wasn't allowed, for after lessons the poor and sick parishioners must be seen to, although I didn't mind this so much, for they were always kind and appreciative. But then the church and rectory had to be dusted and polished, so they too might reflect the pure, clean-heartedness of God's love. My guardian was definitely a man of purpose, and he filled up not only his own life, but mine as well, with duty and discipline, if not with love.

"God punishes those who fail to seek His truth," the deep raspy voice would boom out across the church each Sabbath. Then he would turn his lean, gaunt face toward me, and looking down his long, beak-like nose with coal black eyes that pierced the very core of my being admonished. "Children must overcome the sins of their parents! This is God's will!" His face seemed to me rather hard and cruel for a man of God, but the congregation didn't appear concerned, and each week the pews were filled, although it may have been due more to fear of that gray-headed tyrant than of God.

He must have come to despise me more and more with each day that passed, for I grew to be everything he was not. A man who surrounded himself with blandness and simplicity, his home was sparsely furnished, meals little more than barley bread and cheese, clothes always black. Never, never did I see him wear any color at all, even at Christmastide, when a dash of red or green would surely have been permissible.

And yet, somehow, I became a happy, affectionate creature, who longed to be held and cuddled; who knew at a young age the effect a smile and laughter had on most people. As a child, I loved to play in the rectory garden, decking myself with bright spring flowers and shiny green vines. Once, he caught me at this activity and cast them off, shouting as he did, "Vanity is the Devil's tool, girl. You may have been cursed with a pretty face, but I'll not have you flaunting it about my home."

Mrs. Rickett, a dreary, colorless person as well, never in all my growing up years gave me more than the barest essentials. Before I appeared, she worked only days for the Rev. but afterwards, she became a permanent fixture in his household. Someone, of course, had to take care of me, and with the exception of a village woman named May who served for a time as my wet nurse, Mrs. Rickett practically raised me. Her husband had long since died and she had no children of her own--one would have thought she might have just a little love for a poor, motherless child, but somehow she managed to bring me up without ever offering any real affection. May, my wet-nurse, had a kind and smiling face, but she also had five youngsters of her own at home, and once I was beyond the breast, never appeared to give me another thought. And so I faced the world--left in the hands of those who saw to my needs, but had no real love to offer.

One day I braved the wrath of our housekeeper to ask why, and she replied stoutly, "What do you mean no one cares for you, girl? You've got people to feed and clothe you. Some children don't 'ave that much. And wha' do you know about love anyway."

"May loves her children...I've seen the way she smiles and holds them...But no one truly loves me, Mrs. Rickett. Not you, nor Rev. Jaspar. Sometimes I wonder if even God does."

A snort followed. "God loves everyone who obeys His laws," she answered adamantly, "and it's only by His grace you'll get to Heaven, miss. You'd best be rememberin' that when you're countin' your woes."

And yet again we came back to the same argument; I was a whining, thankless child, unappreciative of those who had taken me in. While Mrs. Rickett wasn't exactly cruel to me, I was treated more like an encumbrance who was always underfoot and causing extra work. At least once every day, she would shoo me out of the kitchen, sending me about some task or errand with the words, "Be off with you then, girlie. Hard work and piety alone twill be your salvation. That pretty face uh'll get you naught."

Obviously she agreed with my guardian's notion that the curse of an attractive countenance made me sinful. I had no real way of knowing how I looked, however, for there were no mirrors in my room at the rectory; and the distorted, dull reflection in my windowpanes showed only wide, timid eyes crowned by curls always seeking to peek out from the ugly white cap they made me wear. Whatever my appearance, evidence stated that I'd been cast upon a man who'd have been happiest with a malnourished plain Jane In fact. I was surprised he didn't call me Jane as was the usual case for poor nameless girls, but instead he chose Anne and that suited me well enough.

Occasionally I wondered if my real parents had given me some exotic, fanciful name and were using it when they referred to me, whoever and wherever they were. As a young child, I loved to make up all sorts of stories about my family; how someday they'd return and tell me how sorry they'd been to give me up for a time. "But here we are now, darling, and we're going to make up for all the years you ye spent without us!" Then we'd go home in their fancy carriage, but on the way to that wonderful place, we'd stop at some little shop and buy me a few new outfits, "just to tide you over until we can get a complete wardrobe." Happily, I'd cast off the drab browns and grays of the rectory, and pull off the unseemly white cap, freeing those imprisoned curls at last. My mother would choose a blue-green dress of the softest velveteen for me, "because it matches your eyes" and those same eyes would fill with tears knowing the dismal days were over and finally I was loved.

But things never turned out the way I imagined; and little by little, I gave up those childish daydreams. Continual letdowns and unfulfilled illusions forced me to shut my mind to the fantasy and look elsewhere for comfort.

Growing older, I discovered the world beyond Countisbury, and every free moment found me wandering the valleys and cliffs surrounding our small Devon hamlet. I learned to finish chores quickly or hurry through visits and errands; even, I'm ashamed to admit, to tell Mrs. Rickett I'd be studying my scriptures in the church, then escape after reading only one or two verses. Surely God would overlook this small untruth; the whole universe waited beyond the walls of my prison; and I felt closer to Heaven rambling those hills and vales than I ever had inside the church or rectory walls. Usually I paid dearly for my freedom though. Ironically, the very person who would keep me from that world had introduced me to it. Geography lessons with Rev. Jaspar taught me so much about the area where we lived, I wanted to see for myself the rivers, the sea, the coaches from the towns nearby.

A small inn sat at the edge of Countisbury proper, the Blue Ball, which boasted a bright sign in the shape and color of its name. The mail coach stopped there each day to change the horses, the climb over Porlock Hill being extremely steep and the poor animals completely exhausted by the time they reached the top. In fact, the imposing hills that bordered us kept our village, as well as the neighboring towns, remarkably isolated from any sense of the world beyond. So I loved to creep down among the shrubs encircling the inn to listen to the driver and the innkeeper exchange news about places which-to me-existed only in books or dreams.

"Wha's tha news of the ton, these days?" Old Pete ran the inn, and his raspy voice always made me wonder if he hadn't had one drink--or perhaps one smoke too many.

"Wha' ton?" the driver innocently queried, always holding back the news until Pete was fair to bursting, and me in my hiding spot as well.

"Wha' da ya mean, 'wha' ton'?" Pete would shoot back. "Thar's only one ton worth knownin' the news about? London, my man, London, of course."

Then the driver's laughter burst forth, for of course he had known all along it was the news from London Old Pete was craving.

Would I ever see that world, I wondered? Would I ever go to London and see Queen Victoria or Prince Albert? Would I ever visit a castle or dine at a fine restaurant? Perhaps not, but for now it was enough to know such a place existed, and to content myself with dreams. In reality, I was happy enough exploring the countryside, finding special nooks and crannies, learning which plants grew best in the rocky soil of the moors and which grew best along the cliffs, the different sounds of the birds according to the season, reveling in the rush of the rivers which was never absent from my hearing.

Unfortunately, upon returning to the rectory, cheeks rubbed red by the wind and strands of hair falling from a hastily pulled on cap usually gave my secret away.

"Out again, are you then?" Mrs. Rickett would admonish, "Rev. says you're to go straight to bed without supper," and she would send me off with a swat on the ear. But occasionally, depending on her mood, she might slip me a small slice of bread and butter before retiring. No matter what the price, however, the hours spent outdoors were worth the trouble.

Extraordinary beauty surrounded the drab grayness of my home. The craggy cliffs of the western English coastline stood jagged and white and Foreland Point, being the tallest, towered above the exquisite blue brilliance of ocean waves crashing below. Leading to its culmination were gorse-covered hills, rough and rocky beneath a patchy exterior of brilliant yellow or green, depending on the season. The hills possessed a sweet serenity of their own, and standing on their summits brought me complete contentment. At the peak of Countisbury Hill, just before the Point, a wide, open space beckoned with a view that went on for miles. Some days I'd climb up there, stopping for a time to gaze at that far horizon, envisioning a distant world which certainly must be filled with laughter and love and happy people. Other times, I'd follow a crooked path along the downstream banks of the East Lyn, where trees and vines grew so thick it seemed I might lose myself in their lush green depths forever, thus never coming to know any place beyond.

When I first rambled up those rugged slopes around Countisbury, I discovered a part of me heretofore missing, as if the land and I had always been one, yet were separated for a time. Suddenly I had come home to an old friend. Lying amidst the green grasses, I would whisper to it softly, "What have you to give me today, dearest one? A garland for my hair or perhaps a sprig of golden broom to rest beneath my pillow for the night? Then tomorrow, I'll sew a sachet and tuck you deep inside so you'll rest against my heart and share your sweet secrets all the day long." The plants would sigh quietly and gently brush my cheek with a tender caress, and closing my eyes, I would sleep by their side like a lover.

Following the East Lyn upstream, I came to a place known as Watersmeet, aptly named, for according to my guardian, the Lyn River meets the Hoar Oak Water there. Under large, overhanging trees, the falling water trickles cheerily by over smooth stones, flowing like a carefree, unbothered child. Coming from nowhere, with nowhere to go, completely nonchalant, making me envious of that unrestricted, unencumbered life. How I wanted that total abandon--no commitments, no duties, no God or Rev. Jaspar to appease.

"Why do you have all the frolic?" I'd ask, feigning scorn. The water replied with its merry little laugh, and ran on, undaunted and unashamed.

So I too became unashamed when I roamed. I shook my fair hair loose, letting the breeze toss it about. My high-topped, constricting shoes were unbuttoned and left sitting abandoned under a hedge, freeing my feet to go on alone, liberated at last, through the fields, the stream, the mud or anywhere in particular they chose to go. Throwing off my cloak, I ran with the warm spring air at my back, once again draping myself with flowers and leaves, heedless of vanity, until I felt like a princess awaiting her prince.

While I waited, I fed the animals and birds who lived on the hillsides with breadcrumbs saved from the rectory table. "Are you my prince?" I would gingerly ask a bob-tailed rabbit. "If you are, what shall I do to win your love?" But with a saucy wink and a flick of his white tail, he flounced off without answering, leaving me to wonder if I'd offended or if he were merely as shy and insecure as I.

Walking across the common one spring day, I came across a wild pony looking strangely out of place amidst the fronds of green and gold. He appeared rather startled to see me approaching, but as I spoke very softly and extended a half-eaten apple left from lunch, he began to warm to me and was soon nibbling eagerly from my hand.

"That's a good boy," I purred into his ear as I stroked the dappled gray back. "We're going to be friends, you and I."

As if in agreement, he whinnied loudly. I laughed and scratched between his feather-soft ears. "I'm going to call you Charlie, after the Bonnie Prince, and you shall be my sovereign, and this shall be our kingdom. I do hope Mr. Rabbit will forgive me but you and I seem so much better suited to one another. Aren't we, Charlie?"

Again, the snort of agreement, and I buried my face in his warm coat. "We shall see the world together, shan't we?" and when he tossed his head up and down, I knew I had a friend for life.

Charlie appeared almost every day after that, and eventually kindly allowed me to ride on his smooth, broad back, clutching tightly to the long mane as his gait carried us along. We rode west across the rocky slopes, and I saw the twin villages of Lynton and Lynmouth, one sitting high on a cliff, the other nestled in the shadowy trees below. I waded in the West Lyn, sister to my babbling falls, while Charlie nibbled at grass on the nearby banks. We visited Sillery Sands, and I sat staring endlessly as frothy waves crashed onto a pebbled shore.

This world became my life, but even so, I had to be cautious lest I be seen and reported to my guardian. I didn't know what I would do if he should discover and take Charlie away, I only knew I belonged here, so much more than in that dreary other place. Amid the trees, on the hills, along the cliffs, I found contentment and peace; it was there I first began to hear the voice that would come to change my life. More than the sounds of the earth, or the water, or the animals, they were the voices of the future, and while I didn't realize it at the time, of the past as well. Most were muted and distant, but one came through clearly, singing soft lullabies or comforting me with gentle words of love. A woman's voice, with a mother's tenderness; and though I had come to know companionship and serenity, only when I met and made her my friend did I truly begin to know love.

Chapter 2

Oh my true friend, I am not lone
While thou canst speak with such a tone...
Emily Brontë

Elizabeth Hardgrove Madden was her real name, but to me she was simply "Maddie"--that simple, affectionate, childish name such as one might give to a Nanny or an aunt, or best of all a grandmother, should one be lucky enough to possess any of those wonderful beings--How I loved to call her by it! She became all of them for me. From the instant I heard her voice, singing to me as I rested in the earth's bosom or speaking gentle words of love while I gazed into the blue of the sea, I knew she and I were destined to become best of friends. When we met at last, it didn't matter that she was almost half a century older than I--we were kindred spirits, and between two such souls, age is immaterial. She taught me so much--to accept my feelings, to go beyond them, to see with my heart.

An aura of mystery surrounded Maddie, and even after I knew her well, I felt she held back, that a part of her she always kept to herself. Maybe that in itself drew me--the knowledge that she, like myself, represented the unknown and because of that, stood on the outside, looking into a world that could never be hers. I lived mostly in a fantasy world--resting and daydreaming about my friend and never really questioning her existence or the fact that in some form, she truly existed. I always felt I would someday meet the voice of those dreams, yet the event, when it actually happened, was unexpected.

Charlie and I had ventured farther than usual that day--past Sillery Sands, the rivers, and the villages of Lynton and Lynmouth--to a place called Valley of the Rocks. I'd longed to see it from the moment Rev. Jaspar mentioned the foreboding place, with its stone formations named in honor of the devil, and caves where escaped prisoners and other such riff-raff occasionally found refuge. "An excellent example of Devonshire geography," he'd said, "the cliff wall drops over a hundred feet into a rough, crashing sea. But not a spot for young ladies, mind you. A dangerous place to visit alone."

While his voice droned on with the lesson, I'd thought, "How exciting!" and made a mental note to try and visit there as soon as possible. Perhaps because of the fact that my life with Rev. Jasper presented itself with so few opportunities for fun and adventure, whenever I saw a chance for escape, I took it. But whatever the reason, I knew as I listened to my teacher describing the dangers and folly of those who frequented the spot, that of course I would have to see it for myself.

The moment came at last, a devilish, wet day when my guardian had instructed me to take fresh milk and eggs to Mrs. Bragg, a kindly old woman who was abed with rheumatism and unable to get to market. She was a good soul, always appreciative of things done for her, and any other day, I might have sat for a longer time and exchanged pleasantries. But just then, I wanted to hurry, and Mrs. Bragg seemed to understand. I gave her a fond farewell and wishes for a rapid recovery, then quickly set off for the Hill to find Charlie. He waited at his normal spot, nibbling at the ground, and raised his head in a friendly greeting as I approached.

"Hello, boy," I said, laying my cheek against his soft gray coat. "We're going somewhere special today. A new spot I've just learned of." Charlie snorted his approval, and laughing, I continued, Perhaps we'll have an adventure. We may find fugitives from the law, dearest, and you must protect me if we do. Agreed?"

He tossed his head up and down, and stepping on a nearby rock, I climbed on his back, urging him forward with a gentle prod. The Valley lay west of Lynton according to my geography maps, so I turned Charlie to a high path bypassing the villages, and in little less than an hour, we were there.

The day had grown even grayer; only a small bit of sunlight sifted through the heavy clouds. Rocky hills enclosed us on every side, shutting out even more of the light. The place was strange and dismal, and I almost regretted my decision to come. There truly was something evil about it, and I wondered if I shouldn't have obeyed Rev. Jaspar. Slipping off Charlie's back, I left him eating what greenery he could find in the packed earth and headed toward the cliff's edge. Castle Crag was the place I wanted to see; its name reminded me to romance and riches, and there perhaps, my dreams of a kingdom where I was loved and cherished could be for a moment fulfilled. A large stone formation jutting from the ground drew me inexplicably; I was sure it must be the spot I sought. Upon reaching it I began to climb, curious of the view from the top. Once almost there however, I found I was not alone.

Someone stood at the summit, looking out to sea with arms raised and cape swirling in the bitter autumn wind. I froze, afraid to move or speak for fear the person might be startled and plunge into the depths below. After what seemed an agonizingly long time, the figure stepped away from the edge, inhaled, then head thrown back, began to laugh aloud. I felt my own breath release with a gasp.

Turning, the dark caped figure began the descent down the hill to where I stood, until it faced me at last and I saw the shadows of the hood held the profile of a woman, with eyes so bright at first I thought she must be mad; but then, extending a hand in welcome, she said merrily, "Hello, you must be Anne.

I recognized the voice immediately. It had comforted me on numerous occasions. This was the voice of my dreams--remarkably, standing in human form before me.

"Y-yes," I answered hesitantly, "you know my name." It seemed strange that although I knew her voice, she should know me by name.

"Of course, my dear. I know all about you. You're the mysterious orphan of Countisbury, are you not?"

Light filled her tone, but I failed to notice this as I stared at her silently, not knowing how to respond. While what she said was true, I wasn't particularly proud of the fact, and hated it that she should know so much about me, yet I nothing of her.

"Except her love." The words hit me from out of nowhere and suddenly I knew she had thought them.

Her smile softened and she wrapped an arm around my waist and together led me toward the path down the hill. We walked silently for a time, I finding comfort in her presence. But once at the foot of the steep path, she turned toward me and began to speak in earnest.

"Dearest Anne, don't you know it doesn't matter what others think? It's what you know yourself to be that's important."

Tears started to well up and I choked them back, not wanting her to think me a child. "But I don't know who I am," I sobbed as they began to flow in earnest, "I don't know." Feeling foolish. I brushed a hand across my face, but all the years of pent-up emptiness seemed loosed at once, and through the floodgates of my eyes poured my tears and frustrations, my loneliness and insecurities.

"There, there, my child. Have your cry if you must. Life resolves itself. You'll see. You'll see." She held me close now, speaking in the voice I'd heard so many times, and looking at her, I knew how it must feel to have a mother; wonderful and warm, and I wanted the moment never to end. But her words prodded me gently, "Have your tears, my dear, and when you've done with them, we'll talk. I have so much to tell you. So very much to share."

Soon I felt like myself again and could look at her with clearer eyes. With hair like a white cap, her face, amazingly, was quite unlined, and her cheeks as pink as a fresh young rose. She wore a great dark cloak that looked black at first, but upon closer inspection, proved to be made of deep purple-colored wool. With the hood thrown back, I could see faint traces of sea-mist visible on her loosely drawn bun. But the eyes alone captured me; eyes of age and wisdom, so unusual, the irises like yellow sunflowers nestled in a field of green and burning so bright, like sunlight pouring into my soul. Staring into them, I felt renewed.

"I can see you're much better now," her laughter tinkled in the air, "so we must have a proper introduction. My name is Elizabeth Hardgrove Madden, but you may call me Maddie. I stopped using my other names many years ago.

We're going to be friends, you and I, and friends must have special names for one another. Don't you agree?"

"Yes," I replied, smiling at last, "And I'm Anne as you've said. But I'm afraid I don't have any other name."

"Well, now, we must make up a name for you, mustn't we? Everyone needs a name that speaks to others, says something about who they are. 'Maddie' for instance, is a warm friendly name, wouldn't you agree?"

I nodded as she continued. "Let's see, what kind of name speaks a truth about you. And more importantly, what kind of name would you like to have?"

Thinking of my childhood fantasies, I answered her after a brief pause. "I always wondered if my parents had given me some fancy name when I was born."

"Hmm," she said, "a fancy name. Victoria? No, no, that's too regal. It's simply not you. Edith? Too old, I think. Well, what about Jessica, perhaps? Not old-fashioned, I'm afraid. My, my, this is turning into quite an ordeal."

"Maybe you could add something to the one I've already got," I said shyly.

"That's an excellent idea. But it must be something that will suit you. Hmm, golden hair, rosy cheeks, sea-blue eyes. Quite like a princess, you are, my dear. Like a perfect rose. That's it! I shall call you RoseAnne. Do you think that will do?"

I colored at her compliment, for I had never received any positive notations about my appearance. "Thank you, yes, it's a lovely name," I said softly, rubbing the toe of my shoe into the damp earth in embarrassment. "You're very kind."

"Only the truth, love, only the truth. Now it's getting rather stormy, so let me walk you back to your friend before the rain begins in earnest. On the way you can tell me about yourself."

It never even occurred to me to wonder how she knew about Charlie as we strolled back across the moors, leaving behind the jagged cliff wall. She listened quietly as I talked freely about life at the rectory, shivering a bit when I mentioned my guardian. Her eyes softened when I explained how I had come to discover the world of nature and met my pony. Only when I told her I wasn't supposed to venture out, that my guardian forbade it, did she turn to me abruptly and speak.

"You must never, never let them take your freedom, RoseAnne. It is no one's to give or withdraw. Whatever price you have to pay. It's never too high." Once again her feelings echoed mine, and thus we both fell silent, lost in thought.

As we approached Charlie, waiting patiently for my return, she turned almost formally and spoke again. "Day after tomorrow, then? At this same spot?"

"Oh, yes," I beamed. "I'll be here waiting." Then, I hesitated, afraid of letting her down in the event I could not get away from Rev. Jaspar's watchful eye.

"I understand, child. But you'll find a way."

Impulsively, I reached out and hugged her tight, unable to believe my good fortune in finding such a friend. As the pony cantered toward the village, I wanted to laugh and sing and shout for I'd never felt so wonderful before. "Oh, Charlie," I said gaily, "Life is getting better and better. First the moors, then you, and now Maddie. It's amazing, isn't it?" And once more my answer was an affirmative snort.

After our initial encounter, I met Maddie two or three times a week, depending on how often I could manage to escape. Always, she seemed to know when I'd be coming, and usually was waiting for me somewhere along the way. We spent our time together taking long walks along the rugged cliffs, or when we felt like straying a little, through bluebells growing under forest trees. All my favorite hideaways were visited, and Maddie brought even more life and warmth to them that I'd ever have thought possible. On pleasant days, she might appear with a basket on her arm and say, "Today we're having a picnic," then we'd walk to the overhanging trees at Watersmeet and listen to the sound of rushing water for the whole afternoon, talking only necessary, mostly enjoying the solitude and serenity.

I never told anyone about Maddie. She was my special, secret friend, and I wanted to keep her all to myself; not to mention my fear of being forbidden to see her again. One day I asked Mrs. Rickett if she'd ever heard of someone named Elizabeth Hardgrove Madden. I knew our housekeeper had cousins in Lynton; indeed she spent her days off gossiping with them about this and that. They probably knew everything about everyone in the area.

But when I asked she said, "No, can't says I 'ave. Wherever did you hear of such a person?"

"Oh, I really don't remember exactly where. I must have heard mention of her somewhere. . .at church perhaps." I crossed my fingers behind my back so as to be forgiven for telling this small untruth.

"Don't you be eavesdropping on the conversations of others, miss. What's said is none of your concern, unless it's said to you. Mind you, now?"

"Yes, Mrs. Rickett," I responded meekly.

"Humph," the housekeeper went on almost to herself, and echoing the same thoughts I'd had earlier, "Tis certain I'd know the name if she was from 'ereabouts--being as I've lived here nigh on thirty years." But by this time I barely heard her, for I was slipping from the room, hugging my dear secret happily to myself, glad that Maddie was mine alone.

Never will I forget the first time she took me to her cottage. It wasn't a cottage exactly, hut would be a better word, tucked between two tors that rose from the ocean, invisible except to a trained eye. Weathered and beaten by the raging winds of the sea, her home appeared frightening from the outside with its peeling gray walls and frayed thatch; but once in the door, it was the safest, most secure place I'd ever been.

Reaching Maddie's residence proved difficult, for there were sharp stones and steep inclines to be crossed, but she was surefooted for a woman of her years, much more nimble than I for all my youth. The sea breeze whipped long strands of hair around my face as I followed, and I loved the taste of the salty mist on my cheeks.

The cob-hut was small, only one room, whitewashed, but clean and neat, and very simply furnished. Yet even in her simplicity, Maddie managed to bring more color to that one room that Rev. Jaspar had in his whole life. A narrow wooden bed in the corner exhibited a brightly decorated blue and green coverlet. "I quilted it when I was only 12 years old," Maddie told me proudly. Cream-colored lace curtains hung daintily at the two front windows letting warm sunlight shine through cheery panes of glass. On a table in the center of the room stood a delicate crystal vase filled with bluebells, poppies, and of course, my favorite, bright yellow gorse. Over the fireplace hung a miniature portrait (definitely the thing I loved most in the entire place) of a young, vibrantly lovely, Maddie.

Looking at the picture, I could indeed see Elizabeth Hardgrove Madden in all her glory. In Maddie, my own dreams came true! Long auburn curls piled high atop her head crowned skin, pale as newborn snow; cheeks kissed with a rosy pink, their blush highlighted by the simply yet elegant gown she wore. Oh, to have a dress like that! The tight bodice with its sloping neck and tiny waistline gave her the appearance of a fairy princess, and she only needed, in my humble opinion, a jeweled tiara to complete the illusion.

"Oh, Maddie," I exclaimed the first time I saw it, "You're beautiful!"

'Perhaps so," she replied, "but that was a long time ago, my dear, and the only reason that picture hangs on my wall now is to remind me of how very little I had then, compared with all I have now."

And indeed I saw a sadness about the young Maddie's eyes that didn't seem to be there when I looked into them now. How often I wondered where my Maddie had lived before she came to this place, what kind of adventures had she had? Had she been jilted by a lover, and vowed to live the rest of her days alone? Or had her family been angered by some innocent liaison, and cast her out, to fend for herself the remainder of her days? Somehow, our lives seemed even more connected by the fact that she too was living a life without a real family.

Still, I knew she must have a past, but each time I asked she would refuse to discuss it, and, respecting her wishes, eventually I left the subject alone. The days spent at her home were my heaven; when she took me there, I pretended she was my mother, and we would live there, happily-ever-after. Maddie either worked at the table on her herbal remedies or in a colorful little patch of garden behind the hut where grew the flowers and herbs from which she concocted her medicines. The house itself and several thick hedges sheltered the ground from the brisk sea winds, and I loved to sit among the blossoms and help, or simply listen as she told me about the plants.

"See those pretty red poppies, love? They'll be used to make laudanum, a pain killer; habit-forming if misused, but capable of performing miracles when correctly administered. The marigolds there are good for the ague. I make a special tea of them, and I always add just a nip of peppermint in case it disagrees with the patients' stomach."

"What about those tall pink ones over in the corner, Maddie? What are they used for?"

"Ah, foxglove...that's for people with heart complaints, my dear. I've seen many a person recover from a near attack only moments after drinking a brew made of it."

And so she would go on and on, insisting I learn everything about the art of healing, since I was expected to be of service to my guardian in the parish I found it impossible to believe I would ever know as much about the subject as she did, still I took her potions and poultices back to the village with me and followed the instructions she had given for their use; and always they brought almost instant relief to the patient. I began to have quite a reputation for healing, and even Rev. Jaspar became a direct recipient of Maddie's cures, for once when he had a bad cough, I gave him a syrup made from aniseed oil which helped him in no time.

That was one of the few instances I remember receiving praise from him. "Thanks be to you and the Lord, girl. You have a gift for healing, I believe." After that, he began to seek me out when a villager had a special need, and usually, after consulting my friend, I was able to provide some concoction that soon provided relief.

So, ironic as it was, I became known as the one with a special touch rather than Maddie. I felt a little guilty at claiming this recognition, but although I questioned quite a few townspeople, no one seemed to have ever heard of her, so I left well enough alone.

While she worked, Maddie told me stories in a voice even more cultured than my guardian's, which in itself was quite different from Mrs. Rickett and the village folk. I stayed in a state of continual curiosity as to how she had come to her present circumstances. So entranced was I by her words that I often had difficulty in following what her hands were doing. She talked in riddles and parables, and usually not until much later did the truth of what she said become apparent. She had this uncanny ability of reading my mind and then spinning a yarn that helped me to solve a problem or answer a question in just the right way.

"Did I ever tell you about the old woman who everyone thought was a witch?" she asked me one day after I'd been particularly wondering about Maddie herself.

"No, you didn't," I answered promptly, hoping I was about to gain some clues as to her background. "Why did they think that?"

"Oh, because she was different from them, of course." She laughed merrily. "She didn't go to church on the Sabbath. She liked peace and quiet, and lived all alone, so they automatically assumed she wasn't right somehow." She gave a light tap to her forehead. "Then one day, someone saw her feeding a falcon from her hand, and it was quickly reported she must be a witch, for those birds were so wild that no ordinary person would dream of having one for a pet."

"Then what happened?" I leaned forward eagerly, trying to picture Maddie with a wild bird. I knew of her fondness for animals--always a crowd of different varieties gathered about her door. She fed them and talked to them, but I didn't find that strange at all. Hadn't I always done the same on the moors and in the forest? "So what happened?" asked again.

"Why nothing, of course. People left her alone, not wanting to involve themselves with trouble. Wouldn't you, my dear?" She peered at me intently and I started laughing then. Maddie always had a way of teasing me with her tales too.

"But Maddie," I asked when I stopped laughing, "what was her religion if she didn't go to church? Did she believe in God?" This was something else that had been bothering me about my friend.

"Well, my dear I'm sure she did, for she had an inner peace that enabled her to communicate with nature in a way that most people can't. But you mustn't confuse inner peace with religion. Religion is merely the outer trappings of something most people never have to begin with. Inner peace is, well, a kind of knowledge, a way of understanding; and like a garden, it's planted inside you. The seed is always there, but it must be watered and fed, and, if it's to fully flourish, you must cut the flowers and share them, so that next year the buds will come again. Just like the roses, here."

"That certainly doesn't sound like the kind of religion that Rev. Jaspar preaches. What kind of knowledge does he have then?"

"The kind that dried up long ago and died among the rocks and thorns." Her answer surprised me, for it wasn't like Maddie to speak harshly, but thinking about it, I knew what she said was true. With Maddie, I felt God's presence and wanted to share that fullness with everyone. Rev. Jaspar had never made me feel that way in all his years of preaching and teaching.

As the months passed, Maddie helped me little by little to come out of my darkened shell and see myself as a good, decent human being. Looking back over my life, I often wondered just how she did this, for all she provided was a loving atmosphere. Time and time again, she stressed to me my own worth, that I was a person of value, that I had something to offer others.

Somehow, in doing this, she made me not only want to live, but to make something of my life as well. Suddenly more than just a lonely, abandoned orphan--I became alive with my own possibilities!

I'd had a better education than most, thanks to Rev. Jaspar; and I could cook and sew fairly well, thanks to Mrs. Rickett's not so enthusiastic instruction. And of course, I knew something about healing from Maddie. I could be a teacher or a seamstress or a nurse; it didn't matter as long as I had my freedom. Just knowing that life waited beyond the rectory door made every day worth living.

"You'll find your way, child," Maddie told me. "Remember though, a person needs more than just an education and skills to get by in this world;

you'll needs your sense as well. When you find yourself besieged by troubles, don't forget to come back to nature. Listen to your heart as you walk among the hills and valleys of life. That's where you'll find your answers."

"What answers?" I'd ask, wondering.

She'd laugh then and say, "Why the answers to your questions, of course!"

"But what troubles will I have, Maddie? Once I'm free from that dreary rectory, what could possibly go wrong?"

"More than you'll ever know," she responded mysteriously, "More than you'll ever know." And she fell silent, leaving me to wonder if indeed she knew my future or if everything she said was merely the fancy of an old woman's imagination.

Now I knew at last that Maddie did know the truth about the days that lay ahead, for part of her prediction had come to pass. We had only talked once about the voices of my dreams; nightmares they were really, and they frightened me, and although I'd come to trust her completely, they weren't something I wanted to share with anyone.

I'd had the dreams off and on since I'd been a very young child, but in those days, whenever I felt truly afraid, Maddie's voice had been there to soothe my fears. She'd always erased the memory of the others, but now since I'd met her, it seemed they came more often, and were more intense than ever before. Sometimes in the middle of the night, I woke from tortured sleep, drenched with perspiration, the strange words still echoing in my ears. And on these occasions, Maddie's soothing, gentle tone, which had so often rocked me to sleep on a sunlit spot of grass at Watersmeet, wasn't there to offer comfort. These voices frightened; first there were men, angry, arguing about something; then a woman with a harsh, bitter tone; and occasionally, I heard a baby, crying very softly, pitifully, and that sound made me feel the worst. Why didn't someone help it, see to it, do something, I wanted to scream? But no one ever came; and so I would wake, the sounds just fading, the words gone, yet lurking still as if to strangle me were my own feeling of fear and insecurity.

Yes, only once did I discuss the dreams with Maddie, but that was enough for me to know that she knew... she knew everything. The night before, I'd remembered the words, horrible words, and I had to ask someone what they meant, and who else but Maddie could I trust?

We'd both been withdrawn all that day, but finally I broached the subject. "What did the men say, RoseAnne?" she asked after I'd told her.

"Something about a bastard. They said it would destroy everything. That it must be taken away. That its mother was evil." I started to cry a little. "What does it mean, Maddie? Why did I have this dream, and why does it frighten me so?"

She reached over and patted my hand. She answered in a very still quiet voice, and I had to listen closely to catch the words. "Dreams such as yours are a gift, my dear, but you must remember that even though you see things which may come to pass, the final outcome of any situation will be determined by you, and you alone. We each have choices on the path of our destiny, but inside us, if we listen, the voices of the past are guiding us."

"Are you saying I saw my future?"

"Perhaps, or maybe you saw your past. I cannot say for certain. Life is a circle, and one lifetime may often be confused with another; we live in the present only to correct the past." She smiled at me tenderly. "What I tell you is that soon you will be leaving here, my dear. A man will come for you, and when he does, I'm going to miss you very much...

"A man? My father?" I was suddenly elated, hopeful that my dreams were to come true at last.

Maddie frowned slightly and squeezed my hand. "No, RoseAnne, not your father. You must trust me in this. But still you will go; you won't have a choice.

"But if he's not my father, I'd rather stay with you." I threw my arms around her. "I love you, Maddie. I don't want to lose you too."

"Dearest girl, you'll never always be just a thought away. Yes?" She hugged me tightly and I had a sense of drowning in her warmth.

"I'll remember," I sobbed, thinking of nothing more in that instant than of losing my dearest friend. "But will I come back, Maddie? Will I ever see you again?"

Tilting my chin up, so she could look into my eyes, she spoke, almost in a whisper, "Of course you'll come back; you'll never lose me. Never. You must remember that. You'll return. Of course you will." Then her eyes filled me with that wonderful glow and I forgot my sadness for a time.

***

Tonight as I listened to the voices downstairs, Maddie's words returned and I knew that the stranger had come, and the time for leaving drew near. Who was this man though, and where would he take me? Why did I suddenly have the feeling that Rev. Jaspar knew more than he'd been telling me all these years? Doubt and uncertainty plagued me. Who *was* the "she" they had spoken of earlier?

I felt afraid, but in an odd way, I was also excited; nothing like this had ever happened to me, and I couldn't help but wonder what the day ahead might hold. Had my parents sent this stranger? Maybe I was to find them after all. Of course I would miss Maddie unbearably, but except for her and Charlie, I had no ties here, and I had to believe that whatever was to come would be better than the past had been. How was I to know I would travel a long road before finding happiness, and ultimately that road would return me to these four walls?

Chapter 3

I left him there, unwatched, alone...
Emily Brontë

The following morning I faced my guardian across the breakfast table with eyes heavy from lack of sleep, but mind alert and anxiously waiting for explanations. Meals at the rectory were silent affairs. Rev. Jaspar and I, not being in the habit of making light conservation at any time during the day, remained abnormally quiet during this early morning ritual. Besides, talking with food in one's mouth was an indication of poor manners, not to mention the digestive problems caused by such undisciplined behavior. Probably most important was the fact that the Rev. wanted to read his daily meditation without interruption; with all these things considered, I felt it unlikely my curiosity would be satisfied before he'd finished with either his food or his reading.

So I turned my immediate attention to the matter before me, and with shaking hands poured an over-adequate amount of salt into the steaming bowl Mrs. Rickett had placed indifferently on the table only moments earlier. A simple fare awaited us as always--porridge and biscuits, accompanied by a pot of hot tea, made strong just the way the Rev. liked it. I imagined our housekeeper in the kitchen--topping her own bowl with fresh blueberries and cream, then adding a healthy amount of sugar to both that and her cup of tea. She definitely had a taste for sweets, as her plump, round body and partially toothless mouth testified; but my guardian didn't approve of such luxuries for himself and insisted as well that he would not have my teeth rotting away from too much confectioneries. Still, the berries would be wonderful this time of year.

Between small, indifferent spoonfuls, I fidgeted in my chair, twirling the utensil to make little rivers and valleys in my bowl, then bored with that occupation, began tapping my foot in time with the tune of a meadowlark whose joyful notes were floating effortlessly through a nearby window. Why didn't he hurry and finish, I wondered? The Rev., not the lark; his song added a pleasant pastime to an otherwise interminable meal.

My guardian nonetheless continued his slow consumption, reading with absorption the book open before him, until eventually, my somewhat odd behavior intruded upon his solitude and he told me to "stop squirming and finish your food."

Just at the point when I had decided I couldn't stand another moment of suspense and was about to broach the subject of the strange man myself, he closed the book, laid down his fork, and cleared his throat to speak. "I've just received some correspondence from my relations in London which particularly pertains to you."

"Relations in London?" I echoed, startled by this unexpected announcement. "But sir, I never knew you had relations in London. How..."

"Glenda and I related by marriage," he interjected rather sharply. "For simplicity's sake, you may refer to her as Cousin Glenda. Apparently, she feels it is time you came to the city and learned to become a lady. Having never had daughters of her own, she seems inclined to ignore your lack of parentage and give you a season in town, portraying you as her own niece, of course. I've told her..."

"But you never mentioned a cousin," I interrupted again, unable to stand the confusion, and realizing once again how very little I knew of his background.

"Why haven't I met her before?" I demanded. A thousand questions flew through my disoriented mind, and most of all I wondered what last night's mysterious visitor had to do with all this.

"Need I remind you, Anne," he made my name sound like an unholy word, "that you are not privy to all the facts concerning myself and my relations? I did not mention this woman because she did not concern you in any way. Now, however, she has chosen to make you her affair. So you have been advised of her existence. May I please continue now?" he finished icily.

"Yes, sir, of course, sir," I answered, once again recognizing my place in his household.

"I've told her I felt you were too young, and much too naive to be thrust into London society, but she is quite insistent upon having you. Since she has recently married a man of some standing after having long been a widow, she feels she will be better able to provide for you in the future than I have been. Probably she is correct in that assumption, and therefore, I have decided to allow you to be placed in her charge for the present. I trust that will be satisfactory with you." He phrased it as a statement, and a response from myself was not really expected.

Since he had paused, however, I timidly inserted a question of my own. "Will she be coming here for me?" This new development was becoming interesting. Perhaps Maddie had been wrong in her prediction after all.

"No, it seems she's been ill lately, so she's sending someone else to escort you to London. The gentleman's name is Martin Rollins."

My jaw fell open in astonishment. So here was where last night's visitor fit in! But why had Rev. Jaspar said he'd received a letter when the man had been here only yesterday? If he'd known about this earlier, why was he just now informing me? And was Cousin Glenda the "she" they had spoken of? My confusion grew by the minute.

"Well, why are you sitting there staring like an idiot?" The harshness of his tone broke my reverie, but still I didn't know how to respond.

"I guess I'm just rather surprised by the suddenness of all this," I said weakly for lack of a better reply. "I didn't know you had any other family."

"There are many things you don't know about me because I don't choose to share them with you," he said spitefully, and the sting in his voice brought me to life again. Rev. Jaspar would never tell me anything more than he wanted me to know; there was no point in pressing for further information, so I tried to concentrate on the matter at hand.

"When am I to leave with this Mr. Rollins?" I asked, feigning ignorance of last night's discussion, "and how are we to travel?"

"He comes for you on Friday, and I assume he'll take you by carriage to Barnstaple. From there you'll probably catch the train to London."

"Who's to be our escort?" Odd that he hadn't mentioned this very important factor. I knew my guardian's feelings about men and women being alone together, for hadn't I been berated severely only last week when he saw me talking in the cemetery with Billy Branchfield, one of the village boys. Of course our exchange was innocent--Billy had merely been telling me about his new calf, but no matter to my guardian, I was never to be "un-chaperoned" when speaking with any young man again.

Once more, the Rev.'s angry tone intruded upon my thoughts. "Surely you aren't presuming to say that my relatives representative would be an unsuitable escort for you? Or did you mean something else..."

"Uh, no, uh I didn't mean that he was unsuitable. It's just that, well, I thought you said it was improper for an unmarried man and woman to be alone together."

Sarcastic laughter filled the room, and I blushed and lowered my head. "You are hardly a woman, young lady, and I seriously doubt if Mr. Rollins will see you as one. Besides, I'm sure he is scarcely of the same quality as that dirty boy I caught you with last week. I don't think you need be worried."

"But I don't know this man!" I cried out, unable to believe this was the staunch minister I had come to know. "Who is he? And why *should* I go with him? I won't, I tell you!" So, here was the reality of Maddie's prediction. Suddenly I felt some strong emotion; I wasn't sure if it was anger of fear, but it swept over me and I wanted to lash out at this man who had controlled me for my entire life.

But he on the other hand, seemed to have washed his hands of me already. Was I simply to be turned over to this stranger, inexplicably and absolutely? Not only had I wanted to be free of Rev. Jaspar, it appeared he wanted to be free of me as well. Well, I would fight him with every bone in my body if need be; my reputation was at stake here. But even as the words came to me, I knew my resolution would never come to pass where he was concerned; I was no match for his strength and determination, and in the end, it would be I would lost the battle.

His thunderous voice echoed these thoughts only a moment later. "You will do as you're told, young lady! I am in charge here!" And then, somewhat quieter, "If you must know, he is Glenda's stepson; more than that is unimportant.

Besides, it's totally irrelevant whether you know the man or not. I know him, that's all that need concern you. You'll be packed and ready to leave by Friday." His eyes had been lowered, not meeting my own troubled gaze, but he raised them now, as if daring me to challenge him further. When I didn't, he went on, "By the way, you should probably wear your Sunday dress on the train. Mrs. Rickett will put the rest of your things in suitable trunk."

Somewhat reassured by his announcement regarding Mr. Rollins--after all, this man was evidently a family member, so he must be harmless enough--my attention turned to a new problem. My "Sunday dress" as my guardian so aptly referred to it, would hardly be appropriate for a journey to London.

"But sir, won't I need something new to wear? That dress is extremely tight and already several inches too short for me."

My guardian gave me a long look, questioning, as if he wondered if he'd misjudged me. After a moment, he rose from the table and spoke in the quietest, but coldest of tones. "I see you're counting your fortunes already. That shouldn't surprise me...Unfortunately, I don't have time to be bothered with your apparel needs. Glenda will see to all that when you arrive in London." And with those words, he turned on his heel and strode purposefully from the room.

"That man!" I said it aloud, but at this point I really didn't care who heard. How could he treat me with such indifference? Didn't anyone care what was to become of me? Evidently not. The Rev. Jaspar Cowper had made his decision, and my own opinions or feeling weren't to be considered. Why this should surprise me after living with him for seventeen years I don't know!

Still, there must be more to the situation that my guardian had told me. I had the feeling he was hiding something, and for the first time in my life I wondered just how much he actually knew about my parentage. Not the kind of man to be questioned easily, past experience told me that any attempts on my part to gain further information would certainly be futile. But perhaps this Martin Rollins would be more eager to talk and indeed some safe topic of conversation would be needed to occupy our time from here to London. Perhaps the answers would be forthcoming sooner than I expected.

Just then Mrs. Rickett poked her head through the kitchen door. "If breakfast is over, girl, you can stop your daydreaming and help me with the chores.

Startled from these unpleasant reflections and more than willing to assist rather than have her grumble further, I gathered up the dishes from the table and hurriedly carried them to the other room.

"So miss, I hear you'll soon be leaving us," she remarked contemptuously as I entered her domain. "Little miss London, you're to be, is it? I suppose you'll be giving yourself high and mighty airs now."

By this time I'd had enough of both her and my guardian's assessments of my character, and suddenly something Maddie had once said occurred to me. "Act like you're worthy, RoseAnne, and people will notice that you are. But always remember to do it sweetly, and with a smile, my dear, for as they always say, 'the bright sun opens more flowers than a cloudy day.'"

All right, bright sun, I said to myself, shine for me now "Mrs. Rickett," I turned to her, all sweetness, "I did not ask to go to London. I am being sent away. It is no easy thing, going to a strange, new place, especially in the company of a man you don't even know. To tell the truth, I'm rather frightened about the entire situation. Still, I'm trying to remember to have faith in Rev. Jaspar and trust that he is only doing what will be best for me in the end." Then I gave her just the barest hint of a smile, to assure her of my sincerity.

From the table where she was busily kneading bread, she looked up and met my eyes, and for the first time, I saw something more than irritability or anger there; a faint trace of kindness shown through, or perhaps it was pity. Whichever, for a moment she softened toward me.

"God be with you girl," was all she said.

***

Though I hadn't much to prepare, the next few passed in a flurry of activity--largely because Rev. Jaspar insisted on acting as if nothing different was happening in our lives, and saw to it normal duties proceeded as usual. This meant that every morning after breakfast and chores, I met him in his study for lesson, following came lunch, then time in the chapel for prayers and scripture reading. Later in the day, we visited ill or needy parishioners, taking baskets of food or medicines as necessity required. Upon returning, we would have our evening meal, prepared again by Mrs. Rickett; and then we went to the church once more for vespers. My own preparations for departure had to be squeezed into any remaining time.

Maddie was constantly in my thoughts, but every time I tried to get away to the moors, something or someone stopped me. I began to be afraid I wouldn't have an opportunity to say good-bye to them or to Charlie and Maddie. Although she had already spoken of my going, it wasn't the same as a formal farewell, and I wanted her promise that she would correspond. As for Charlie, well, he would understand in his own way, but I couldn't bear having to leave without giving him sugar cubes one more time. Leaving for an indefinite time would be hard enough without having to go with no word to those I loved most.

Finally, on my last day, came a chance to escape. Rev. Jaspar needed time to prepare for his sermon, so the afternoon was free. I intended to make the most of it, whatever the consequences. Slipping silently out of the house, leaving a pile of mending waiting listlessly, I made my way across the lawn and through the hedge, heading straight for the common where hopefully Charlie would be waiting. A gentle autumn breeze blew in from the sea, and bending to pick a handful of golden gorse, the realization dawned that I might never return to travel this beloved path. There was no way of knowing if I'd ever see this place again, and suddenly I felt forlorn and lost and afraid of the world I had wanted so desperately to see. I breathed in the deep, smoky sweet smell of the heath and wiped a bit of moisture from my cheek.

"I will come back someday," I said aloud, "I promise I will. I'll find a way." And the wind whistled over the hills, wrapping gentle, feathery tendrils of reassurance about me.

Sure enough, the pony waited just where I'd hoped. Brushing my face against his soft, gray coat, I smiled as he tickled the hand extended with his treat. "I'm going away, Charlie," I told him quietly, "but I won t ever forget you. You'll always be my prince. And one day, I'm going to come back, and take you away to live at my new homewell, that is if it's a good home. One you'd like. I would never want you to be unhappy, you know? Will you miss me, Charlie?" he tossed his head and I laughed through tears, then found a rock and climbed on his back, pointing him towards Maddie's.

The salty ocean wind felt warm against my cheeks as we galloped across the familiar hills and vales. The colors of the moor were in full bloom, and they blended into one another, giving the place a muted tone like a medieval tapestry. There will be no moors in London, I thought dismally, and wondered again if I shouldn't try and find a way to stay. In spite of my unhappiness at the rectory, this was my home, especially here, beneath the hazy, blue-gray sky where I could breathe in the fresh scents of heather and gorse, and communicate with something akin to God, whatever that some might be. Whether I could continue to exist beyond all of this I didn't know, and it wasn't something I was sure I wanted to find out. But unfortunately--or would it be fortunately?--life moved on.

Coming to the Valley at last, I slid from Charlie's back and went to find my other friend. I hurried along the path to her hut, wanting us to have as much time together as possible; but reaching the place, windows silent and deathly dark were all that greeted me. When no response came to my knock, I hastened to the back, thinking perhaps she was working in her garden, but found only a lonely patch of ground, still and quiet except for the gentle rustle of blooming buds tossed about delicately by the breeze. "Maddie!" I called, filled with the fear of not finding her. "Maddie!"

The wind sighed across the water in reply, and I ran from the darkened hut to the edge of the cliffs, looking desperately left and right, hoping to catch a glimpse of her somewhere along the coastline. Nothing met my vision but the waves crashing against a wall rock below. Running back up the path, I headed toward Castle Crag--the place she'd been on the day we met. Upon reaching the spot, I threw out my arms, wanting her warmth and strength, the sensations of vitality I'd experienced so often when we came here together.

All that met me today was a strange emptiness as if I'd drunk the cup dry and there was nothing left with which to fill it.

"Maddie, where are you?" I cried out in anguish.

I felt unbearably sad and not able to believe she wasn't here for me when I needed her most. "I need you, Maddie. Please." I fell to the ground, and weeping rose up from within, forcing salty tears to flow down my cheeks.

"Remember, RoseAnne, I'll never be more than a thought you won't forget?" I heard her as clearly as if she were standing by my side. I looked around and found only space; yet a hovering, golden glow had descended over Somehow I knew her spirit was here, even if she wasn't. So it would always be.

"I won't forget, Maddie. I promise." My tears had stopped and I spoke aloud, tilting my chin up and she'd done so many times in the past.

"Ah, yes, my dear. That's much better indeed. Everything will turn out well. That's my promise to you." Then there was nothing more than the sound of wind and water; the brightness and warmth that had surrounded me a moment before were gone.

"Au revoir, Maddie, until we meet again," I said as I sadly walked away.

Shadows had gathered in silent corners when I entered the church some time later. Seldom did I have need of its solace, normally I found my comfort among the hills and away were vales, but tonight I wanted to somehow reassure myself that peace could also be found within four walls. As a child, I'd come here crying because I'd fallen and scraped a knee or been bitten by a wasp, and there was never anyone else to turn to with my tears. My favorite place was a little bench in the south chancel wall, with a graceful swan carved intricately in its wooden end. The poor bird was wrapped in heavy chains, and I used to imagine I was that swan, an unhappy prisoner, bound to a life of bitter emptiness. But then, I had discovered the moors, and they had given me my freedom. Was I now to be chained once more?

Curling up on the bench, I looked around at the church for what might be the final time. How many other young girls had sat in this same spot and cried tears of their own? I wondered. Light flickered in creating eerie shadows against the screen that was my guardian's pride and joy. "Jacobean," he'd told me, "Dating back to at least 1700. We are blessed to have a screen like this one in our church." Gazing at it now, I felt sad because I knew he loved that screen more than he'd ever loved me. In a way, I was sadder for him than for myself.

Tonight the church seemed darker and damper than usual, and I shivered with a chill that cut deep beyond the outer layers of my flesh. My body trembled, and for the first time, I was afraid to be in this place. I felt I couldn't breathe--that I must escape or I would be suffocated by these thick gray walls.

As I turned to leave, however, a movement caught my eye and I noticed abruptly that I wasn't alone in the chapel. A man was kneeling at the alter head bowed, and it surprised me to hear weak, pitiful sobs coming from him. I watched, willing my vision to let in the light, then with great astonishment, I realized it was Rev. Jaspar. Never in my life had I seen him display any kind of emotion, yet here he was, alone and in tears. I wondered if I should rise and go to him but what was I to say or do? My own sense of terror left me feeling totally inadequate--I couldn't meet my own needs, much less his.

Presently, he began to speak, and I've never forgotten the words, or the sheer dread they brought to my soul.

"God forgive me," he prayed. "forgive my sins, the child is innocent. She's innocent, she doesn't even know. But I have to send her, she must go, she must. But please, oh Father, please, forgive me the lie, the crime..."

And with that he broke into a fit of racking emotion and I took the opportunity to hasten out of the church, afraid, alone, and once again, with nowhere, or no one, to turn to.

Chapter 4

...but hard as hardest flint the soul that lurks behind
Emily Bronte

Night tossed and turned about me--a storm had crept upon us--but its thunder and lightening paled in comparison with the churning turbulence in my own breast. The world had crumbled before my very eyes as I watched, powerless to prevent its fall. All that I thought I knew so well--where had it gone? In a days instant I had experienced Mrs. Rickett's compassion, Maddie's disappearance, and the Rev.'s exhibition of emotion--each of these things I would never have dreamed possible. There'd always been a certain amount of security in my unhappiness. I'd known what to expect from the people in my life. Yet suddenly that had changed. The sorrowing man I'd seen in the church last night was a stranger, and I wasn't sure I wanted to know the secrets he held.

Perhaps I should have approached him in his weakness, but at the time I'd felt weak myself, and afraid--afraid of discovering the truth about who I was. Now, I knew I'd missed the chance, for certainty possessed me that with the morning's light, all would be as it had been before; the pitiful man of the evening banished by day.

Between these fitful preponderances, I slept a little, only to be awakened by dreams of voices again. This time, though, a face crossed their shadows: a gray, off-colored reflection, masculine, lean, with a gauntness that reminded me of illness, and death. More than this I couldn't see with the blurred vision of sleep, but he laughed and the sound was horrible, frightening, evil--and with the laughter came a recollection, but from where, I didn't know. He spoke no words of his own, but seemed to be listening to those of others; and when he turned towards me, I woke with a start, to hear only pattering against the panes, words lost once more, but the echo of his image remaining to haunt me.

***

As the first slivers of daylight lit my darkened chamber, I rose with weary resignation. The day of departure--leaving was upon me. I splashed icy water from a pitcher onto my face, then shivering, turned to look out on the morning. Dull and cloudy; the rain had stopped but the misery hung on, left behind, a reminder of the nights woes.

"I won't be a reflection of this day," I said aloud, summoning brightness. Today I was going to London, and it had to be for the best...

My dress hung in the wardrobe--navy blue linen, let-out to the full extent--and taking it from the closet, I dressed quickly, hurrying against the cold and my own unpleasant thoughts. How nice to be wearing color for a change, my mind sang out; but buttoning the bodice, I couldn't help but notice once more the tightness, for my breasts had definitely filled out since its purchase three years ago. No matter, it was all I had; luckily my long cloak (handed down from Mrs. Rickett) would cover it for most of the journey. Then perhaps my new guardian would be kind enough to loan me something else to wear.

Just as I was adding the finishing touches to the thick braid I'd knotted at the nape of my neck, there was a quick rap at the door.

"'Es 'ere," Mrs. Rickett announced solemnly, and we both knew who the "he" she referred to was. "Seems rather anxious to be off, 'e does, so I've brought you some tea and toast, and told 'im you'd be down in a bit."

Setting the tray she carried on a table by the bed, she moved away from it and came hesitantly toward me. Awkwardly, I was enclosed in her heavy arms, clasped tightly to the ample bosom. "I'll be prayin' for you every day, girlie. Keep your eyes on the Lord and all will be well with you." A half-sob escaped her, and I thought with amazement that perhaps she did care for me a little after all.

Entering the parlor some time later, I was even more unprepared for the shock that awaited me there. My guardian sat stiffly on the sofa, while another man stood nearby, leaning impatiently on the mantle; at the sound of the opening door, both turned to face me and I grasped the knob tightly, a small gasp of disbelief escaping my lips. The man in my dream! I felt faint with remembered fear, but somehow I managed to extend a shaking hand. Somewhere in the back of my mind, I thought I heard Rev. Jaspar introducing Martin Rollins, but drowning his words was the mocking laughter that had followed me from the night. Oddly enough, it occurred to me to wonder if that dream had been a premonition from the past or the future?

'Perhaps both', a whisper of air quite like Maddie's voice breathed against my unspoken question.

Pushing thoughts away, I tried to concentrate on the person standing before me now. The hand clasping mine was lean and hard, and cold-icy cold. Tall, with the gauntness I remembered, he looked sallow by daylight, and even more pale and deathlike than the vision. While I realized that some might find him handsome in a dandified sort of way; to me, everything about him seemed faded. Limp blond hair was slicked back away from his forehead; his clothes were stylish, but drab, and the gray eyes that met mine like an overcast day held danger. I shivered inwardly, drawing my hand away as quickly as I could without being obvious.

"So Miss Cowper, we meet at last. I'm delighted to make your acquaintance." The voice, though low and charming, filled me yet again with fear.

"I trust your stepmother is feeling better?" I asked weakly.

"Ah, yes my stepmother..." Was I mistaken, or did he turn questioning eyes to my guardian?

"She's much better actually," he continued almost without a pause, "and so looking forward to meeting you." Emphasis fell on the "you." What kind of game was he playing with me? That smile on his face, I shuddered again, a frozen smile; it reminded me of one of the gargoyles I'd seen in a drawing of the cathedral at Wells.

Turning away abruptly, I faced Rev. Jaspar. "I shall write to you, sir, and I thank you for all you've done for me over the years. I'll not forget it." I meant these words more than he could ever have known -- I'd never forget how it felt to be unwanted or unloved, but because of those feelings, I knew I would always have more to give others. Some good things had come of my time here.

Sharp words stung me back to reality, however. "I'm sure you'll be much too busy with you new social calendar to remember an old man. Just try not to forget that your life belongs to God. Only by walking in His path will you come to righteousness.

"Well," Martin interrupted, "if the sermon is over, I suggest we be on our way. After you, Miss Cowper." Gallantly, he gestured toward the door and my guardian made a quick move to open it for me.

"Goodbye, Anne," he said, eyes lowered, refusing to meet my gaze.

"Goodbye, sir," I replied directly, "And thank you again." Holding my head high, I picked up my umbrella and bonnet and swept past him and a solemn Mrs. Rickett waiting in the hall to the carriage standing at the gate beyond.

***

Once outside the rectory walls, breathing became easier, despite the uneasiness I felt toward my traveling companion. The damp morning air smelled of sea salt and leftover rain. Inhaling deeply, for a moment I let go of all my troubles, and leaned back comfortably against the cushioned seat of the rig. Whoever owned this carriage must have money, I thought, for I'd never seen anything so luxurious. It was painted a deep burgundy with gold trimming, and our heads were protected from the weather by a roof, so the bonnet I'd brought still lay across my lap, forgotten. The day had only a light chill; the breeze pulling loose strands of curls from the braid at my neck felt wonderful, and I shut my eyes, forgetting, and enjoying the ride.

Without warning, laughter rang out from Martin Rollins, and my contentment shattered. The fears of the night returned.

"So, Anne," he said with mock cheerfulness, "I'm sure you don't mind if I call you that since we're to be in close proximity for such a long while..." He paused, and seeing I wasn't going to respond, continued, "So, Anne, what can I tell you about your new life? I'm certain you must have quite a few questions." Sarcasm filled his voice. He could care less whether I had questions or not, I felt certain. However, I wasn't going to pass up the opportunity to have my answers, so I proceeded quickly, before he had time to change his mind.

"You could begin by telling me why your stepmother would want to go to the trouble of taking in a poor, abandoned orphan of questionable origins?" I asked, adding to the words my own touch of sarcasm. "I don't imagine London will be waiting for me with open arms."

Head thrown back, the malevolent laughter with which I was becoming familiar filled the air once more, bringing again my own inward shudder.

"Direct and to the point, aren't you, my dear girl? Actually, I like that quite a lot. Adds some depth to you." He gazed at me intently, with new interest. "In answer to your question, Mother is rather fond of renovating, improving, restoring, if you will, things which might otherwise be considered as having no value."

I winced at this remark, but he smiled slyly and went on. 'You, my dear, are merely another project. As to your reception in London, well, we'll see how receptive they are to you after a year at Chattingham's. In the meantime, I'm sure Mother dear will come up with a suitable explanation for your background."

I gaped at him, wide-eyed and innocent. Not only was I totally unaccustomed to such an irreverent manner of speaking, complete confusion had set in at this statement

"Chattingham's?" I said almost to myself. "I thought we were going directly to London?"

All at once, I looked around and realized with dismay that at some point during our conversation we had turned off the road to Barnstaple. We had taken the ocean road, towards Somerset and Minehead, away from the nearest train depot. Where was this man taking me?

Martin obviously found my surprise amusing. "Of course you're not going to London right away. Why, you'd be the laughing stock of the town. *Mother* would be horrified if she could see you. Your hair is falling down, that dress is too short, and unless I miss my guess, much too tight as well. But in a year, after finishing school has put the proper finesse on you, well, old girl, you'll be the talk of the city."

"But Rev. Jaspar said..."

"That old man is a fool," he interjected sharply. "Besides which, my mother has reasons of her own for not wanting him to know exactly where you are. She'll explain it all to you in time. Actually, I doubt he cares much one way or the other."

A protective wall began to close in around my feelings, something I'd learned to do as a child feeling lost or afraid as so often I did, it helped to shut out the pain and emptiness. Since I'd met Maddie, I never cried, and I wouldn't now, especially in front of this vile person.

"I thought your Mother was anxious to meet me," I said, biting my lips, but forcing fullness into the words.

"Oh but she is, my dear, she most definitely is. But all in good time. She'll like you much better when she sees you at school properly attired." The grotesque laughter rang out again, and I turned my head away, not wanting to give him the satisfaction of seeing my fear.

We rode for some time in silence. The day was spoiled for me and for the first time since I had woke that morning, the clouds reflected my feelings.

***

Eventually he turned the rig away from the sea, and our journey began to take an inward course. The rugged hills of Exmoor were all around, and I made a concentrated effort to ignore Martin Rollins and enjoy the scenery. I'd never been this far from the village; in fact, I'd never been farther than Maddie's valley in my entire life, so in spite of everything, here was a rare treat.

After we crossed into the county of Somerset, the incline of the lanes lessened and fewer trees lined their paths. Hedgerows patterned the lush green landscape, various shades of autumn wildflowers nestled gaily amidst their briars, peering out at these two strangers who traversed across their isolated byways. If only I could be experiencing this new world with Maddie or aboard Charlie's handsome back! How happy I should be then!

We passed through little hamlets with tiny houses, covered by roofs of thatch and behind whose half-opened doors peeked the faces of children curious as the blossoms had been earlier. I hadn't the vaguest idea of where we were; occasionally a signpost would name a village, but having never ventured this far from Countisbury, none of the names were familiar. I did notice that we came to no large cities or towns, and I began to wonder about this Chattingham's.

Where was it and what kind of place would it be? I was seventeen, a little too old to be sent to school. What type of things would I learn there? Or be expected to do? If worse came to worse, I could run away. There was always Maddie to turn to, but perhaps I might find work, and a way to make a place for myself in the world as I'd always dreamed of doing. Then when I returned to visit my friend, she'd be able to say, "I knew you could do it, love. I'm so proud of you...

"You're a thousand miles away." The man at my side interrupted the happy daydreams that had been carrying me along in time with the horses' gait. I scowled a reply and was given an insolent grin.

Deciding to make use of the intrusion, I asked him abruptly, "Where are you taking me exactly?"

The look he gave me made me feel chilly in spite of the day's sultry warmth. "Anne, my dearest, where exactly would you like to be taken?"

When I turned my head away again and didn't respond, he continued in a more serious manner. "The school's near a town called Somerton, but we'll stop for the night in Taunton, for it's too long a trip to make in one day. So, my dear Anne, we'll get to have our night together after all. His jeer took me in, then he jostled the horses reins sharply, spurning them forward with a crack of his riding crop.

I didn't like that look or the way he handled the animals; it must have been apparent for he turned an ugly smile on me and spoke again.

"It's almost dinner time, old girl, and I'm an impatient man. When I want something, I want it now..." Then the whip flew through the air once more, and for the second time that day, I sensed danger.

***

After a silent lunch in a village pub called the Lion's Den, we resumed our travels. Throughout the meal, Martin had observed me intently, from head to foot, and I'd had the odd sensation of being unclothed in public, and wished my dress weren't so revealing. I was beginning to understand why Mrs. Rickett referred to a pretty face as being a curse. If indeed mine was attractive, I certainly didn't want this man to be the one who noticed it. Perhaps it was only my imagination, but didn't his cold hand rest on my shoulder just a little too long when he helped put on my cloak? And a few moments later, getting into the carriage, it seemed I was held just a bit too close, and nausea rose in me at the odor of him, musty and dank.

"Dear God", I prayed, "Be with me. Take care of me. Please." Rev. Jaspar would have been pleased to find me obeying his final request, but at this point God appeared to be the only one to whom I could turn for help.

I wanted desperately to remain alert for the rest of our trip, but the emotional strain of the past few days had taken its toll, and I drifted into a light sleep. Upon awaking, body stiff from the bumpy roads. I found that my cloak was open and two buttons of my bodice popped so that the bare skin beneath was revealingly exposed.

Sitting up quickly, I rearranged my garments carefully, but not before I saw the repulsive look in Martin's eyes. He wanted something from me, and I didn't think I wanted to know what it was.

Finally, we reached the inn, a sad-looking place called Ram's Head on the outskirts of Taunton, which appeared to be a large bustling town, and I wondered why, if his stepmother could afford this expensive carriage, she couldn't get us better lodgings for the night. Still, exhausted as I was, sleep would probably come the instant my head met the pillow, so what did it matter where we slept? All I cared about at the moment was getting as far away from Martin Rollins as possible. Even if it was only in another room.

The inn smelled of ale and tobacco and one or two heads raised from conversation as we entered. The place appeared to serve as the local tavern as well, but the hour was still early, so it was quiet.

I noted with distaste the torn paper lining the walls and the worn quality of the furnishings. A large, poorly dressed man was behind the bar, and as we approached, he looked up, then brightened considerably at the sight of my traveling companion.

"Well, well, well, if it ain't Mr. Martin? Been nigh on a year since ah've seen yer face. An' who's this pretty little thing?" He gave a leering stare in my direction that was blandly returned. "Will it be the usual, Mr. Martin, lodgin' fer tha night only?" He turned toward Martin, a knowing look passing between them.

"Yes, Tom, I think that will do fine. And if my old room is available, and Miss Cowper could have the one directly next to it, I'd be most appreciative."

The man smiled a toothless grin and moved a fat hand to his head, slicking back the remains of a balding scalp. "Course ya can have yer ol' room, sir. T'wouldn't do fer me ta rent it ta anyone else, now would it?"

He came from behind the counter, taking our valises in each hand, and proceeded to lead the way upstairs, muttering as he went about this and that, all the while giving Martin those knowing looks.

I wondered exactly when Martin had been here before; this didn't appear to be a reputable place, but then who was I to know of these things? My life had been sheltered; for all I knew, this inn might simply be indicative of those along the road. Perhaps I should feel lucky I wasn't obliged to spend the night outside with this man.

"Now, Anne, dear," Martin turned to me when we came to my door, "I'll just be in the next room should you need anything Tom will bring up a hot evening meal for you shortly, then I know you'll want to get a good night's rest before we leave in the morning. So until then I'll bid you good night." With that he swept the door open for me, made a low bow, then turned away, leaving me to my own devices.

I never got to enjoy the "hot meal" Tom was to bring, for the moment I lay down on the bed, I fell asleep. I passed the night in the sleep of the dead, then woke to streams of daylight and sounds of movement in the next room.

Was it time to leave? I wondered; and if so, why hadn't Martin called for me? Surely he would want to get an early start...and I, what did I want?

My thoughts turned to the trick that fate appeared to be playing on me once again. I had actually believed I was going to be cared for by someone, and now it looked as if I was only to be abandoned once more. How easy it would be to let myself fall into a state of despair, but Maddie's gentle voice came back to soothe away my troubles as it always had in the past.

"You'll find love, RoseAnne. I can promise you that."

I clutched at the feather pillow beneath my head. "Oh, Maddie," I whispered into the morning's half-light. "When will that moment come? When?"

"Soon enough," I felt her reply, "soon enough..."

I must have drifted off again at that point, for when I next opened my eyes, the room glowed with full sunlight. Goodness, I thought, it must be midmorning at least. And here I was lying abed.

Rising quickly, I dashed cold water from the pitcher onto my face, and then proceeded down the narrow dark stairway. Why hadn't Martin called for me, I wondered once more?

As I entered the large room downstairs, I noticed again the shabbiness of the place. And no one was here. I supposed this wasn't a popular spot for travelers to stay overnight.

I looked about, and seeing no one, called out, "Mr. Rollins?"

After a moment Tom's balding head peered out from a curtain behind the bar. "Ah, then, you re up, are ye?"

"Yes, thank you. Have you seen Mr. Rollins?"

The man gave me his knowing leer. "'E be gone since dawn, 'e has." My face must have reflected my amazement.

"Aye, miss. 'E said 'c'd be back in a few days."

"And what, pray tell, am I supposed to do in the meantime?" I demanded, beginning to feel angered by the entire situation.

The man let out a throaty laugh. "'Ah'm sure we can find somethin' to keep us busy," he replied, coming around the bar and close to where I stood.

Suddenly. I began to feel afraid, left here alone with crazy man. Just then, however, another voice burst onto scene.

"What's all this racket? Can't a person get any sleep around here?"

A woman larger than any I'd ever seen entered the room, and at her entrance, Tom paled visibly and backed away as if in fear of his own.

"Mornin' Dottie," I heard him mutter.

"'Ou the 'ell is this?" she wailed.

"Rollins left 'er," Tom muttered. "'E said to good fer 'er, an' 'ell be back in a few days."

"Oh, 'e did, did 'e? An' jus who does 'e think 'e is, jus waltzin' in here after a year and thinkin' 'e can leave one of 'is women? 'E never paid the las' time 'e wuz here, now did 'e?"

"Yes, 'e did, Dottie. Tha lady paid, remember?"

"Yeah, after I went to London to git tha money. I ain't takin' no chances this time. If she's stayin' 'ere, she can damn well take care of 'erself."

"'Ere," she threw a towel my way, "start wiping down that bar, and be quick about it."

I watched in dismay as she waddled out of the room, and then, for lack of anything better to do, I began to wipe angrily at the counter.

Chapter 5

Like a false guard false watch keeping...
Emily Brontë

The reality of my situation failed to arrive until the next day. For the first few hours after my life's second abandonment, I was furiously angry with fate for casting such misfortune upon me. I determined to fight back in whatever manner I could--even if it meant running away and finding my own place in the world.

Then, after a few boxes to my ears from the gargantuan Dottie, I began to feel somewhat sorry for myself, wondering why bad luck always seemed to be in the neighborhood when I was there. Every time Tom gave me a leer, Dottie grew a little more angry and resentful, and by the end of the morning, not only were my ears red from her slaps, but my arms were bruised black and blue as well.

By afternoon, exhaustion threatened to overwhelm me from both her physical abuse as well as the work of sweeping and mopping each of the vacant upstairs rooms. At one point Dottie came into the room I was cleaning and found me about to drift off. She yanked me up by the hair.

"Lazy wench," she wailed, "git off yer arse and finish this room. Ah've customers downstairs waitin' for it. An' there's bar to be tended this eve. Now move yerself.'

Tears began to brim up in my eyes, but I refused to let this vile person see me cry. I'd rather die first. 'Be with me Maddie,' I prayed vehemently, feeling a warmth at the very thought of her.

When evening came I was expected to keep the bar clean and dry, as well as carry ale to the coarse filthy men that seemed to have appeared out of nowhere during my cleaning spree upstairs. They laughed and jeered at my tight dress, swatted at my behind every time I passed a table, and muttered obscene comments beneath their breath when I handed them their mugs.

Humiliated and alone, as the evening passed I began to be more than a little afraid. What if Tom and Dottie sent me away with one of these men? What would happen to me then? No one would ever care to look for me except Maddie, and how would she ever know where to begin? The thought of their fat, groping hands on my body made me ill. In fact I felt nauseated every time one of them touched or breathed on me.

Finally the day was over, although by the time I fell into bed it was well into the early hours of the next. Oddly enough, Dottie allowed me to stay in the room where I'd slept the night before--I'd felt sure she would lock me away in some secret little garret where mice and spiders ran rampant and the light of the sun never shone.

But she led me to the same room, slammed the door behind me, locking it from the outside. To keep me in, I wondered, or someone else out. No matter, I certainly didn't want Tom or any of those other obnoxious men in my room.

That night I must have fallen asleep before my head even touched the pillow, because the next thing I knew, Dottie was banging at my door announcing "daylight was burnin', and I'd best get myself movin'."

So arrived my second day at the Ram's Head, where hopelessness became my reality.

***

A week went by, much in the same manner as the first day, except with each passing hour I grew more tired and less certain the future would ever see me away from this place. Where *had* Martin gone? I wondered by the hour. What was this place to him that at one time he had come here often, but hadn't for the past year? Was I destined to do menial labor forever? I couldn't believe this was to be my end, certainly I didn't want to believe it.

My hands grew red and chapped from scrubbing the floors and bar; my already battered "Sunday" dress was soiled with the grim and dust of the old inn; my hair became matted with a week's accumulation of dirt, for Dottie, unlike Rev. Jaspar, didn't believe cleanliness was next to godliness, and refused to let me bath at all, so sometimes I felt ill with my own stench.

I tried to think of good times and good days, but more often than not any thoughts of my own were interrupted by the landlady's battering voice. And it seemed the dirtier and grittier I became, the more liberties Dottie's customers seemed to think they could take.

"Look at this one, lads," a particularly lewd oaf would yell out, whirling me into his hairy arms and slobbering against my neck. "Ain't she a pretty lass under all the muck?"

And I would pull and tug away, heading back to the bar in shame, where Dottie would attack me with, "Let 'em 'ave their fun, the lads. Quit yer snooty ways, miss.' Then she'd pinch my arm till I bit back the tears, and push me back out among them, an easy victim.

One evening, when I thought I couldn't take another minute of their abuse, and was about to run into the night, taking my chances against its darkness, someone came to my defense. I didn't recognize the man--apparently he was a traveler, not a regular visitor at the pub.

He'd come in quietly and I heard him discussing rates for a room with Tom on my way to and from the bar. The men had gotten their wages on this particular day and were in an especially rowdy state of mind and body.

"'Ow pretty yew look tonight, Annie?" someone said to me. "Ah 'specially like 'at pretty dress."

"Yew jus' like it 'cause it's so fittin'" another yelled out.

"An so wha' if I do," the first yelled, pulling me close to him and pinching my breast.

"Stop it," I screamed, "Stop it this minute."

"Oh, a feisty one. Ah likes my women feisty, I does. An' what'll yew do if I don't?" the man jeered.

"Please," I begged, hoping a softer tactic might work.

The man guffawed, and pinched me again even harder. "Yew like it an' yew know it. All women like it," he breathed against my neck with his putrid breath.

Then suddenly I felt myself wrenched free from him. "The lassie asked you to stop it," a full, heavily-accented voice charged.

I turned my head and looked into the darkest eyes I'd seen, and in this instant, the coldest. For the longest instant all I could see was those eyes, the light within their deep depths drawing me, but then at last he spoke again, breaking the spell that seemed to have caught us both.

"When a lassie asks you not to do something, you should nae do it. At least this is the way I was taught. You, on the other hand, perhaps were not taught at all."

The voice commanded authority and dared his opponent to challenge him. At that point I noticed what a tall, broad man he was, and I knew that most men would think twice before opposing his wishes.

But these brutes had been drinking for hours, so of course felt invincible. Before another moment passed, the man who'd been fondling me was out of his chair, his right fist drawn for a punch.

But in only another second, the stranger somehow had him on the floor, with his arm twisted behind his back, and a drawn pistol daring any others to come forward.

"Now I suggest you all leave the lass alone," he repeated in a barely audible tone whose authority came through like a cymbal. Slowly he rose, and after giving me a nod, turned to Tom, "I'd like to go to my room now, if you please."

And Tom, always the quickest to bow to authority, hastened from behind the bar with his keys and ushered the stranger from the room.

After he'd gone, I closed my mouth, which must have been gaping for the last ten minutes. No one had ever come to my defense in such a manner! Who was he? I was, unable to reflect for very long, because in the next instant Dottie was hollering for me to replace some empty mugs.

The remainder of the evening passed in relative quiet compared to its normal pace. Everyone left me alone, but I could only guess at what tomorrow night might bring when my protector wasn't in the vicinity. Oh well, I could always hope that by tomorrow evening I, too, would be gone from this place. I still had a small belief in miracles, despite all that had happened!

I mounted the staircase during the wee hours of the morning, oddly hopeful that perhaps my luck was about to turn. Had the dark stranger given me that hope?

Just as I was about to turn the handle to my door, a movement in the corridor caught my attention. Thinking it was Dottie coming to lock up after me, I turned back to my room, but a moment later a large hand touched mine.

Shivering with some unknown emotion, I looked up into the dark eyes for the second time that evening.

"Did I startle you?" he whispered.

"Perhaps a little," I replied softly.

"I'm sorry. I didn't mean to. I just wanted to assure myself that you were alright." His voice was gentle and concerned, and the Scottish lilt sounded almost musical against the night.

"I'm quite alright," I told him, "and I appreciate your concern."

His eyes seemed almost to caress my face, and there was something so familiar about him, with his wavy dark hair and stern yet gentle features. "You're a bonnie lass, and you should nae be in a place such as this."

I started to speak, but something about his gaze was drawing me in, closer, as if I'd known him forever, and I ached to be in his arms. I knew in another instant our lips would touch--and not only that, but that I wanted that touch.

Inadvertently I must have drawn closer to him, yet with the movement he drew back and stared at me in surprise.

"Ah, so that's how it is then?" he demanded quietly. He pulled away and I shuddered against the chill of his withdrawal.

"Tis not what I'm looking for lassie. I'm afraid I want something more." His voice seemed almost sad.

"What do you mean?" I asked, sensing his meaning, but not wanting to believe he could suspect such a thing of me.

"A night's pleasure may suit some men well enough," he answered, "but I want a life of loving. Not just an interlude."

"And what makes you think I wanted an interlude?" I bristled at his words.

"Ah, lass, there's a way with some women. A man can tell. May be tis why those lads downstairs were drawn to you. I thought you something different, but apparently I was wrong."

Without thinking, my hand struck out, hitting hard against his face. "How dare you!"

Ignoring the shocked stare on his face, I spun around and entered my room, slamming the door and hoping I'd caught his hand or foot or some other vital body part in its closing.

The nerve of the man, I thought as I slipped between the icy bed sheets. Who on earth did he think he was?

Well, he was no one to me, that was for certain. And with the sudden realization that indeed I didn't even know his name, I fell asleep against my pillows, unaware that my cheeks were wet with silent tears.

***

I dreamed again that night. It was the first time I'd dreamed since the night I'd had the vision of Martin Rollins. My ghosts had stayed away since then, giving me some peace of mind, but tonight they returned with a vengeance, giving me little rest, but no specific clue as to their purpose in tormenting me.

I tossed and turned against the voices of angry men, and kept seeing the face of the stranger in the pub; his eyes filled with concern and tenderness one moment, and with hatred and anger the next.

The light of morning brought me no relief, and rising from the bed, it seemed I had reached the darkest point of my life. No stranger would rescue me today. I wanted to somehow find the strength to save myself, but an ache had crept into my bones, leaving me drained and empty.

The stranger apparently left early, and I didn't see him again. I felt a twinge of regret at our disagreement, but still stung with his insinuation. I wondered if all men were so self-righteous, and thought that if they were, I would do well to spend a single life, learning to depend of myself. And yet, the safety and warmth of his arms had been so tempting. Well, that moment was over, and I must leave it behind and face this new day.

So with the exception of my extreme weariness, the day passed as all the others, but evening brought an unexpected surprise. I was unsure if it was a welcome one or an unwelcome one, but whichever, Martin Rollins had returned.

"Anne, my lovely," he cried out as he swept into the tavern, "did you miss me? I missed you." He came behind the counter where I was filling a mug and threw his arms around me, placing a dry, musty kiss against my cheek.

"What *are* you doing down here?" he asked appearing somewhat dismayed at my disheveled appearance.

I was startled at seeing him, so tired and angry, I couldn't speak.

"Tom," he yelled, "why is Anne filling ale mugs? And why is she so dirty? Haven't you let the girl bathe?"

"Well, Dottie, she said..."

"I don't give a damn what Dottie said," Martin ranted, "I told you to see she was well cared for in my absence. Now you tell Dottie to run a hot bath for her this instant!"

And ten minutes later I was soaking in a tub filled with luxurious scent and steaming water. For once I was grateful to Martin. Maybe he would turn out not to be such a bad person after all.

Dottie had snorted and hissed about the bath, but I had it all the same. It did much to ease my aching body, and no sooner had I gotten out of the tub than Tom knocked quietly at the door and appeared seconds later with a tray laden with food.

I suddenly realized for the first time how long it had been since my meager lunch (Dottie believed one worked better on an empty stomach for some odd reason). Each bite tasted wonderful--at least Dottie was an excellent cook. The ham was broiled to perfection and the potatoes and carrots practically melted in my mouth, not to mention the hot bread fresh from the oven. It was the first meal I'd enjoyed in days.

Perhaps Chattingham's wouldn't seem so bad after this. I thought, sipping the hot wine Tom had provided. Surely

Martin had returned to take me there, and now I was more than willing to make the best of it.

The drink was strong, and after the hot bath, I felt sleep creeping over me much quicker than I'd anticipated. Before I even had time to ring for Tom to collect the tray, my head began to nod.

I must be dreaming. I thought later. I heard voices arguing in my room, but couldn't seem to move or call out. My body felt oddly disconnected from my mind.

"Ah'll not have you keeping 'er here," a woman said. "Yew expect us to bow and scrape to her, an' she ain't nobody. I mean it, yew hear? Tha days are over when yew kin come in ere bringin' all sorts of women. If yew ain't stayin', neither is she."

"You'll do as I say," the man replied. "I play you both well."

The woman sneered. "The lady pays well. So doen be tellin' me wha' ah'll do. Jus wha' would the lady say if she knew about this one. Ah bet she wouldn't like it none too well."

"Don't you threaten me."

"Then take that one away from 'ere. On the morn."

Heavy footsteps echoed away, but the man's form moved toward the bed where I lay. He stood over me, towering, his face clothed with the night. Without warning, his hands started to fumble with my nightgown; I tried to move, but heady with the wine I'd drunk at dinner and my extreme weariness, my body refused to obey.

Roughly, he yanked the fabric open and bent his head, sucking fiercely at the tender breasts beneath. God, I must be dreaming! But then, he was on me, forcing a hard knee between my legs, probing, pushing, and I knew this was no dream.

Drawing all word the power within me, my mind screamed out a word--"Maddie!" And, as if released from its spell, my hand found the pitcher standing on the table beside the bed it down forcefully on the head of my attacker, who fell back, dazed senseless with the contact.

I must have climbed out a window, but still in my groggy and disoriented state. I wouldn't swear to it. My cloak was on the bedpost, and somehow it occurred to me to grab it, never even looking back at the man on the bed By his shape and build, I guessed it to be Martin Rollins, but at this point all I cared about was escaping from whoever it was. To safety. Wherever safety might be.

Chapter 6

...weary with the long day's care...and lost and
ready to despair.
Emily Brontë

Martin didn't find me that night. But he couldn't be dead, I reasoned. My feeble attempt at protection surely hadn't been capable of extinguishing his life. But I don't believe I'd have been sorry if it had-- for surely it was he who'd come to my bedchamber--who else did I know who was vile and despicable enough to try such a thing? And from the conversation I'd overhead, having his way with women must be a regular routine with him. But who was the "lady" they'd discussed. Cousin Glenda perhaps? Did she support her stepson's ugly habits?

Such thoughts ran through my mind as I made my way through the dismal night. A steady drizzle had started to fall, and the damp air hung chilly and thick with its moisture. My long cloak offered some protection from the weather, but without a bonnet, long strands of hair soon framed my face in sad ringlets.

The fatigue I'd experienced earlier had grown beyond control. The events of the past few weeks had caught up with me, and each foot forward cost great effort. If only I could lie down for a few minutes and rest. I'd take no chances though; Martin might only have been dazed and could already be setting out to find me.

But where was I to go in the middle of the night and only half-clad at that? Maddie said she'd never be more than a thought away but now her presence evaded my call, and the only sound around me was the dripping of rain from tall, solemn trees, and the still quiet of nighttime. A forest bordered the inn, and I'd immediately sought shelter there. Now, lost for sure, my body quivered under the shadows of old, gnarled oaks, their branches reaching like threatening hands toward me, to grab, choke, suck me into their depths. With each crack of a twig beneath bare heels, new terrors arose; and although soon my feet were numb cold, the echo of footsteps still reverberated through the woods, haunting me. Shivering from both fear and the damp, somehow I kept moving, and after what seemed an eternity, the trees began to thin. Once past the darkness, I saw a sight that filled me with never-ending gratitude--a road--and with it came the hope that just perhaps, someone would come along.

Almost before finishing the thought, I heard before I saw the approaching wagon, a horse's bell jangling loud as a town crier and creaking sides belying the age of the conveyance. An old man with a graying beard and wide straw hat held the reins slack, clucking his overweight nag onward; the only youthful thing about the entire scene was the cheerful whistling of the man, but even that stopped abruptly when I stepped into his path, waving.

He pulled the horse to a halt and stared as if he *were* seeing a ghost.

"Whoa, Angus, whoa boy. Saints be to God, what on earth is this? A specter from the grave, or a real little lady? If ye be real, then why on airth be ye wanderin' about this dreary evening?"

"I'm real, sir, and please, could I beg a ride with you to the next town?"

While the man continued to gape, I realized suddenly I had no excuse for being out, half-dressed, in the middle of the night. If I told him why I'd run away, he might insist on taking me back, or calling the sheriff-- and then what? At best, I'd be returned to Rev. Jaspar; I knew I didn't want that. And the worse, well, Martin could deny it all, and once again I'd be left at his mercy. Much as I disliked telling untruths, one seemed called for at this point, at least until I could decide what to do.

'I missed the train at Taunton and I must be in Somerton by morning." These were the only names I knew to give him, so I prayed I was on the right road.

"An wha did ye think, young miss, that ye could walk the 20 miles to Somerton in one night?" His gaze took in my bedraggled appearance and I could imagine the questions running through his mind. 'An where might yer bags be, girl?" His suspicion was fully aroused now, and I noticed the white of my nightgown peeking from beneath the cloak.

Thank heavens for Mrs. Rickett's hand-me-down cloak, I thought, drawing it closer. At least my feet didn't show.

Answering aloud, I summoned what I hoped was an air of innocence. "I sent them ahead yesterday. I hadn't expected to miss the train, sir. I promise I'll be no trouble if you'll just let me off at the next town."

"Well, now that'd be Langport, miss, and as I'm goin' there to market, don't see why ye shouldn't ride along. It's only a stone's throw from there to Somerton. Grab a hand, lets get ye up, then climb under the tarp ere, and keep out of the wet. Hope ye don't mind the smell of scallions, miss."

I didn't mind the smell at all. So grateful was I to be dry and moving under someone else's guidance, it wouldn't have mattered if a corpse lay next to me. The last thing I heard before falling into a deep sleep brought a smile even in the midst of my weariness.

"Bloody fool woman," the old man said.

***

Sunlight had already crept playfully under the corners of the tarp when I awoke, warmed by the golden glow. The wagon stood, not moving, and sticking my head from under its cover I found we had parked near the market stalls of a small town, its early morning hustle and bustle already in full swing. The smells of fresh fruits and produce filled the air, or perhaps I only imagined this to be so (after all, I'd been sleeping next to scallions the entire night, thus their odor not only covered my outer apparel, but permeated my nostrils as well! And my eyes! How they burned against the bright sky!)

There was another smell, too; one I'd have recognized anywhere--river water! Scanning past the town, I saw for the first time a wide canal, water traffic filling up its narrow banks. Langport must be situated on a river. Which one? I wondered thinking briefly of the Lyn and wishing myself there, safe and secure and dreaming of my handsome prince.

"You've got no time for pitying yourself, girl," I could almost hear Mrs. Rickett saying, and that was true enough. My driver had disappeared and unfortunately, the rest had not refreshed me, for my head throbbed, and a raw burning tormented my throat. Not wanting to tell any more untruths and hoping to avoid further questions, I adjusted my garments and climbed down, looking left and right, wondering what to do now.

Hunger gnawed at my stomach, but I wouldn't have felt right about taking from the old man even if he'd had something besides scallions, which I doubted he did; after all, he'd been good enough to give me a ride, and I couldn't even pay him for that. Weakness, however, was beginning to overcome me, and the headache and soreness of my throat weren't helping in the least. If only I had some drinking water...

A little to the left of the market area, I noticed a grove of trees and what appeared to be a small stream running past them. Stumbling across a dusty road over to the spot, I sank down in the fresh scented morning grass and drank the sweet, clean water, then splashed a bit on my forehead in an attempt to cool it. Afterwards, sleep slipped in, uncalled.

Faces drifted in and out of my vision. Rev. Jaspar's cold, angry eyes. "Stupid girl, I've done for you all your life, and what do I get in thanks for it? Ingratitude and disloyalty."

Then Martin's leer. "Anne, my dear. . .What lovely breasts you have. Just let me touch..."

And the stranger. "I thought you were a lady."

I jerked up, wide-eyed and afraid, but no one was there, only the sun, a little higher in the sky than when last I'd looked.

Looking back toward the area from which I'd come, roadways jammed with carriages and horses seemed to indicate the popularity of this particular place; and the market now literally brimmed with people, scurrying about, livestock in leash or toting large baskets, the sound of laughter and bartering ringing through the day. Still feeling a little dazed, I shook my head to clear it, but doing so only made the ache worse. Langport. Somewhere I'd heard the name before. What told me about this town? Had Rev. Jaspar mentioned it in my studies? I shivered at my own lunacy and waited for my head to clear. Why in the world should my studies come to mind at this particular moment? Here I sat, alone, probably being followed, no one to turn to for help, and ill at that, contemplating a history lesson about the village of Langport!

I had more important things to concern myself with: such as what to do to get out of this predicament? No clothes, no money. I couldn't even get back to Rev. Jaspar without those things. Not that I wanted to go back there. I wouldn't even be in this mess if it weren't for him. Some guardian he'd turned out to be. I shook my head to clear it, but it was useless, I felt so tired, I couldn't go on, couldn't think. What to do? What to do? I closed my eyes against the pressure.

"Oh, Maddie, where are you?" I asked weakly, "Why aren't you here?"

"Some things I must let you do on your own, my dear." I sat up quickly, looking around, but there was no one. Only a gentle whisper of a breeze. But just feeling of her nearby made me a little stronger. All right, Maddie. I'll try. I will try.

Taking note of the market again, my gaze caught sight of a glint in the mid-morning sunlight, red and gold glistening against the day, and I realized I knew that particular carriage; I'd ridden in it only a short time ago. Parked a little beyond the vendor stalls, it stood, waiting, beckoning. I quickly looked around, but saw no sign of its driver. Thank God, I thought. My bag will be there! My shoes, my clothes! Surely if he had come in search of me, he had brought them as well. Maybe not, but it was the only chance I had. I'll get them quickly, before he returned, then decide what to do. One step at a time. Fate had presented a perfect opportunity! If only I didn't feel so ill.

Rising on shaky legs, I put up Maddie's brave chin and crossed the dusty road again, to the spot where the carriage had been left. Nervously, I searched the sea of faces for some sign of Martin, but found none. The crowd pushed and shoved around me, but I was in a daze, weak and feverish, unaware. I approached from behind, still watching, but feeling less capable by the moment. He must have changed horses, I thought, noticing that the dark browns had been replaced by two dappled gray roans. And no wonder, the way he treats animals! The poor things were probably tireder than I!

My valise should most likely be on the floor inside; that would have to do, I couldn't very well carry a trunk. Fortunately, however, the bag would at least have my old dress, and hopefully, my shoes. Oh, no, the thought suddenly occurred that Martin might have left in such a hurry as not to have brought anything. Surely this wouldn't be the case! Please, Lord, let the bag be inside, I prayed.

As I pulled open the door, I realized with dismay this wasn't the same carriage! The leather stood out in front of me, black leather, not deep red as ours had been. Shock set in. This couldn't be! I needed that bag! Oh, no God! Please, no! Now what was I to do? Everything seemed to be going wrong. Closing the door quickly, I heard voices from behind. "Hey girl! What are you about there?"

Spinning around I saw two men approaching, fighting their way toward me. I panicked. They'd arrest me. Take me away. And how could I ever explain who I was with no clothes, no papers?! I turned and ran in the opposite direction.

"Stop! You there!" one of the men called out.

The trees in the distance beckoned like a safe harbor. Get to the trees. If I could just make it to those trees! Splashing across the stream, the fog swirled thicker around, taking control. I must escape. Must get away. Run. Run. Brambles tore at my face, nettles stung my legs; and although the cloak, my one protection against total exposure, fell unheeded to the ground, I ran on. Fire coursed through my body. I've gone to hell, terror screamed, and the force driving me could only have been fear. The very trees soon choked and smothered as they'd done in the night, only this time, despite daylight, their threat was greater.

Finally, strength and breath exhausted, I could run no more. Gasping for each mouthful of air, I stumbled into a clearing, and feeling an ankle twist beneath me, fell to the ground. I reached out, clutching uselessly at stands of grass, begging for help from Maddie, God, or anyone who might be listening to my pitiful cries.

Suddenly, the snap of a branch behind and beyond the cover of trees brought silence, and forced my head up, searching fearfully for some sign of the men. The pain in my throat, head, and ankle merged into one agonizing throb. If the end had indeed come at last, perhaps it would be a blessed relief.

As the sound of the footsteps moved closer, I covered my face, wanting to shut out the ugliness to follow. A figure loomed over my shivering form all too quickly, and I dared to look from behind half-closed lids. Dark hair, dark eyes, dark, dark, dark--the fury of a storm blew across his face. For one brief moment I experienced a sense of incredible joy such as I had never known. Past, present and future merged into one instant and I knew them all--they were here in this man--my stranger had returned. Then abruptly darkness took over, and the world went black.

Chapter 7

Beyond the town his mansion stood,
Girt round with pasture-land and wood...
Emily Brontë

Semi-darkness shrouded the room into which I awoke, but a soft, carefree humming brought the shadows to life. With vision blurred and unclear at first, several moments passed before I managed to make out the figure of a woman, bustling about, straightening bedclothes and drawing curtains. Light poured into the grayness as she did, blinding me further with its intensity.

Eventually my gaze focused on a short, plump person wearing a full white apron that bounced gaily over a dark-colored dress when she moved. Graying hair slipped from under her white cap and curled about dimpled cheeks. After a time, she lit at a large bureau and began to pour water from a pretty porcelain pitcher into its matching bowl. Dipping a towel into the liquid, she wrung it with a hard twist, then turning, noticed my wakeful state.

"Blessed be the Lord! So you're finally with us! We thought we might have lost you for a time there, child, but twould seem you're to live after all!" She crossed herself, towel and all, and though her full, resonating tone might otherwise have frightened me, kind eyes and the smile that lit her face offered reassurance. Moving beside the bed, she placed the damp cloth across my head, gently bathing dry skin.

"Where am I?" I asked weakly, speaking with effort only to find my throat parched and sore. Sensing this, she reached to a nearby table for a glass of water, then helped me drink a little. Replacing it after a moment, she straightened the plump pillows behind my head.

"Nice and easy, lass. There'll be time later for all that. First you must get your health back, which means you need a bowl of good, steaming broth. You've not eaten much these past two days. Now you rest easy while I go and see to the meal and tell the family you're awake at last. There's those who've been worried about you, miss." With that she patted my shoulder gently and danced away like a bubble on my brook at Watersmeet.

With her departure came the opportunity to look around the room and take in fully my surroundings. The chamber was large, with furniture heavy and dark which appeared to be very old. Plush green draperies adorned the windows, drawn back now to let bright sunshine pour in through beveled panes of glass. In one corner stood a small sofa of some soft golden fabric and a matching chair. An accent table complemented the arrangement, graced by a delicate crystal vase filled with a bouquet of red roses. On the wall adjacent to the bureau a rich-looking dressing table with a curved mirror reflected the morning light. (Or what I assumed was morning light since I had no idea whatsoever of the time! Did the woman say I hadn't eaten for two days? Could I have been here that long?)

Drawing my sights back to the present, I let out a small sigh. This was truly the most beautiful room I'd ever seen in my life! Lying small and weak in the gigantic canopied bed, I felt like a queen--I just hoped I really was alive and hadn't died and gone to Heaven!

I remembered nothing of how I'd come to be here. Thinking back, I saw myself in Langport, very weak and ill, but I wasn't sure what had happened after that. Something...I should remember...still, it's no use, I thought. My head had started throbbing again, and instinctively, I knew better than to push myself. Hopefully, it would all come back later.

Without warning, the bedchamber door swung open and a girl of about fourteen rushed into the room. "So, you are awake! Mrs. Blum said you were! I'm so glad! We've all been terribly anxious about you. And so curious! Who are you? I'm Sarah. How do you feel? What's your name? And where on earth did you come from?"

The flow of words seemed endless, and in my disoriented state, I wasn't sure I comprehended half of what was said.

"Sarah, enough." A stern masculine voice admonished from the doorway. Turning toward it, I saw framed in its entrance the most amazingly handsome man I'd ever seen in my life. In my confusion, I felt quite certain he must have come directly from Heaven. Golden curls swept across a broad brow, gracing an angelic, almost feminine facade. Eyes clearer than the sky on a summer's day turned from reprimanding authority to gentle concern as he looked at me. Whereas the girl was frail and plain with mousy straight hair, this man glowed sunlight, making the day appear dull in comparison.

I thought I'd never be able to drag my sight from him when another man walked into the room. Then it all came back to me. The carriage like Martin's, running from two men, fainting in the forest--everything--with painful clarity. This man had found me. This man I had met once before. The dark brooding stranger from the tavern. The man I'd believed I'd known once before in some other life...

Yet now, in the daylight I saw only a stranger, and the joy I'd experienced faded into nothingness as I gazed into his face. Where the other shone fair, this man shadowed, but a warm earthiness pervaded his presence, and somehow with him, I knew the forest would be a safe place. Just as the tavern had become...

"Look, Ian, our guest is awake at last," the fair one smiled to the dark. "Really Sarah, must you start badgering the poor girl with a thousand questions the minute she opens her eyes?" The girl's eyes began to fill at his words, so I held out my hand and spoke to her gently.

"It's all right. I'm Anne."

She came to the bed and clasped my outstretched palm. Suddenly she seemed quite shy and spoke with downcast gaze.

"I didn't mean to b-badger you, Anne," she stuttered a little, "it's just that I was so happy you were awake finally, and I wanted, well, for us to become friends." She smiled at me hopefully and I smiled back and squeezed her hand.

The blond man spoke again. "Yes. Sarah, we're all glad Anne's awake, but you'll have to wait until she's stronger to begin a friendship. She needs her rest." Then to me, "You've had a bad time. We nearly lost you, but you're on your way to recovery now."

He approached the bed timidly, and now gazed at me with tender eyes. The other, Ian, remained silent at the door. "I think we could have a quick introduction, then we'll leave you in peace. Is that alright?" He smiled, slow and easy, and I nodded an affirmative, then waited for him to continue.

"I'm Lyle Leighton, and you've met Sarah, who is my one and only sister, imp that she is." He tweaked her hair playfully and I saw he wasn't upset with her anymore.

"You are, at present, a guest in our humble home, Leighton Hall." He gave a short, friendly laugh. "Oh, and this dear girl, is your rescuer, or shall I saw pursuer, Ian McCrae." He turned to the other man, gesturing him forward. "Come and meet Anne, Ian, don't be shy.'

Now was certainly the chance for Ian to say that we'd already met, and where. But for some reason, he kept silent as Lyle continued.

"Ian feels certain you're a thief who meant to rob us blind at the market, but what, I asked him, would a thief be doing in her nightgown, and surely you must be a 'damsel in distress.'"

Ian strode forcefully across the room and the picture I had was not of a shy man at all. Certainly he hadn't been shy the evening he came to my rescue in the tavern. I noticed now he stood several inches taller than Lyle, with a more muscular build. His tanned features told of many hours spent in the sun. While they both wore riding clothes, this man's betrayed a lesser quality. Could he be employed on the estate, I wondered? He stopped beside the bed and stared down somberly and despite his outward appearance--the rugged strength, the hard line of his jaw--what captured me once again were his eyes...

"'Tis glad I am you're mending, lass," he said with that singing Scottish lilt, all the while his dark brown gaze bearing such warmth into me that suddenly I was reminded of Maddie. But something seemed to be lurking behind that gaze. A warning perhaps? Why hadn't he told that we'd met before?

Feeling the need to say something, I began uneasily, "I should tell you...

"Later, Anne," Lyle said firmly, "it's obvious you're a person of some quality, and I don't believe you're going to steal the silver in your present condition. Ah," he looked toward the opening door, "here's Mrs. Blum with your broth now." The plump, cheery woman I'd spoken to earlier bounced back into the room.

"And what are you all doin' here," she demanded, and I noticed for the first time she spoke with an accent less pronounced, but similar to Ian's. Could they be related?

Mrs. Blum continued to glare at them disapprovingly. "Tisn't proper for gentlemen to be in a young lady's bedchamber, as you all well know. Now off with you, every one; you too, Miss Sarah. I've half a mind to tell your mother how you're actin' in her absence."

I couldn't help but smile a little, for her words had nearly succeeded in replacing the tears in the girl's eyes, Lyle looked cowed, and even Ian refused to meet her gaze directly; yet she'd done all this with a tone of love, and I suspected she'd not trade this family for any other.

"Well, Anne," Lyle said, "I suppose you've already met Mrs. Blum, our beloved housekeeper. Now, I think we'd best be gone before we're eaten by this dragon," he gave the woman a fond smile, "but have no fear, there'll be time for talking later." He drew his sister from my side and moved toward the door, while the woman moved to set her tray in front of me.

"I can't thank you all enough," I said softly in a voice heavy with emotion.

"We're glad to render aid, my lady," Lyle said gallantly, bowing as he ushered the others out. Only when Ian turned to look back at me for a moment did I remember I hadn't thanked him for rescuing me in the forest.

***

The next morning, after a refreshing night's sleep, I woke feeling much more like my old self. Sitting up, I was just beginning to adjust my bed pillows when the housekeeper bustled in with a breakfast tray.

"'Tis good you're up then! And ready, I imagine, for a hearty meal." Cheerfully, she placed before me a tray laden with food. Then she began adjusting the bedcovers.

"Yes, I am rather hungry today," I admitted, realized as I looked at the heaping platter that I was ravenous. The aromatic smell of eggs and ham actually made me feel faint. Besides that, buttered toast with jam, freshly squeezed juice, porridge, and a pot of steaming tea completed the meal.

I began eating with relish, while Mrs. Blum went singing about the chamber, dusting and drawing curtains as she moved.

"Eat as much as you can, love, and don't feel bad about it. You need solid food to get your strength back. Master Lyle and Mr. McCrae are out and about the estate this morning, and I'll not let the likes of 'em back in your room, but Miss Sarah wonders if you'd be feeling up to a visit later?"

"Oh, yes," I answered between mouthfuls, "I'd like that. She seems such a sweet girl. I'd like to know her better."

"Aye, lass, Miss Sarah is a good child, but plain as a Derby mare and rather frail. Doesn't get enough fresh air and sunshine, if you ask me. She's lonely too. Children should be out and running about, not cooped up in a dreary old house such as this." She clucked her tongue in disapproval as she spoke.

"Why doesn't she have any friends?" I asked, spreading jam on a second slice of toast. Inwardly, I was thinking a girl like Sarah, from a good home and family, ought to have lots of friends. But I kept this to myself.

"Humph, tisn't for me to question the ways of my employer." I smiled a little at this as she continued. "But some folks set themselves above others, and since the Leightons own most of the land hereabouts, Sarah is set apart from the other children. Tis a shame if you ask me."

"Perhaps her health is part of the problem?" I ventured. "Children can be rather rough and unruly at times."

"Humph," she said again, "nothing wrong with her health that a good dose of play wouldn't cure! Well, dear, I must be off about my other duties now. This is a big house, and I'm charged with seeing it runs well! When you've finished with the tray, just put it on the table by the bed, and Nell'll fetch it later."

Then she swept out as quickly as she'd entered. I liked Mrs. Blum very much, and despite her complaining, I couldn't imagine her ever being really angry with anyone.

Finally, I'd finished every bit of food on the tray, and was beginning to wonder what I was going to do with the rest of my day, for I didn't feel in the least bit tired. Turning to set the tray on the table, I noticed a small leatherbound book lying there. I picked it up, and opened to the title page. *Le Morte d'Arthur*, it read in a finely lettered gold print. I'd never heard of this particular story-- Rev. Jaspar wasn't fond of literature-- but I had heard of a King Arthur when we'd studied Geoffrey of Monmouth's *History of the Kings of Britain*. But this book, from what I could see after scanning through it, seemed to be some sort of French romance.

Wondering to whom it might belong, I returned to the front cover. "You reflect the true meaning of the word friendship," it read, and was initialed I.M. So, did the book belong to Ian, or had he perhaps given it to Lyle or Sarah? Surely one of them must have put it here, but when, for no one had a book when they came in yesterday? Somehow, I didn't think Mrs. Blum had brought it. Who'd been in my room then?

"How ridiculous," I said aloud, "surely it doesn't matter who left the book. It's obviously here for me to enjoy, and so I proceeded to enjoy it.

Within minutes I had immersed myself in a tale of kings and queens, lords and ladies, and Knights of the Round Table. Never had I read anything so fascinating! Only with great effort did I manage to tear my gaze away to respond to a quiet knock at the door.

"Come in," I said, and immediately saw Sarah's solemn blue eyes peering around it.

"Do you feel like having company for awhile?" she asked politely.

"Yes, of course. I'm feeling much better today. I've been looking forward to your visit." I set the book aside and held out my hand. She came to the bed and clasped it warmly in return.

"I'm so glad you're better. I've been so excited about having someone near my own age in the house. I do hope we can be friends."

"I hope so too, Sarah."

"Oh, you've been reading. What's the book?"

"It's about King Arthur and the Round Table," I replied, "it's very enjoyable. I thought perhaps you'd left it for me."

"No, twasn't I. It's my favorite story though. You mean you've never read it."

"No, I haven't."

"Gosh, that's something. Lyle's been telling me the story since I was a baby. Have you got to the part about Lancelot and Guinevere yet? No, well, just wait until you do. It's so romantic. He's the most dashing, handsome, wonderful knight there is and she simply can't resist his charms even though she's married to the king."

"How sad for Arthur," I murmured, questioning inwardly how any woman in the kingdom could resist his charm.

"Wouldn't it be wonderful to know a man like that?" She sighed wistfully, lost in young dreams of her own knight in shining armor.

I immediately thought of Ian, then brushed that picture aside, for while he might seem to be a knight in shining armor, his true self was not so pure as I knew from my encounter with him. But Lyle, that might be another story...

"He reminds me of your brother," I said at length, remembering my first impression of him, so handsome and angelic.

Sarah giggled. "That's funny. Lyle, like Lancelot? He's not a bit like that. Lyle is definitely a King Arthur, if you ask me. He's much too conventional and gentlemanly to sweep anyone off their feet. Now, Ian," there was that sigh again, "Ian is really a man of passion. I could easily imagine him as Lancelot."

I smiled, wondering what Sarah could possibly know of passion. I sensed she had a schoolgirl crush on Ian McCrae, and perhaps was holding on to the hope that he would wait until she grew up and marry her. And who knows, maybe she was exactly what he was looking for?

I, on the other hand, couldn't remember ever having a crush on anyone. No one in Countisbury had ever seemed worthy of girlish daydreams; never before had I known men of any stature. Besides, love hadn't been a consideration for me; I'd always expected to remain single, to be forced to make my own way in the world. My dreams had held a prince, but what prince would want a woman who knew nothing of her origins? They were nothing more than a young girl's foolish desires. For a moment in a tavern in Taunton, I'd let myself believe a real man might want me. But that hope had been quickly shattered.

Was Lyle married, I wondered? He hadn't mentioned a wife and surely she'd have been introduced if she lived here too. It seemed a little odd for him and Ian to be alone here with Sarah. Where were her father and mother? Curious, I prodded her for more information.

"Well, most of the time they're in London. You see, Father's in diplomatic service at the Foreign Office and Mummy finds the country tedious, so she stays there with him. The city air is bad for me- I'm always sick when I go to

London-- so Lyle usually remains here to manage the estate and look after me."

"And what about Mr. McCrae?" I asked, growing more and more intrigued. "Is he related?"

"Oh, no," she stressed, "he and Lyle went to Oxford together for a year, but Ian had to leave when his family lost their money. That's why he's here. He's working to rebuild his fortune. He has a beautiful old castle in Scotland, but it's closed now because he can't afford the upkeep."

"How sad for him," I said softly, thinking I sounded like a repeating parrot.

"Yes, it is, but he'll be rich again some day. He can always marry someone with a lot of money." She gave me a knowing look, confirming my impression that her sights were set on him.

Just then a young servant girl of about fifteen whom I assumed was Nell popped her head in the door. "Air ye done with ye're tray yet, mum?"

"Yes, I am. Thank you, Nell."

"Ye're welcome, mum," then to Sarah, "Ye're wanted in schoolroom, Miss Sarah. Rev. Little is 'ere for yer lessons."

"Oh, dear, I'm afraid I must go see that boring man now, Anne. May I come back later?'

"Of course, my dear. I'll be eagerly waiting," I answered as she and Nell exited the room together, closing the door on me and my thoughts of poor Ian's misfortunes. At least Sarah's story had helped me put aside my own troubles for a bit, but now I began to think once more about what I should do when I recovered. And what should I tell them about my plight? Sooner or later they were bound to ask.

"Oh, well," I said aloud, "time enough later for figuring that out." Perhaps there would be a job for me somewhere in this house, a maid or seamstress perhaps. I certainly possessed the skills for tasks such as those, and Lyle Leighton had seemed a kind man. For now, the visit with Sarah had tired me more than I'd imagined, so turning over, I lay my head against the soft pillow, and closed my eyes to the worry and frustration I felt certain lay ahead.

The forest was all around, and I ran through it, surrounded once more by suffocating grasping trees. Suddenly, right before me, loomed Martin Rollins, hands outstretched, eyes gleaming. The malignant laughter, and then, "Think you've escaped me, don't you my dear Anne? You haven't, you know. I'll find you. Just wait and see. Just wait and see."

Again the laughter then stumbling away, I fell into the arms of another man. A man's golden curls bent to touch mine as our lips met The embrace turned from gentle caress to passion, and opening my eyes, I saw it wasn't the blond man who'd kissed me at all, but the dark one, the brooding Ian, whose gaze frightened me with its intensity. Once more, the suffocation, and I pulled away, struggling against its death.

"No!" I cried out, "No, No!"

From out of the darkness I heard a familiar voice, Maddie's voice. Her words were muted, and strange, and I didn't understand their meaning.

"Choose carefully, my dear. Choose very carefully."

***

A strange noise startled me into wakefulness, and a room filled with moonlit shadows. With trepidation, I looked toward the door, and saw that it was partially open. That same door had been shut earlier! I distinctly remembered Nell closing it after she took out my supper tray. Had someone come back after that? Surely not, as I'd told her I felt tired and planned to go to sleep immediately. I slipped out of bed, shaken by a slight dizziness as I did, but determined, I moved toward the opening.

The hallway beyond my chamber stood dark and ominous, and appeared to be empty. Perhaps the noise had only been my imagination, working overtime after such a vivid dream. But no, it couldn't be; for abruptly, out of the dark, came the distinct sound of footsteps on a hard wooden floor. Stealthy, quiet footsteps--as if someone didn't want to be heard. Who could it be? And why had he or she come here in the middle of the night?

Feeling a sudden chill, I closed the door, locking it securely, then returned once again to the warmth of the canopied bed and restless, troubled sleep.

Chapter 8

. . .What sweet thing can match with thee,
My thoughtful Comforter?
Emily Brontë

The next few days passed gray and sluggish as I felt; I had no desire to do anything more than stay in the canopied bed and recuperate. After my strange nighttime experience, a sense of foreboding remained and I fancied I heard sounds in every dark corner. During the morning hours I often had a visit with Sarah, but afternoons she spent in lessons with Rev. Little so I, left to my own devices, either read or did a little needlework, amply supplied by Mrs. Blum. Occasionally Sarah would return after the evening meal and bring her own sampler, then we sat in serene solitude, passing the time quietly and without event.

The housekeeper, true to her word, did not allow Lyle or Ian to visit the bedchamber where I had taken residence again. "You need to rest, lass. There'll be time for the likes of 'em when you're recovered. They've their own work to keep them busy anyway."

So I, resigned to her well-meaning interference, began to look forward to the day when I could share their interesting companionship once more.

From my evening visits with Sarah I learned quite a lot about the estate and was eager to be up and about on a tour of the place myself. The house sounded magnificent, dating back to the 1600's, and her descriptions of the grounds were oddly reminiscent of Countisbury's landscapes. Rolling hills and hedgerows, and a battleground not too far away where, although she couldn't remember the name, she told me an important military action had occurred.

My curiosity strong as ever, I wanted to see it all myself, including discovering exactly which battle had been fought there. I tried not to think about the fact that I might never have a chance to see more than this one room. They'd all made me feel so at home here, the idea of leaving was almost more than I could bear.

My friendship with Sarah was progressing especially well; in fact she actually did confide to me that she thought perhaps her parents might have 'plans' for her and Ian, and this didn't disappoint her at all. Of course she worshipped her brother but, next to him, Ian was probably the most wonderful man in the world, and she couldn't wait until she was old enough to marry.

I guarded my tongue carefully on this subject, and indeed, I wasn't sure exactly how the thought of Sarah marrying Ian made me feel. Actually, I couldn't imagine any two people more mismatched than the dark, brooding man and this mousy little girl.

At any rate, I kept my own counsel and simply advised, "Don't grow up too fast, Sarah. You should enjoy your youth while you can. Not everyone has so much as you do to be thankful for.

"Did you, Anne?" she asked.

"No, not really," I replied. "I never really knew my parents."

"How sad for you. . .was your adopted family good to you?"

I laughed a little at this. "Well, I wasn't really adopted by a family. I was taken in by a minister. Unfortunately, he wasn't particularly fond of children."

"Oh, Anne, how dreadful for you." She rose from where she sat and came to my side, giving me a kind embrace. "Well, I love you, and I'm so very glad you're here. I never had a real friend of my own before."

"Thank you, Sarah," I said, feeling a bit misty eyed. Having you say that makes me very happy." And indeed, I did feel loved but more than that, content, in this place which again made my thoughts leaving all the more painful.

On the third day after I'd 'come back to the land of the living,' as Mrs. Blum so aptly put it, I found myself feeling much better and planned to get out of bed. Dismayed, I realized I had no clothes! The nightdress I wore seemed a little too big for me, and I'd assumed it was borrowed from Sarah's mother. Perhaps they'd left something else for me. So that particular morning the housekeeper entered with the breakfast tray to find me diligently searching an empty wardrobe for something to wear.

"Mrs. Blum," addressing her politely, more than a little embarrassed at having been caught rummaging about in someone else's closets, "would it be too much trouble for me to borrow some type of dress from you?" I looked at her short, plump form doubtfully. "Until I can get something of my own. I guess you know I didn't have my own bag when they found me."

"Aye, child, I noticed that indeed, but far be it from me to question the actions of others." She shook her head back and forth while settling the tray on a table. "Ye've naught to worry though. Master Lyle brought down some of his mother's old things from the attic, and while they're a wee bit out of the mode, I've 'ad Nell take 'em up for you, and I think they'll be a good fit. I'll 'ave her bring them now if you like."

Moisture gathered at the corners of my eyes. I reached out to her and she came to where I stood and hugged me warmly. "Everyone here has been so good to me," I said, "and I'm a stranger, discovered in rather unusual circumstances. I don't know how I'll ever repay you."

"Well, child I've always been something of a mother hen, and from the looks of you, a bit of mothering wouldn't hurt." She brushed a spot of wetness from my cheek. "You'll tell us all when you've feeling more capable."

"Yes," I said softly, "I promise I will."

"As for the others, dear, well, Master Lyle always seems to be takin' someone under his wing, if you will. When e was but a boy, 'e'd bring home stray dogs and cats to torment me and 'is poor mum, but now it seems to be people 'e gathers in. Why, look at Mr. McCrae and all 'e's done for that one."

My curiosity perked at the mention of Ian's name. "Yes," I said, "Sarah mentioned his family had lost their fortune."

"Humph, lost indeed. Gambled and drank away by a no-good father, it was. Then 'is grandmother who had some money of 'er own took off to God knows where and left them without a word. 'Er fortune might 'ave helped Ian rebuild, but she did nae even bother to stay and see what was to become of her grandson. Tis a cryin' shame if you ask me."

"What happened to his parents?" I asked, better able than Mrs. Blum to understand abandonment.

"Well, they lived in the family castle for a while, even though the money was running out. 'Is mother caught pneumonia in that big, cold place and died these five years past, and last winter, well, 'is father came to a bitter end." She shook her head in disapproval causing me to wonder about the end of Ian's father. "That's when Master Lyle persuaded 'im to close the castle and come 'ere. 'E pays him a decent wage for helping manage the estate. Maybe someday Mr. Ian will be able to go back to 'is homeland."

"Does he miss it a lot?"

"Aye, 'twould seem so. My own mother was Scottish, so we've shared a tale or two. I know he'd love to put aside the pain and make his home into a happy place again." She paused and we both fell silent, each lost in thoughts of our own. I wasn't the only one who'd had a difficult life--others had suffered too. My heart gave in to Ian a little in that moment.

"So, lassie, I can't stay 'ere gabbing all day. Must be off to my duties now. I'll send Nell with the clothes. Later perhaps you'd feel like sittin' in the garden for a spell. Nell can 'elp you downstairs if you need. And I know of two young gents who'd be especially glad of your company." She gave me a grin and a wink, and I laughed in return.

"Yes, that would be very nice, Mrs. Blum. And thank you again, ever so much."

Some time later, seated comfortably amidst a sea of later summer roses and brilliant rhododendrons in my lovely 'new' dress, I couldn't stop thinking about my good fortune in being brought to this house. Perhaps fate had decided to be a little kinder to me.

When Nell had entered the room earlier, bearing a gown of rose-colored linen, I'd drawn my breath in at its loveliness. Never had I owned anything so attractive--it reminded me of Maddie's portrait with its tiny gathered waist and sweeping full skirt. Not only that but she'd also brought a full white petticoat to wear underneath, and tiny satin slippers a shade darker than the gown.

"I'm afraid to wear all this finery," I told her slowly, gently fingering the delicate beauty of each item.

"Well, mum, I jus' hopes yew doen mind wearin' a dead woman's clothes," Nell said as she helped me put the garments on.

"Dead woman?" I asked, startled. "But I thought these things belonged to Lyle's mother?"

"Oh, and for certain they did, mum. 'Is mum was the first Lady Leighton. Sir Roderick remarried some fifteen years past. Lady Gwendolyn's Miss Sarah's mum, but not Master Lyle s 'Is mum 'uz Lady Caroline."

"Oh," I responded dumbly. "How did his mother die?"

"'Twas awful sad, miss. She 'ad consumption, tha' fever, yew know. Took 'er in a flash, poor thing."

"I'm surprised Sarah never mentioned it," I said.

"Well, you know Miss Sarah She idolizes Master Lyle, and if she ad 'er way, 'e'd be 'er brother for sure, and not jus' ahalf. As for 'imself, Lady Gwendolyn's pretty much the only mother 'es ever known. 'E wuz only a wee lad when 'is real mother died, least that's what Mrs. Blum says, and she's been 'ere long enough to know. I've only been 'ere three years, meself."

She gave a final brush to the soft fabric, looking pleased with the results. "Now miss, shall I 'elp you with your hair?"

"Oh, would you Nell? That would be very kind of you. I'm not very good with it, and I'm sure it must look an awful mess right now."

"Sure miss, no trouble tall. I do Lady Gwendolyn's when she's 'ere from London, so ah've' 'ad a bit of experience. Not that anything ever pleases that one, for sure."

Still, Nell's voice was full of pride at doing the lady of the house's hair. "'Ah'll pull it back with this ribbon," she said, magically producing one from her full apron, "then a few curls at the sides, and you're ready."

A few moments later, I met a stranger in the long mirror. A pale girl, with wide timid eyes and a small pink mouth, slipped into a fairy-princess dress with a waist so tiny a man could have spanned it with his hands. Its tight but charmingly cut bodice highlighted not the bust of a girl, but of a woman, and my blonde hair curled delightfully at the neck of the gown. I felt reborn and wondered if I would ever be that lost abandoned child again.

Now, sitting in sunlight strained through gray clouds, I marveled at the recent changes in my life. In less than a fortnight I'd gone from someone with only one person in the world that cared about them, not counting Charlie, to someone who had a whole family! Or so it seemed. These people had been so good to me, but soon I must tell them the truth, and surely that would mean leaving. Perhaps if I explained to Lyle and asked for employment he would be generous. But I was only 17, a minor, and my guardian could demand me back at any time. What was I to do?

I breathed deeply drawing in the fresh fragrance of the garden as I tried to recapture my happiness of only moments before. Gazing around, I let myself slip from the present into the world of nature, the world I loved so well, and watched in wonder as a graceful delicate-looking butterfly lit on the edge of the settee inches from my hand. I closed my eyes. High above in one of the elms, I heard two sparrows debating the problems of the day, and a cool, refreshing breeze barely stirred the leaves of shrubs and plants around me. What a wonderful spot! How happy Maddie would be for me to be in such a place!

At the thought of her, my mind went back to the dream of a few nights ago. "Choose carefully," Maddie had said, but what did that mean? Then it had seemed she meant choosing between Ian and Lyle, but that was ridiculous, for the choice was not mine to make. "Oh, well," I said aloud, "it was only a dream, after all."

But if I ever did have to make such a decision, was there really any question whom I would choose? Opening my eyes, I stared up at Leighton Hall. Here stood all I'd ever dreamed of in a home. Ancient brown, moss-covered stones had held up these walls for hundreds of years. The house itself, according to Sarah, was Elizabethan. It would give you a real sense of pride to belong to a house like that, I thought. Slender turrets reached upward, tall and stately against the sky, and the long mullioned windows twinkled in the early sun. A glass covered dome shone at its west side, probably the conservatory where all kinds of plants and herbs were grown, according to my young friend. From what I'd seen of the inside on my way downstairs with Nell, Leighton Hall was nearly as big as the village of Countisbury and filled with more valuables than I'd ever thought existed.

But none of it seemed to have gone to Lyle's head.

Someday he would be lord of all this, yet he remained able to see the needs of others and offer them shelter and comfort in their times of trouble. How wonderful it would be to be cared for by a man like that--and to live in such a home! I sighed a wistful sigh when suddenly someone spoke from behind me.

"Dreaming of your knight an shining armor?"

Turning, I saw Ian standing nearby, a slow smile playing at the corners of his full mouth, as if he found my reverie amusing. I took a moment to study him before answering, noting again his dark features, sensing a warmth even from where I sat. The heavily lashed eyes surveyed me in like a hawk, intent on every movement of its prey.

I won't be intimidated by him, I thought. Who is he to intimidate me, anyway?

"Yes," I said in response to his question and, stretching my arms, pulled myself into a sitting position. "Even I have dreams. But how did you guess what they were?"

"I noticed the book," he answered, indicating the open volume that lay forgotten in my lap.

"Oh, yes. I'd planned to read but became so involved in enjoying the day I forgot I'd even brought it down."

A lengthy silence gathered around us. "It's about King Arthur," I said finally. "Did you leave it for me?"

"Perhaps," he answered evasively. "Are you enjoying it?" I nodded. "Quite. He was a king but he never forgot to be a person first. He was strong but generous and warm as well."

"How true. But unfortunately his generosity led to his downfall. Because of his giving nature, he lost not only his wife but his kingdom as well."

"You're very cynical, Mr. McCrae." I said bluntly. "Still, if he hadn't been so generous and trusting, neither could he have been the great king that he was. Don't you agree?"

"Touché, my dear Anne, and you may call me Ian since I've yet to discover your last name. Even so, it was his downfall." His words held a warning undertone, and I felt he was talking about more than just the book.

However he continued, outwardly calm, "You seem very educated, which is surprising for a tavern wench."

I bristled. "I am not a tavern *wench*, Mr. McCrae."

"Oh, and what are you then, lassie?"

"A girl left in unfortunate circumstances," I replied, determined not to share my story with him. Just then I was rescued for further comment, for Lyle entered the garden.

"Ian, there you are. He stopped abruptly and stared at me, eyes taking in every inch from head to foot. His mouth opened in surprise, then after a moment a smile spread across his face.

"I knew you were lovely, Anne, but I hadn't suspected anything such as this. You are definitely the most ravishing creature I've ever seen." He bowed gallantly and I blushed, confused and embarrassed by such flattery.

"I am yours," he went on, "to command."

Suddenly I giggled, thinking of the conversation between Ian and me a few moments earlier. The knight had appeared! Looking Ian's way, I noticed that his skepticism had been replaced by a half-hearted grin. "Sir Knight," I laughed, "go forth then, and do battle with yon wicked dragon, and if you win, I shall grant you a favor."

"At once, my lady,' Lyle replied, grabbing a garden hoe and moving toward Ian. "Back, evil dragon. Thou shalt not harm my lady fair."

The scene had an odd familiarity about it, as Ian sidestepped Lyle then cheerfully came at him from behind, playfully capturing him in an easy vise then relieved him of the hoe. Soon they were both laughing at their own antics and I wondered at the bond between them, how they'd come to be so close for they seemed to be such different types of people.

"Well, fair lady," Ian teased, "your knight seems to have failed you."

"Oh, but I haven't, old friend," Lyle answered, still laughing, "I'll rescue this fair damsel from distress yet." Then, turning serious, he came to where I sat and kneeled next to me. "Anne," he said softly, "I'd like very much to help you with whatever situation you're in. But I can't do that until you tell me about it."

I lowered my gaze, trembling.

"Won't you trust me, Anne? Please."

"I do trust you," I said, meeting his eyes. "It's not that at all. It's just that it's so very difficult. I don't really know where to begin."

Ian cleared his throat and suddenly I remembered he was still present. I paused uncertainly.

"I think I'll leave you to talk alone," he said abruptly, then spun around and left the garden.

"You don't have to be afraid of Ian, my dear," Lyle said gently. "He's as concerned about you as I am. He wants to help, too."

I wasn't sure this was the case but I certainly couldn't share this feeling with Lyle. "I'm afraid it's a very long and complicated story," I said instead.

"And I have all the time in the world." He settled himself casually on the ground near my feet and waited patiently for me to speak.

Hesitantly, I proceeded to tell him my tale, beginning with life in Countisbury, my unknown origins, growing up in Rev. Jaspar's household, and finally my trip with Martin and its outcome. The only portion I omitted, and I'm not sure why, was my encounter with Ian at the tavern.

He listened in silence and with utmost interest until reached the part of the story where Martin tried to attack me, and then his anger burst forth unrestrained.

"That stupid old man!" His eyes gleamed as he spoke, surprising me with the intensity of their passion. He rose from his reclining position and began to pace back and forth in front of me. "How could he have sent you away with a stranger? A grown man at that! And you, a young woman, defenseless! I'm appalled at his insensitivity. A man like that has no right to be called your 'guardian.'

"I suppose he thought it would be all right since Martin was his cousin's stepson." I put in softly, feeling a little obligated to defend Rev. Jaspar.

"That's no excuse whatsoever! You're a woman, attractive and innocent of the world. He should have known that and seen to your protection. Goodness, Anne, you saw how Mrs. Blum watches over Ian and I when you're around! She's probably peering at us from some window right now!"

I had to smile at his allusion to the housekeeper. Indeed she was a gentle tyrant and I knew Sarah would be well-protected in her care. As for Lyle, I was amazed at his defense of me. We hardly knew each other, yet here he stood, proclaiming me a woman, not a girl, and not only protesting my treatment but ready to do battle for me if need be. My knight in shining armor indeed! Yet I knew I shouldn't allow myself to become too attached to Lyle. Soon I'd have to leave this place, or at best be reduced to a serving position, in which case it would never do for us to be friends.

Finally he spoke again, calmer, pulling me away from my thoughts. "I leave it to you to decide whether or not to tell him where you are. I cannot in good conscience return you to such a person. Until you fully recover and decide what to do, you're welcome to remain here as our guest."

I smiled at him gratefully, and he approached the settee once more, kneeling at my side. Taking one of my small hands in his large strong ones, he gazed at me for a long time, and I wondered if what I saw was the beginnings of something more than friendship. But surely not, for he and I scarcely knew one another.

"You're safe, Anne. While you're in my care, I'll see to it no one harms you. I promise you that." Something about his look confused me, and I turned away.

"Perhaps you might have work for me. I sew very well and have had a good education. At least my guardian saw to that."

"Hm," he said thoughtfully, and his stare still devouring my face, "we might have something. But later, my dear. There'll be time for all that. First, you must make a complete recovery. Agreed?"

"Agreed." I smiled, feeling much happier and at ease. Someone wanted to look after me and suddenly my future seemed brighter and better than ever before.

Chapter 9

The desert moor is dark; there is tempest in the air...
Emily Brontë

And so I began a new life, growing stronger as the days passed, but facing with each more and more uncertainty about my future. At first it was enough simply to be cared for and accepted, to experience having a family since I never had before; but eventually concern began to set in, for I didn't believe this wonderland existence would continue forever. Living in such a beautiful home, wearing lovely clothes, being cared for and protected--everything seemed so perfect. Surely it must end.

Fortunately, this was my only worry for the present. The frightening nightmare in which Maddie had told me to "choose carefully" hadn't reoccurred, nor had I been bothered further by dreams of Lyle and Ian. The footsteps in the corridor faded into the past; I simply started locking the bedchamber door against intruders and therefore was not disturbed again. In fact, I realized with rather subdued surprise, since leaving Countisbury I hadn't even been plagued by my "voices", except for the night at the tavern. I felt grateful for this; my current worry was enough. Not knowing when the nightmares might return, though, made my relief rather wary.

***

The day following my confession to Lyle, Mrs. Blum entered my room, came straight to the bed, and pulled me to her breast. "You poor lass," she cooed. "Master Lyle confided a wee bit o' your troubles, but don't you concern yourself, I'll kept 'um to meself. My heart just breaks for you, child, but have no fear, you're safe here, and Master Lyle will think of some way to help you out. I've known him from knee-high and he's a good man, that one."

My eyes brimmed. How could I respond to such kindness? I found on attempting to speak a voice shaky, groping for words. But the housekeeper merely shook her head, patting my shoulder gently. "No need to say a thing, lassie. I understand. We all do."

"Oh, Mrs. Blum, "I muttered, returning her hug. "You don't know how much that means to me."

"Well, at's about time you had some love in your life, I'd say. It's been pretty lacking in that area up to now."

I smiled a little. "Except for my friend Maddie, I guess it seemed it was. But I certainly feel cared for now. And I can't ever thank you all enough."

"Humph," she said in that way of hers, "no thanks needed. We're all glad you're here lass."

But were they *all*? I wondered later. What about Ian? I had the distinct impression that he was suspicious about my coming here. Thought me a fortune hunter, no doubt. Oh well, perhaps in time he'd come to know me better. That is, if there was to be time for knowing me better.

A day or so later Mrs. Blum suggested I might like to begin taking meals with the family. In the absence of the master and mistress, she explained, they usually bypassed the formal dining room for smaller eating quarters near the kitchen. I was glad about this, for although Nell had presented me with two other dresses, courtesy of Lady Caroline, my wardrobe still wasn't adequate for formal dinner attire. I soon felt quite comfortable, however, eating in the quaint setting which Sarah referred to as the Breakfast Room. Sunlight poured through large windows, cheery flower boxes framing their view, as we sat around a white oval-shaped table. The whole place normally seemed alive with light, situated directly next to the conservatory as it was, but if the day was gray, Mrs. Blum lit glass lanterns with daintily painted globes, making the room shine once again.

During my second meal there Lyle asked if I would be up to a tour of Leighton Hall. "You don't mind taking charge of things this morning, do you Ian?" he asked the other man.

Ian scowled, but continued to eat. "No," he said quietly. Lyle turned to me once more. "What do you think? Are you up to a long walk about the place?"

"I'd love it," I responded enthusiastically. "I'm staring to feel a little like a caged bird. Normally, I spend quite a lot of time outdoors."

"Do you ride then?" Lyle asked.

"If one could call it that... I guess I do. I had a pony named Charlie in Countisbury. But he was wild-- not a thoroughbred. I've never used a saddle."

"No matter. When you're stronger, Sarah will help you learn. If you've ridden a wild pony, you can surely handle our gentle mare Betsy." He laughed. "However did you manage to catch a wild pony?"

I smiled wistfully remembering Charlie and missing him more than a little. "I didn't catch him actually. We just, well met. There seemed to be a mutual attraction between us from the beginning." I looked toward Ian for his reaction and saw, as I might have expected, skepticism. Lyle however, and Sarah, were fascinated. They insisted I tell them all about Charlie, and soon I was immersed in a tale about my home--the home I loved--the moors, Watersmeet, the bluebell laden forest--and feeling more and more homesick for Maddie and the happy things I'd left behind.

Lyle seemed to sense this and after a few minutes changed the subject back to our day's activity. "If you like, we can start after breakfast," he told me.

"Oh, Lyle, may I come too?" Sarah chimed in.

Sternly, he reproached her. "No, you may not. As you well know, Rev. Little will be here at ten and you have examinations today. I expect you to spend time studying for them. Really Sarah, your grades are atrocious, and you promised me you'd try to do better."

"I do try," Sarah wailed, "But Rev. Little is so boring. Why do I need to study anyway? Someday I'll have a husband to care for me, so what do I need lessons for?" She looked in Ian's direction but, head down, he appeared to be concentrating on his meal and nothing more.

"Gracious, Sarah, you're much too young to be thinking about marriage. Don't you care about learning at all?" Lyle sounded exasperated.

"Maybe I would if it was interesting, but all he ever does is drone on and on about mathematics and history and stupid old grammar."

I couldn't help but smile as I listened to Sarah's description of her studies. It brought back vivid memories of my own with Rev. Jaspar. How I'd wanted a teacher who could bring the knowledge to life for me!

"Sarah," I said timidly, "perhaps I could help you with your lessons. I understand how boring they can sometimes be. but I think I might know a way to make them a little more exciting."

"How?" she asked sullenly.

"Why don't you come and see me this afternoon and I'll show you?" I replied.

"All right," she said, brightening, then jumped up from her chair, running from the room.

Ian, too, rose from where he sat, mumbled something about his work, and exited. So Lyle and I were left sitting alone at the table.

"You have a way with her," he told me. "Have you worked with children before?"

"Only helping out some in the village," I answered. "My guardian was an excellent teacher but still, I'm afraid, as boring as Sarah's Rev. Little. I wanted to know everything, however, and apparently Sarah doesn't. I think children like her must be given a reason for wanting to learn. It's just an idea, though. I haven't had an opportunity to practice it."

"So you've considered teaching then?"

"No, not exactly. But I've always seen it as an option. My friend Maddie taught me that each of us has many different choices in life, that we should never feel trapped into becoming one thing or another. Since I've had a good education, I've always known that teaching could be one path I might take."

"Not the one that included marriage and family?"

"I suppose that is another road I might take. But that would depend on someone else as well. Maddie always said we should learn to depend on ourselves first that way we would never be too dependent on anyone else."

"This Maddie of yours sounds very wise." Lyle said, and there seemed to be a wistful note in his voice.

"Yes, she is," I answered softly.

"Well, my dear, perhaps someday you will have the opportunity to pick the path of your choice--should it be in teaching or love..." He gave me a smile. "Would you like that?"

"Of course," I said returning the smile, "I suppose everyone likes to think they will have many opportunities to choose from in life."

A short while later we began our tour of Lyle's home. I knew from what little I'd seen already that it was a grand place, but I hadn't suspected the actual "grandeur" of it. Lyle explained proudly that it had first been constructed during medieval times and updated as the years passed, the additions giving it the present E-shaped floor plan.

From the breakfast room, Lyle took me on a quick inspection of the kitchens at the back of the house, "modernized quite a lot since the 1600s" he told me as he proudly pointed out the large black ovens where meals were cooked, an indoor pump, and shiny brass utensils hanging about the room.

I met "Cook", as he called her, a fierce-looking older woman with steel gray hair and a perpetual frown who appeared even more cross at our entrance into her domain than she'd probably been moments earlier. She did cheer up a little, however, when I commented on the delicious meals I'd partaken since arriving at Leighton Hall.

"You certainly know how to charm people," Lyle said, grinning when we left the room. "You'd make a wonderful politician's wife." We both laughed, and I think I must have gone quite red at his compliment.

Since I'd already seen most of the west side of the ground floor, my guide then led me across the tiled floor of the Great Hall toward the east part of the house, pointing out as he went his family crest, a stag and unicorn, horns locked in battle, which he said was quite ancient, tracing back to Roman occupation in Britain. Although the Hall was chilly, something more than cold penetrated my bones as I looked at that crest. Some flicker of recognition, something I knew but had forgotten.

Moving on, I looked again at the twisting oak staircase with its lovely carvings, and remembered the first day I'd come down those same stairs, marveling at the magnificence of this place. I still felt awe at the splendor and wondered how Lyle managed to be so nonchalant about all this.

"This is the formal dining room," he told me as we entered a cold room with high, vaulted ceilings, paintings of cherubs and angels gracing its walls. "My step-mother redecorated most of the house after she and my father married. She has very good taste, don't you agree?"

I nodded, although inwardly I shuddered, feeling almost overpowered by the tall marble columns, heavy dark furniture, and magnificent chandeliers; in fact, even the angels appeared to be unhappy about something. How could anyone ever feel comfortable eating in these quarters, I wondered.

Next, Lyle led me down a long hall adorned by what I was certain were priceless paintings in gilt frames, to the library. The rectory in which I'd grown up could have fit easily into this one room, its walls lined with more books than I'd ever seen in my entire life. Though it was daytime, dark red velvet drapes shut out most of the light, giving the chamber a dark and foreboding cast; and whereas in the dining room I'd felt overpowered, here evil gathered round, teasing, taunting me, and I breathed a sigh of relief when Lyle suggested we move upstairs toward the gallery.

There I came face to face at last with Lyle's ancestors. He led me slowly past each one, recounting a little of their history, until finally he stopped before a somber fortyish-looking man with clear blue eyes, who reminded me very much of Lyle himself.

"Sir Andrew Leighton," Lyle said proudly. "He led a brigade against Monmouth's Rebellion. I come from a long line of military heroes, as you can see. But this man... he's special to me." He paused briefly and I waited for him to continue. "You see Anne, Sir Andrew didn't want to be a soldier. He wanted to farm the land, bring it to life, help his tenants help him. Unfortunately, his timing was all wrong."

"Why was that?"

"Most of those same tenants were fighting against him in the Rebellion. He had to go to war or lose his lands forever."

"What finally happened to him?"

"What happens to most soldiers?" Lyle asked bitterly. "He was killed in battle. And so his sons took up the cause and continued to fight, thus his dream was lost."

"And what about you?"

Lyle had a faraway look in his eyes. "My dream too is to farm this land. Ian is helping in that respect, and for now, my father is content to let me be. But some day I, too, will most likely be called to do my 'diplomatic duties'

I touched his arm. "Remember, Lyle. You do have options."

Again I saw the wistful, sad smile. "Unfortunately, it's not so easy for me Anne. Because of all this" He indicated the room and the portraits around us. "I'm my father's only son and heir. I have obligations, and I must, to a certain extent, follow his wishes."

"An unwilling ruler," I said, "like King Arthur."

"Yes," he said quietly, turning inward for a moment, "yes, something like that."

His light eyes penetrated mine, searching, asking. We stood very close, so close I could almost feel him breathing. Suddenly, I knew he wanted to kiss me, and I thought I wanted to kiss him too; to know complete safety, complete warmth, to share a man's love as I never had.

Remembering what had happened with Ian though, I held my ground, and in the next moment fate intervened in the form of Nell. "Master, Lyle," she said, curtsying quickly, "Rev. Little's waitin' for yew in the library. 'E said yew wuz expectin' 'im, sir."

The glazed look faded from Lyle's eyes. "Yes, thank you, Nell. Tell him I'll be right down." Then he turned to me, patting my hand gently. "I'm sorry, Anne, but this shouldn't take long. Do you mind waiting?"

"Of course not," I responded. "I shall spend the time better acquainting myself with the rest of your ancestors."

He laughed. "Or you could take your exercise here, which is what they used to do. At any rate, the three portraits on the end are my father and his two wives. They have name plates, so if you'd like, you can acquaint yourself with them while I'm gone then we can finish our tour when I return."

"They sounds fine," I answered, smiling as I watched his retreating form. Lyle was such a good man, I couldn't help thinking. Truly my life had been blessed when he entered it.

Slowly I moved out of my reverie and toward the paintings at the other end of the hall. Focusing on the woman to the left, I read below the picture, "Lady Caroline Leighton." Lyle's mother. She'd been a lovely woman, all sunlight and brightness like her son. Soft, golden curls fell gently around her neck, and her cheeks blushed against pale white skin. There was a sad look in the blue eyes, wistful, like the one I'd seen on Lyle's face earlier today. Had she known she would die young, I wondered? She looked like a person I might have enjoyed knowing, and I wished for Lyle's safe she'd lived a full life.

The man next to her had little of Lyle about him. Sir Roderick was large--a sturdy, strong man; a determined, impatient look glared across the bearded countenance. He wore fashionable dress and was well groomed, but aside from that, I saw nothing distinctive about his appearance, except the bluish-green color of his eyes, which bothered me for some reason.

On his other side was a body-length painting of Lady Gwendolyn. This picture both drew and repelled me. Of course she was beautiful--thick auburn hair flowed to her waist, loose, and she wore a dressing gown cut so low I wondered why her full, pale breasts didn't tumble from it. Her green eyes glittered, following my gaze over the portrait, and her mouth curved into a tight little smile, teasing, tempting, yet somehow hard and unyielding. The artist must have known her well, for he'd captured an intimacy that seemed more than casual acquaintance. I shivered under this visage, undeniably afraid.

Suddenly, I couldn't breathe. The gallery had turned to winter, and my chest heaved up and down. I drew in large gulps of air, but they dissipated before filling my lungs, and struggling, I moved toward the window. Locked.

Then the voices started. Louder than I'd ever heard them. I covered my ears, wanting to drown their clatter. Two men again, fighting, arguing violently. A woman, between them, pleading. And someone else was there, I felt a presence then a loud uncertain but deafening noise, followed by silence. Utter, complete silence. I had to get out of here. Now...

I ran down an unfamiliar corridor; hadn't Lyle mentioned that this part of the house wasn't used? Thank God. I didn't want to be seen and stopped in my endeavor. I had to get out. To nature. To air. To Maddie. There must a door somewhere. Sure enough, at the bottom of a length of stairs it beckoned. Please, dear God, don't let it be locked too. But strangely, it flew open easily when I turned the knob, and just beyond it, hanging from a peg on the wall as if waiting, was a heavy, dark cloak. Without thinking, I took it down, throwing it across my back as I ran.

The crisp, cut lawn seemed to stretch on forever, but I flew across it, past the garden, over a bridge, finally through the thick, green hedges that enclosed Leighton Hall. Only then did I begin to feel the air rushing back into my chest. Slowing my pace, I inhaled, thankful for the simple joy of breathing, for being free, for the safety of the moors I hadn't even known were there. Granted, they weren't the same as mine, but moors they were, and my heartbeat slowed as I stood amidst the heather, letting the familiar scent of it carry away my fear. Why I'd felt so unreasonably frightened in the gallery, I didn't know. Under the open sky, it seemed rather childish; now, almost giddy with happiness, I dropped to the ground, gathered my arms full, savoring the soft silky caress of the flowers against my cheeks, content. A fine mist hung in the air, but I didn't care. The cloak was warm, though yards too large for me; still, only the warmth mattered at the moment.

I lay in the heather for a long while, never noticing the expanding grayness of the day. My breathing became an easy rhythm and dream waves flowed over me--of Charlie and Maddie, my other animal friends far away on the Devon coast--What might they be doing today, I wondered? Thoughts of Rev. Jaspar and Mrs. Rickett even crossed my mind at one point, but I brushed them aside, only happy things today. No more sadness or anger or fear or uncertainty. Here I was free from all that--here I was complete. Hadn't Maddie said I should return to nature to answer my questions? I was beginning to understand what she meant. Walls would never hold me. I somehow knew I would always be afraid of walls, of captivity, but among the hills, I could experience peace--even in the midst of grayness and rain.

Just then I realized that indeed a storm was brewing; thunderclouds gathered like an army grouping itself for battle. The sky had grown darker, lower, and threatened to burst forth in fury any moment. God, how I loved it! In Countisbury I'd never been allowed out during a thunderstorm, but here, there wasn't anyone to tell me no. Still, I had been ill and the others would be worried, especially Lyle, who had surely returned and discovered me gone by now, so I decided with little joy to head toward the manor.

As I rose from the soft cushion of ground, it occurred to me abruptly that I wasn't sure from which direction I'd come. Several little groves of trees bordered this open space; Leighton Hall might be through any of them. How had I managed to lose my way? I felt rather foolish. Heavy droplets had already started falling from the sky, so, turning toward the nearest grove, I began to run. Just as I neared its edge, a black form loomed before me, rearing, whinnying loudly, as startled and surprised as I.

"Easy, Titan, easy boy. Whoa, now." Ian's voice remained calm, but his eye burned their fury into me. When at last he had the animal under control, he took me to task. "Damn you, lass. You could have killed us both. What on earth are you doing out here?"

"I...I went for a walk," I stammered.

"A walk? In this weather? You've been ill, fool girl. What did you hope--to kill yourself?" His look enveloped me--wet hair, clinging cloak, thin slippers--

and I returned his stare, taking in the dark curls already damp across his brow, the firm line of his square jaw, the long lashes that framed the angry eyes.

Finally, he held out a hand. "Get you up, now, and I'll see you home before the storm gets worse."

"Thank you." I said, thoroughly embarrassed that he, of all people, had caught me in this predicament. He pulled me up in front of him, and I felt his strength as he curled a sturdy arm around my waist.

For a moment he sat without moving, and after a second I realized he was breathing deeply, his face almost pressed into my hair. At length he nudged the horse forward, never speaking, and the slow, easy rhythm of its gait lulled and relaxed me. Then abruptly, without warning, I had an almost uncontrollable impulse to turn around and throw my arms around Ian, to hold him, kiss him, not as I wanted to kiss Lyle earlier, but intimately, passionately, to be devoured by the very heat of him. With the greatest effort I fought against this urge. Just as I felt certain I had lost, was out of control, would further make a fool of myself before this man who thought little enough of me as it was, the moment passed. We had reached the relative safety of Leighton Hall, and Lyle stood anxiously waiting by the gate.

Chapter 10

All day I've toiled, but not with pain,
In learning's golden mine
Emily Bronte

"Where on earth have you been?" Lyle's concern was etched on his face, while I stood, still shaken, and watched Ian's silently retreating form. He hadn't spoken a word when helping me down from his horse, and merely gave a curt nod in answer to his friend's questioning gaze.

Turning back to Lyle now, I tried to put my thoughts into perspective. "I went for a walk." I gave him a feeble smile. "I'm sorry, Lyle. I honestly didn't mean to worry you. But it wasn't storming when I left, and well, I simply felt a need to get out. It seemed rather stuffy in the gallery. Can you forgive me?"

He'd taken my arm and led me through a massive oak door at the front of the Hall that I hadn't seen before. Despite the queer sensations lingering behind from my odd encounter with Ian, I couldn't help but notice this further indication of the house's magnificence.

Lyle responded as we passed through the doorway. "Of course, my dear. You're free to come and go as you please while you're here. I just..." he broke off, and we paused, facing each other in the cold hall. "It's just I thought perhaps you'd run away. That you hadn't believed I truly want to help you" He gestured around the room. "That all this had frightened you. But mostly that you'd gone." His eyes dropped to the floor; I stood, openmouthed, marveling at his sincerity.

Automatically, I reached out and touched his arm. "I won't run away." I whispered, "You don't know what your kindness means to me. I have no desire to flee from it."

He met my look then, and in that moment, I knew with certainty he thought of me already as more than just a friend; that I was beginning to be special to him thought I couldn't imagine why he should feel that way. We'd known each other less than a fortnight--how had he come to care for me in that short amount of time? He knew so little about me. I knew so little about myself.

But it was all there in his eyes, and again I knew he wanted to kiss me, but this time held himself in check. "You must get out to these wet things right this minute. I don't want you to have a relapse, my dear. I'll send Nell up to your room with hot water for a bath, and some warm broth, then we'll talk at supper." He paused for a moment as if debating whether or not to say more. "I have some rather interesting news to tell you. Do you still think you'll feel up to seeing Sarah later in the day?"

"Of course," I answered. "I really am fine. The cloak kept me fairly dry. Thanks for the use of it." I removed the garment, noticing briefly the long curious look that Lyle gave it.

Slinging it over his arm after a moment, he went on. "Why don't you rest for an hour or two after lunch, then I'll send Sarah up to show you the way to the schoolroom." He grinned. "We didn't finish our tour. No matter though, there'll be time for that. Anyway, I'll meet you both in the schoolroom and escort you to dinner. I can share my news with you and Sarah both then. All right?"

"That sounds fine, Lyle. You have me quite intrigued."

"So you should be, my dear. I hold the key to your future in the palm of my hand." That look again, but for some reason I felt the first stirrings of discomfort and lowered my own head this time. I heard Lyle's voice, as if from very far away. "I promised you'd be safe with me, Anne. And safe you shall be." Then without further adieu, he pointed me in the direction of the room that I'd almost come to think of as my own.

Dry, rested and refreshed, I could nearly believe the experiences with both men existed only in my imagination. Now the only adventures that interested me were those of King Arthur, and I sat reading when a light knock announced Sarah's arrival.

"Lyle says I'm to show you to the schoolroom?" she told me glumly, then noticing my book, "Couldn't we just sit and talk about Lancelot and Guinevere instead? That's much more romantic."

"Your brother says he has a surprise for us. It may be something we don't want to miss."

Intrigued by the thought of a surprise, she swept me out the door and into an unfamiliar corridor toward the schoolroom. For some moments it was all I could do to simply to concentrate on the twisting turns the girl took--and keep her in my sight. I noticed, however, the delicate brass and crystal lamps that graced the paneled walls leading into the unknown oblivion. Glad I was for their light, too, for I couldn't quite shake the eerie feeling that crept over me when I walked the darkened halls. I felt both drawn to and repelled by this house-its grandeur impressed and drew me in, yet at the same time a gloom pervaded it that I couldn't seem to shake.

When Sarah finally pushed open a door that led into a room with large airy windows, several desks, and shelves laden with books, I breathed a sigh of relief. At last we'd reached our destination.

Since my host had yet to arrive, I moved toward the shelves of books, searching until I found what I was looking for. Pulling it down, I opened to a large world map, then turned to Sarah, still sulking near the window. "So you want to talk about King Arthur now?" I asked her.

Facing me, her look registered surprise that I'd heard her question at all. "Could we, Anne? It's my favorite story, you know."

"Yes, I do know, Sarah. But haven't you ever wondered how it all came about--why the country needed Knights of the Round Table, where Lancelot came from, what started another war?"

"Well, sort of," she said, approaching the desk and the open book warily.

"Look, here we are on the map. Now, as legend has it, King Arthur was born here, at Tintagel on the coastline. Have you even been to Cornwall, Sarah?"

She shook her head.

"Neither have I, I'm afraid. But look, I'm from Devon. It's also on the western coast. See, just here," I indicated the spot, "and not so far from Arthur's birthplace. So I can tell you a little about what it's like there. Then we can talk about some of the history behind Arthur's rule and why he ended up befriending someone like Lancelot, who was from France and came all the way across the Channel to serve with Arthur."

By this time Sarah was enthralled and for the next hour we sat side by side at the desk, pouring over the large atlas, discussing the king's travels, what his life must have been like during that time period, why he went to France, and on and on. When Lyle finally arrived with an announcement that it was almost time for the evening meal, we'd both forgotten the present existed so immersed were we in a world of the past.

Lyle stood over us for a moment, smiling strangely at our intensity. "I knew I'd made a good choice," he stated, beaming at us both.

"What?" Sarah and I "Choice about what?"

"Your new teacher."

"I didn't know I was to have a new teacher." Sarah grew glum again.

"Oh, but indeed you are." Lyle teased. "Did you like Rev. Little so much you wanted to keep him forever?"

"No," she said sourly, "but at least I'm used to him."

Lyle laughed out loud and I, too, had to smile at the girl's predicament. "Well," he went on, "I think I have someone better in mind."

"Who?" she frowned, unable to imagine such a thing as a 'better' teacher.

"You're studying with her right now!"

At this we both looked up sharply. The words, "Me!" and "Anne!" rang out simultaneously, causing Lyle to break into a fresh peal of laughter.

"Yes to both of you," he said gleefully. "Yes, yes, and yes! Remember this morning, Anne, when Nell came to say that Rev. Little was here? Well, I spoke with him about it then, and was coming to tell you when I discovered you'd disappeared!"

"Anne disappeared?" Sarah interrupted.

"Yes, but she only went for a walk," Lyle said impatiently. "That's not important. What matters is *what* the good Rev. and I discussed. You see, Anne, his duties in the parish keep him very busy--he doesn't have a curate at the moment--and he's only been helping Sarah as a favor to me. So when I told him about you, he was overjoyed!"

"But Lyle, you hardly know me, much less whether or not I'm qualified to teach your sister!"

"Don't be ridiculous! Of course I know you! I know I've never met anyone as kind, caring and intelligent as you in all of London society. And as for your educational qualifications, well, Rev. Little has already agreed to test you regarding those, and prepare you to take up with Sarah where he'll leave off."

"Oh, Anne, please say you'll do it!" Sarah begged. "It would be so wonderful! You'll be my teacher and my companion. Please Anne."

I looked at the two happy faces before me. How could I ever refuse such kindness? "Well," I said, "I'll try. But if I don't pass the Rev.'s exams, I couldn't possibly accept. And Sarah must agree to work very hard and not let you down, Lyle. Agreed?"

"Yes!" they said together, all smiles.

Dinner that evening was a gay affair in all but one quarter. Ian's scowl became even more obvious at Lyle's announcement of my upcoming appointment as governess to Sarah. He remained silent for the better portion of the meal, but Lyle and his sister, oblivious to anything other than their own excitement, continued laughing and planning for my prolonged stay at Leighton Hall.

"You'll need some other clothes," Sarah pointed out.

"You can't go on wearing Lady Caroline's old things forever. Lyle," she turned to her brother, "I think you should advance Anne part of her salary, so she can purchase new things."

I gasped at her forward behavior, certainly something to be worked on in my future sessions with her, and turned to Lyle at once to countermand the suggestion.

He, however, raised his hand in rebuttal. "Sarah is absolutely right, Anne. You will need new things to wear. And soon I'm sure you and she will be going on outings together which will most definitely require some suitable attire."

Ian surprised us all by interjecting a statement own at this point. "Why doesn't Miss Cowper retrieve things from her guardian?"

Lyle turned a disapproving glare on his friend. "You know the situation Ian."

"All right, I know the situation. But surely her guardian needs to know she's safe, that she's found work. And," he looked directly at me as he added, "that she needs her things. Unless perhaps there's some other reason you don't want to contact him, Miss Cowper?"

I was about issue a retort to this when Lyle spoke again.

"And what if he should insist that she be returned to him?" he demanded.

Ian shrugged. "Why should he? Sounds to me like he wanted nothing better than to be rid of the lass."

"Ian!" Lyle snapped.

By this time I was sure I must be beet-red, for listening to their argument made me angrier by the minute. How dare they act as if I wasn't present? Wasn't I capable of making my own decision? And Ian--the man had some nerve to make such a rude, uncalled for remark in my presence. It incensed me. He was right on one count, though. I should let Rev. Jaspar know where I was. And ask him to forward what little I'd left behind. At least I could make due until I accumulated enough income to purchase new apparel on my own. I'd accepted enough from Lyle already.

Turning, I said to him with a controlled tone, "Ian's right. It's time I wrote Rev. Jaspar. I'll do so first thing in the morning." The dark-headed man at the opposite end of the table raised a curious eyebrow at my statement.

"It isn't necessary, Anne." Lyle's tone conveyed irritation. "I've told you how I felt about that. The man doesn't deserve to hear from you after what he put you through."

"I know Lyle, but I will send word. Don't worry. I'm sure he'll be satisfied knowing I've found employment."

"And if he isn't," Sarah chipped in, "we'll tell him we're holding you ransom, and then ask for so much money he'll never be able to pay."

With that we all laughed--even Ian managed to emit a small chuckle--and the unhappy mood was broken for the rest of the meal. I wondered though, what response I might receive from my guardian when he learned what had become of me.

The following fortnight was a busy, happy one for me. After writing my dreaded letter to Rev. Jaspar, I pushed thoughts of its response aside and concentrated on the task at hand. We'd agreed I should have some time to prepare myself for Rev. Little's examinations, so I spent afternoons in the schoolroom, reviewing Sarah's textbooks after she and her teacher had finished morning lessons. During those mornings I occasionally retreated to the library to do research of my own. I still didn't like that room, and avoided it as much as possible, often borrowing large volumes and laboriously toting them back up to my bedchamber to study. I saw very little of Lyle or Ian--both appeared to be very busy about the estate and had usually gone out by the time I appeared for the morning meal. Evenings, I often took a tray in my room. Passing the examination had become very important to me; I wanted to live and work in this house, with these dear people, and in order to accomplish that goal, I must do my best on the test.

The hectic activity of the passing days provided little opportunity for me to think of anything besides my studies. I forgot the encounter with Ian, even refused to believe that

Lyle might have deeper feeling for me than I was ready to accept. Occasionally, if these memories threatened to creep in, I pushed them back just as the child who had been myself had done when unbidden thoughts of the past attempted to sadden me. The future would take care of itself, I thought. And for the moment I was free--free as I'd always dreamed of being--with people who cared about me, who laughed and lived as I'd wanted to live.

When the day of the exam arrived and I passed with flying colors, I actually felt all my dreams had come true! That event behind me, I began to spend several hours each morning in the schoolroom with Rev. Little and Sarah, watching his instruction. We'd agreed that it would be easier for me to have lessons in the morning and other activities in the afternoon. Then, after the lessons, I reviewed with him what she had covered thus far and we decided which direction her studies should proceed. In looks, Rev. Little reminded me somewhat of my guardian, but in disposition they were as different as night and day. His kindness to me was remarkable, but he seemed almost relieved that his time with the girl was nearly at an end.

"There are people in the village who need my attentions," he told me one day, "and Sarah is a daydreamer who isn't interested in lessons at all. Half the time her thoughts are elsewhere, as I'm quite certain you've noticed. You'll have to find a way to control that, Miss Cowper, if you want to make any progress with her." He spoke in a kind, helpful way, for he knew I was young and inexperienced and this was my first post. "Any time you need me, feel free to call at the vicarage. I'll help in any way I can."

"Thank you, sir," I told him sincerely. "I'm sure I'll be needing your advice often."

"Oh, you'll come along well, my dear. Just remember one learns by one's mistakes, so have no fear on that count." And so he left me to finish preparations for my first day as a governess.

"Are you with me, Sarah?" I paused expectantly. "Sarah!" I moved to her desk abruptly, rapping on it. "Your head is in the clouds again, I fear."

After two weeks of teaching, I was beginning to realize it wasn't as easy as I'd expected. Some lessons simply weren't interesting, no matter how hard I tried to make them so. And my student, disinterested as she was, often let her mind stray beyond the open window, shutting out both my words and form. The gray silk (Lyle's other contribution) rustled as I bent over my pupil's blank page. 'You're supposed to be doing arithmetic, Sarah, not gazing at the sky."

"Oh, Anne, but it's such a gorgeous day. Couldn't we take a walk now? Please?" Another drawback of being on friendly terms with my student was that she expected leniency.

"Sarah," I said, summoning authority, "you know that mornings are for lessons, afternoons for exercise. If we go out now, you'll be too tired later to work and the whole days' studies will be lost."

"Please, Anne. I promise I won't be tired. Just this once. Please." Her eyes implored, and I felt like a mean, spiteful old woman instead of someone only a few years older than she, who would like to be out enjoying the day as well.

"I'm sorry, Sarah, we just can't. You're already behind in your lessons and I don't want to waste any more time. Rev. Little is trying to keep you in pace with other children your age, and it's important we stay on task. I tell you what though, I have an idea that might appeal to you."

"What?" she asked glumly.

"How would you like to be rewarded for your efforts and attention?"

She looked at me suspiciously. "Rewarded how?"

"If you promise to concentrate and work very hard for the rest of the week, on Saturday we shall stop our lessons and ask Mrs. Blum to prepare an alfresco luncheon for us. How does that sound?"

"Could we do it every Saturday?" she asked, suddenly interested.

"Every other Saturday," I compromised, "provided that you've worked hard the previous two weeks." Delighted with my momentary flash of brilliance, I continued, "and perhaps you could choose a good spot for our outing. Agreed?"

"Oh, yes, I know just the place. That sounds wonderful. Do you think maybe Ian could go with us? And Lyle too, of course?" She smiled at me knowingly.

"Perhaps," I answered hesitantly, "but first you must prove that you're willing to work for the treat, then we'll do the planning."

"Of course," she said importantly, then busily set about proving what a good scholar she was. I smiled as I watched her work.

A short while later, we were again interrupted by Lyle's entrance into the schoolroom. We both looked up, surprised to see him at this hour of the day.

"Lyle!" Sarah said excitedly. "Guess what? We're going to have an outing on Saturday. I have to concentrate and do well with my lessons, then Anne will let me off on Saturday for an alfresco luncheon. And you and Ian are invited."

Lyle raised a curious eyebrow and I laughed. "Sarah and I have a bargain," I told him.

"Oh. I see. Well I for one shall look forward to the event."

I blushed and turned my gaze toward the window.

"So what brings you in this early, Lyle?" Sarah asked.

"Ah, my pet. I've been in the village to retrieve the post, and I have a letter that I thought might interest you. And perhaps Anne too, for she's mentioned in it."

I shrank inwardly. Word from Rev. Jaspar had come.

What if he insisted I return to Countisbury? I didn't think I could bear to leave Leighton Hall!

But before I could speak, Lyle continued, setting my mind at rest. "A letter from Mother. Sarah. To you and I. Shall I read it aloud? That is, if Anne doesn't mind the intrusion?"

"Not at all," I said, breathing a sigh of relief. 'Please do."

Lyle seated himself casually on the corner of a desk and began reading. "Dearest children," Lyle seemed a little old to be referred to as a child to me, but no matter. "I was pleased and excited to hear of your new friend," the letter continued, "and look forward to meeting her when I return to Leighton Hall. Take good care of her and make certain she doesn't leave before I am able to make her acquaintance.

'Your father and I are well, although he's been a little tired as of late, and I'm sure would profit from a visit to the country. I plan to speak with him and will let you know our plans.

Until later, my loves, kisses to you both, and give my regards to Miss Cowper. All love, your Mother."

An interesting letter, I thought, and wondered that she should mention me twice, and asked them to be sure I didn't leave before she met me. What kind of person would Lady Gwendolyn be? Would she and I get along? I hoped so, for I had a feeling one would not want her for an enemy. Something about her look had troubled me in the gallery, and just now I had once again felt the stirrings of disquiet as Lyle read her letter. I didn't believe I would relish her return, and said a silent prayer for Sir Roderick's health.

Lyle and Sarah, however, had fervently begun to discuss their parents and both seemed eager to see them once more.

Sarah turned to me excitedly. "Perhaps Mother will be able to go on one of my outings, Anne."

"Perhaps," I answered, "but first you must prove yourself worthy of the event, and I think we should attend to your lessons now if you're going to be able to accomplish that feat.'

"Hint taken," Lyle said gallantly and, giving me a friendly wink, swept from the room, leaving my pupil and I to complete our morning's work.

***

Shadow fairies danced along the corridor as I made my way to the library later that day, loaded down with borrowed volumes. The evening meal was just over, and I'd decided to take this opportunity to return some of the books I had been using for my study. Reaching the library, I realized the room was not empty; voices sifted out the partially opened door, and I turned away, planning to complete my errand some other time, when I recognized that Ian was speaking.

"I don't trust her," he was saying, and I knew at once he must be talking about me. "You need to be wary."

Who could he be speaking with? The other voice was muffled. Was it Lyle?

"Damn it!" Ian exploded, "You can't mean that. Do you realize what that would involve?"

Again I failed to hear the response, then both voices fell to a lower level and, not wanting to be caught eavesdropping--which is exactly what I was doing even if I hadn't meant to--I slipped back down the hall toward my chamber.

Ian must be very suspicious of me. And yet, if he wanted to check my story, all he had to do was write to Countisbury. In fact, if and when my guardian's letter arrived, it would be proof of my sincerity. Now that it came to mind, I wondered why I hadn't heard from him. I'd written almost a month ago. Could it have been lost in the post?

I've been so happy, I thought I don't want it to be spoiled. I'll wait a bit before I write again.

Tired from lugging the heavy books around, I sat down on the stairs for a moment, resting. I still found myself a little weak from my illness.

"Anne, are you all right?" Lyle's voice interrupted my thoughts.

I looked up, surprised to see him. Had it been someone else in the library after all? "I'm fine," I said, "just taking a rest."

He took note of the volumes beside me. "You shouldn't be trying to carry heavy things about. One of the servants can do that. Or me, for that matter."

"It's all right. I borrowed them. I should return them."

Lyle laughed. "You're wonderful, my dear." He seated himself beside me on the steps. "I don't think I've ever met anyone quite like you. So self-sufficient and determined." He gave me a long look "And yet, you have a sort of elusiveness, a mystery that's more than just your curious background. It's part of your essence, I think."

"I hope that's a compliment," I returned.

"Oh indeed, it is!" His voice took on a more serious note. "Anne, I'd like to know you much better as a person." Reaching over he touched my arm, then clasped my hand in his gentle grasp. "I've seen that you're intelligent, kind, sincere, but I still don't feel I know you as well as I'd like. There's still the mystery. I'm very much looking forward to the outing with you and Sarah."

Again I felt the odd panic that seemed to close around me when I was alone with this man. I shivered a little.

Lyle, mistaking the movement, went on. "You're cold. And here I am-- letting you sit in a drafty hall." His arm went around my waist, gently, and he helped me to my feet. "We'll talk more later, my dear." And with that he took the books from the floor and heading in the direction of the library.

***

I suppose it was only natural I should dream that night. I'd had a strange day after my overheard conversation, then the experience with Lyle. The dream was brief, but I woke in a sweat, still shaking with fright and that other treacherous feeling. I'd been with a man; I don't know who, his features were unclear. There had been ecstasy between us, shared lust, passion, and the heat of his embrace had carried me away on a tide of some unknown emotion. I'd known it was wrong but had only pulled him closer, tingling with the pressure of his hands on my breasts, his kiss against my neck. And then I'd felt the evil, the danger, death, closing in, smothering, smothering, destroying. And suddenly, behind the stench of it all, I saw my own face.

Chapter 11

Waking sounds revive, restore again,
The hearts that all night long have throbbed in pain.
Emily Brontë

The hour was early; I crossed the garden like a wraith, fully dressed and draped in a shawl loaned to me by Mrs. Blum when I was ill. The chill of the morning air signaled the nearness of winter, but the cold within me was greater I'd had to get out, away from the house, to clear my foggy brain before beginning lessons with Sarah. Last nights dream had still been with me when I woke; in fact, I'd never really slept after it, merely tossed and turned in anguish and confusion. Finally I'd risen with the sun, hoping that the fresh bloom of heather and the sounds of birds and trees in the breeze might calm me.

I knew nothing of passion, nothing of love--except for Maddie--and yet the previous evening I'd dreamed of being with a man. In a very physical way. I wasn't that naive--I lived in the country--I'd watched animals. I knew what happened between men and women. But it had never happened to me, so how could I know the ecstasy of such an encounter? And yet, I knew, at some point, at some time, the events in that dream had happened.

As I walked along a rose-laden path, I began to remember my last conversation with Maddie. We had spoken of another dream I'd had. It could be a vision of the past or the future, she'd said. Why did I know last night's experience had been from the past? Or was it simply that I wanted to believe that? Surely I wasn't evil, I couldn't be a bad person.

But the dream must be an indication of something awful from the past. I felt this with certainty and it frightened me. I'd wanted that man, wanted him more than I'd ever wanted anything; and yet it had been wrong. "Maddie," I said softly, more to myself than anyone else. "I wish you could help me now, Maddie." I crossed a little wooden bridge leading into a grove of birch trees.

Suddenly I had the feeling I wasn't alone.

"Will I do instead?" Ian's voice asked from out of nowhere. "You startled me," I said, as he fell into step beside me.

"I'm not surprised. It's awfully early to be wandering about, isn't it? But then, you seem to wander quite a bit, don't you Miss Cowper?" I heard the suspicion in his tone once again.

"I walk when I haven't slept well." It irritated me need to respond to his unspoken accusations.

His head jerked around, and he stared at me for a moment. "Neither did I," he said finally. "And I felt the need of a walk as well. Now that we're both out, we may as well go together, hadn't we?"

"I suppose so," I answered reluctantly, and for a short while we strode in silence, enjoying the quiet of the morning. The grass was still damp with the early dew, glistening like tiny diamonds against a velvety case. A gentle breeze stirred the trees and I glanced up, strangely content, to gaze at sunlight streaming through their branches.

"It's a lovely day," I said to Ian, smiling as the beauty of the day swept away my irritation.

"Yes, and what knight in shining armor will you attempt ensnare on this lovely day?"

Something in the way he asked the question indicated he was plying me, sarcastic and inquisitive. "You don't like me, do you Mr. McCrae?" I inquired bluntly, tired of all this nice pretense with him.

Stopping, he turned and faced me. "I want Lyle to be happy."

"And why shouldn't he be?" I asked.

"I don't know, but he seems to have become taken with you rather quickly, and he really doesn't know much about you, does he? Probably not even as much as I do..."

My temper sparked and I glared at him angrily. "And just what is that supposed to mean?"

"I think we understand each other quite well. I'm referring to a certain night at the Ram's Head, when you made your intentions all too obvious."

I wanted to strike him for that, but determined not to let him see any sign of my emotions, I turned and started to walk away, towards the manor. I could feel his eyes burning into my back, then abruptly, he turned and quickly was upon me. He grabbed my wrist, his fingers tightening as I struggled to free myself from his grip.

"Not so fast my pretty lass," he said, the dark eyes bearing into my own. "Didn't you want something like this that night?" With that he pulled me to him, crushing his mouth to mine, bruising my lips with his harshness. For an instant, we clung together, drawn by some animal force such as that passion I'd felt in my dream. Then, breathless I managed to draw back, summoning strength as I did to strike out at him in fury.

At first he looked surprised, then he laughed, mocking and cold, and his voice reminded me hauntingly of another. Martin Rollins. The fear of the night and my dream and the man who'd tried to attack me before were all upon me at once. Would I have to flee now as I'd done then? Please, God, no, I thought. I wanted to stay here. I didn't want to run away again.

Suddenly Ian seemed to be aware of my distress, he stopped laughing and looked at me steadily. His dark eyes studied, then he spoke in a voice so soft I could scarcely make out the words.

"I'm sorry, Anne. That was inexcusable. It won't happen again." Then he turned, a dark form disappearing through the trees, and after a moment, the garden was so quiet it seemed difficult to believe he'd been there at all.

I sank down on a bed of soft grass, breathing a little more evenly now, letting my composure slowly return. Recalling Ian's accusations, my anger began to stir anew. How dare he imply that I was attempting to seduce him that night at Ram's Head? Or that Lyle need be cautious of me? I shuddered violently. This man had saved my life once, rescued me from humiliation yet another time--why had he bothered at all, I wondered.

My tongue flicked across lips still tender from his roughness. My first kiss, I thought indignantly. Why couldn't it have been from Lyle? He would treat a woman with respect. Ian McCrae. The name was etched in my mind. His troubles didn't seem to have mellowed him. He was brutal and unkind, and to my way of thinking, no better than Martin Rollins.

At that thought I shivered once more. Why then, had I felt something when Ian kissed me? There had only been revulsion when Martin tried the same thing. Yet with Ian, I could almost believe I was dreaming despite the morning's light. But I detested the man! Could that be why I'd sensed evil in my dream? It wasn't I--it was *he* who was evil--he and Martin both. The dream had been a warning. Surely that must be it!

Still, I wouldn't let either of them drive me away from here. I was beginning to think of this as my home--Sarah needed a friend, I provided that for her, perhaps Lyle needed one as well. God only knew what a man like Ian might want from Lyle. His suspicions of me might only be a cover- up for his own treacherous activities. Yes, Ian would bear watching. I was beginning to discover I, too, could be fiercely loyal to people I cared about, and if pushed, Mr. Ian McCrae might find in me a worthy adversary.

As Lyle, Sarah and I stretched out like lazy cats in the shade of several ancient oak trees enjoying our luncheon, nothing could have been further from my mind than Ian McCrae. No troubles would be allowed to torment me today. I wanted only to feel the warmth of the sun on my face, the cool breeze across my skin. No thoughts of untrustworthy men, nightmares, or future uncertainties would be allowed to disturb my composure. This hour was to be held for enjoyment alone!

Thanks to several afternoon riding lessons with Sarah, and an old habit, courtesy again of Lady Caroline, we'd been able to ride horseback across the moors to this lovely hillside. The sidesaddle didn't particularly appeal to me; I missed the freedom of galloping Charlie over rugged slopes--Betsy was a rather fat, slow old thing--but oh, how wonderful it was to feel my curls pulled loose by the wind, and the solid earth swaying beneath the horse's gait!

Sarah had chosen the spot, and I had to admit she'd done well, for not only was it shady and quiet with a babbling brook just down the hill, there was also an excellent view of the Hall and grounds from this spot. Pale blue flowers dotted the fields between us and the trees of the manor, and the house itself was shaded by their green, yet standing stately and grand like a proud defiant

Briton. From our perspective I could see that its east side was covered with thick coats of ivy reaching almost halfway up the walls. Mullioned windows set within the turrets reminded me of sparkling jewels in the noonday sun, and flowery gardens surrounded the place, a circular rainbow, that made the scene look more like a painting than an actual setting.

"This is the best place on the whole estate," Sarah told me gaily, twirling around like a top while I stood next to her, gaping at its splendor.

"Like it, Anne?" I heard Lyle whisper at my other side.

"It's like a fairy tale castle!" I replied sincerely.

He threw back his head and laughed. "Now how many fairy tale castles have you seen, my dear? But thank you all the same. Sarah and I are proud of our home, aren't we Sarah?"

"Truly, we are," she said, returning his smile. I was glad to see that she'd recovered from Ian's refusal to accompany us. I'd been afraid she wouldn't for a while.

"But why, Ian?" she'd asked, "Can't your work wait until tomorrow?"

"Tomorrow's the Sabbath, lassie," he'd told her, pulling a strand of her hair, "I must get to Langport today, for we've a shipment coming in. Perhaps next time I'll be able to go with you."

"Do you promise?" she asked glumly.

"I promise, lass," he said, giving her straight hair another tug. Then he'd stolen a quick look across the room toward me; we both knew the reason for his refusal to accompany us. That suited me--I had no desire to spend the day in his company.

Now, Sarah seemed much better, happy and ready to enjoy her hard-earned day. She had worked her fingers to the bone preparing for this outing, and I was pleased and impressed with her efforts.

Mrs. Blum had certainly cooked up a feast for us. The basket had been filled with smoked venison, still-warm bread coated with butter and laced with cheese, and fresh strawberries and cream to top it all off. We washed our spread down with gooseberry wine, the best I've ever tasted, after which Lyle and I were content to simply recline beneath the trees, while the girl, free from the confines of the schoolroom, roamed about with her large setter, Nero.

"May I follow the stream for a bit, Lyle?" she asked.

"All right, but don't go too far."

"I won't," she responded happily, grabbing the dog's leash and bounding away.

When she'd gone, Lyle turned toward me, propping himself up on one elbow. His eyes devoured me with tender caresses, and I closed my eyes, uncomfortable under the power of his gaze.

"Having a good time?" he said finally.

"Oh, yes, it's lovely here."

"I think you're lovely." He said softly, and moved to take my hand as it roamed idly among some bluebells growing near our blanket. He brought it gently to his lips, and I trembled a little at his touch, feeling the beginnings of tears.

"What's this?" he asked, sitting up and drawing a hand across my cheek. "I'm sorry, my dear, I didn't mean to upset you."

I wiped my eyes with the corner of my shawl. "No, Lyle, please don't think that. It's nothing you said or did. Well, actually, it is in a way. You're so good to me. So kind. I'm not used to feeling cared for. My friend Maddie is the only person I ever felt really close to." Another tear fell at the mention of her name.

Lyle pulled a handkerchief from his pocket and wiped it away. "You miss her, don't you?"

"Yes, dreadfully. Though sometimes she seems as close to me as you are right now. But I miss talking to her and having her nearby to share my thoughts and feelings."

"I hope you know you can share them with me, Anne. I mean that. I'm here for you." He squeezed my hand tightly then reached up tracing the path of the fallen tear. I smiled, feeling better, at peace with the moment, no uncomfortable stirrings of passion or fear, just simple serenity.

I think Lyle might have kissed me on the lips just then, if Nero hadn't come bursting through the trees, closely followed by Sarah from whom he evidently had broken loose. A dirty piece of cloth hung from his mouth, which she grabbed from him, laughing.

"You silly dog," she admonished, "you should be ashamed of yourself for running away like that. You're a bad boy." She swatted him playfully and he licked her in reply.

"He got away, Lyle, and then he went snooping all over the place and when I caught up with him, he was growling at this stupid old rag." She threw it down and began scratching behind his ears as he continued to lick her face.

Lyle reached down and picked up the cloth, which appeared the shredded remains of a man's handkerchief. "Looks like I've dropped another linen," he said, then after a closer inspection went on, "No, this one isn't mine. Wonder whose it could be?" He was thoughtful as he laid the cloth down next to me, then suddenly, as realization dawned, he reached to pull it away. It was too late, however, for I'd already seen the initials and could feel the nausea rising. Sewn in gold embroidery across the dirty fabric that Nero had found not more than a mile from where we sat were two letters that made my skin crawl--M.R.

Alone in my room later that evening, I tried to make sense of the event. Lyle had been most comforting as we rode back to Leighton Hall.

"Try not to worry," he told me. "It could have belonged to someone else. Besides, Ian found you on the outskirts of the estate not far from Langport, miles from where we were today, so if Rollins were on the grounds, it's possible he was only hoping to pick up your trail. I'm sure he would have come directly to the house had he suspected you were there."

Sarah, listening intently, asked, "Is Anne in some kind of danger?"

"No, little one, not with us around to protect her." He gave me that slow, easy smile of his. "But all the same, let's not be telling any strangers about her, just in case. Can you remember that?"

"Of course, Lyle," she said importantly, "I'm not a baby, you know. Anyway, I'd never do anything to put Anne in danger." Sarah reached a hand toward mine. I squeezed it tightly. "You're my best friend in the whole world--if anything happened to you, I couldn't bear it."

"Nor I you, Sarah." I responded, filled with a warm glow at her words.

But lying alone now, that glow was replaced by an icy chill. What if Martin found me? Could he force me to leave Leighton Hall and go to Cousin Glenda's? Why hadn't he come here directly to inquire about me? And why hadn't I had any response to my letter to Rev. Jaspar? Surely Martin would have returned and told him of my disappearance. He must know they'd all take his word over mine concerning that night at the inn. What was going on?

Maybe Lyle was right and the handkerchief didn't belong to Martin after all. Or perhaps he'd dropped it after losing my trail. For the moment, all I could do was stay here and be watchful. But for how long could I stay? I wasn't going to let them take me away. Not back to Rev. Jaspar. Ever. Not when I'd had this taste of freedom. Shivering at the thought, I pulled the comforter tightly around me and fell into a fitful sleep.

***

"RoseAnne, can you hear me? RoseAnne?" Maddie's voice was calling, but my eyes refused to open. "RoseAnne, you must listen. Listen to me carefully."

I forced my eyes to open halfway and found myself standing in a swirling mist. A few feet away, a cloaked figure stood with a hand outstretched.

"That's better, my dear. I can only stay a moment, so heed my words carefully." The voice seemed to be coming from the robed figure. I tried to move toward it, wanting to see and touch what I knew must be my friend, but my legs seemed disinclined to obey me.

"Don't struggle, child, just listen. You are in grave danger here, but you cannot leave. No matter what happens, you must stay. But be on your guard, RoseAnne. Be very watchful. Your destiny lies in this house, and you must follow its course or you will never find happiness. Do you understand?"

I managed to nod an affirmative reply and struggling to find my tongue, was able to at last utter one word. "Who?"

"I cannot tell you more than I have, my dear. You must follow your heart, but listen with care. Now I must go, go, go..." her words echoed as she faded into the mist, leaving me alone and desperately trying to reach her before she was gone completely.

***

The darkened chamber was aglow with moonlight when a noise from the gravel drive below shook me into wakefulness. The sound grew louder and louder, and as my mind began to clear, I realized it was a rider approaching the manor. I lumped across the cold wooden floor to the window. A rider was indeed nearing the house. How odd, I thought, for nudging from the shadows, it must still be quite early in the morning.

The rider slid from his horse and ran to a side door used by the servants. Urgently, he began pounding against it. Several moments later he was admitted by a white-capped figure. Who on earth could be calling at this hour? I wondered. His horse was in a lather, so he must have ridden rapidly for some distance. I was in the process of contemplating whether or not I should dress and go downstairs when I heard a soft knock at my door.

Mrs. Blum stood in the hall with a candle in hand when I opened the chamber door. "Lord, Miss Anne, you must 'ave been woke by all the commotion. You answered so quick." Her eyes were still heavy with sleep but I could tell something was amiss for she seemed nervous and upset.

"What's wrong, Mrs. Blum? Did something happen?"

"Lord, yes, child. Sir Roderick is ill in London and Master Lyle must go to 'im immediately! 'E said 'e'd like to talk with you for a moment, however, if you don't mind comm' down at this hour. No one's about, so just put on your robe. I think you'd best get your slippers too, afore you catch your death of cold."

She waited in the doorway with her candle as I hastened to don both robe and slippers. Following her down the massive wooden staircase, I noticed for the first time that Leighton Hall was even eerier at night than it was in the daylight. The candlelight cast long, frightening shadows against the walls as we moved along quietly. I imagined it would be terrible to be lost in this house after dark with nothing to guide the way. I shivered both from chill and my own apprehension.

Lyle, fully-clothed by this time, was pacing up and down in front of the fireplace when Mrs. Blum opened the door to the library. Of course this room was worse by degrees than the rest of the house. Tiny, dark figures crept across rows of books and heavily curtained windows, mocking, teasing, threatening to surround me like little dancing demons in an ancient ceremonial rite. I shrank from them.

"Anne." The sound of my own name caused me to start. He crossed the room and came toward me.

"I'm sorry. I didn't mean to startle you. Is something wrong?" The housekeeper had tactfully retired to just outside the door, leaving us along in the semi-dark. I turned and clasped his arm. "No, I'm fine. It's you I'm concerned about. Mrs. Blum told me you father is ill. Is it serious?"

He moved from me and began to pace the room again. "I'm afraid so. I received a very strange note from him. He said he must see me immediately, had to tell me something important, that I should come right away for he was very ill. His writing was shaky. Not like him at all. I'm very worried." Lyle rubbed his temples as if it pained him to think. "I'm also concerned about you. Especially after what happened today."

"I'll be fine. Your father should be your main concern at the moment." I walked to him and touched his arm again.

"Damn it, Anne," he said more roughly than I'd ever heard him speak. "Don't you understand that I'm falling in love with you. If anything happened..."

"Nothing's going to happen to me, Lyle. Martin doesn't want to hurt me, only to take me away. And I'm not going anywhere."

For a moment we stopped speaking, then I added lightly, "Remember, my friend Maddie is watching over me."

He smiled. "And don't forget Ian. He always seems to be rescuing you from one predicament or another. By the way, I'm stopping at the gatehouse before I leave to ask him to keep an eye on you."

I grimaced inwardly at the thought of Ian McCrae watching me but, not wanting to add to Lyle's immediate problems, said nothing.

At any rate, I couldn't leave without letting how I felt and telling you not to worry. I'm sorry awakened you." He took me tenderly in his arms.

"I'm glad you did," I said. "All my prayers will go with you."

Before I could move out of his embrace, he bent his head to mine and began to kiss me with a passion I hadn't suspected in him. His mouth devoured mine, and I felt myself slowly beginning to respond as we stood thus for several moments. Suddenly, he pulled back and stood, enveloping me with the light in his eyes.

"Dear Heaven, but you're beautiful!" He ran long fingers through my unbound hair. "The fire is dancing in your curls, and I wish I could stay here and watch it forever. But if I don't go now, I never will. It's a long ride to London, but I promise you, I'll be back as soon as I can. An arm gently encircled my waist and he walked with me to the door.

"Take good care of her, Mrs. Blum. She's becoming very important to me."

The woman had tears in her eyes, as did I, and turning, we both watched him stride quickly down the hallway. She patted my shoulder sympathetically.

"Don't worry, child. He'll come back to you. He's a good, honest man, Master Lyle. And he deserves to be happy."

Sniffling, I nodded my agreement. Lyle would be back, I was certain of that. What Mrs. Blum didn't know was that my tears were as much for my own uncertainty about his return as they were for my fear at his departure. For once back, Lyle would surely expect to pursue our relationship; and while I definitely cared for him a great deal, I didn't think I loved him. Love was an unknown, uncharted territory, and before I plunged into its depths, I wanted to be sure I understood exactly where that path might lead.

Chapter 12

And sometime the loved and the loving,
shall meet on the mountains again.
Emily Brontë

"But you promised, Anne! You promised!" Sarah's voice was petulant, her eyes pleading as she looked at me across a bolt of fabric from which I was cutting a dress for myself. My first month's wages had allowed me at last to buy a few much-needed items. "So did Ian," the girl went on. "I bet he won't break his promise!"

"Sarah, your father is terribly ill. Surely you must realize how serious that it."

"I know he's very ill, Anne. Truly I do. And I am very anxious about him. But this house has been so dreary lately with news of Father and fall setting in, and well, I need to get out. I feel smothered in this place."

A chord in Sarah's tone touched me; how very well I could understand that feeling of suffocation. Hadn't I experienced the same thing not so very long ago in the gallery of this very house? Lyle had been gone over two weeks, and each day seemed longer than the one before. We'd received word shortly after he arrived in London, but nothing since. According to his letter, after arriving at their flat, he found his father drifting in and out of consciousness, unable to communicate at all with his concerned son. Lyle said he intended to stay on there until the doctors knew something more definite about Sir Roderick's condition. I could tell from his words he felt grave concern for his father.

For the most part, Sarah and I had continued with our daily routine of lessons in the mornings and riding or other exercise in the afternoons. Just now, however, when she'd entered the sewing room to question me about Saturday's alfresco, my suggestion that it should be postponed until her brother's return met stark rejection. I knew she was tired and worried, yet she had kept at her lessons. Perhaps an outing would do her good.

I made myself face the truth--the idea of Ian accompanying us was what truly bothered me. After my last encounter alone with the man, I had no desire for a repeat episode. Perhaps a compromise with Sarah would work.

"Sarah," I countered, "perhaps we could have tea in the village with Rev, and Mrs. Little? I should like somewhere to wear my new dress when it's finished. And I know they'd both enjoy seeing you again."

This plan didn't cheer the girl at all. "But I want an outing, Anne. You said we could. Soon it will be winter, then we won't be able to go. Please, Anne."

Now she was beginning to cry, which really caused me to feel alarm. "You're a liar," she burst out, "and I hate you!" With that she turned and fled from the room, leaving me stunned at her open display of hostility.

Poor child! I walked out, intending to find and comfort her, when I saw Ian standing on the landing below with his arm about her shoulders. Sarah was still sniffling, but her tears were no longer flowing and she gazed at him with shining eyes.

"I'll talk to her, lass," I heard him saying. "Leave the day to me. I promise twill be a fine one indeed." Glancing up at the railing where I stood, he caught my look of doubt and sent me a charming and unexpected smile. What was he planning, I wondered?

After another minute he gave Sarah a quick hug, and pointed her in the direction of the kitchen. "See if Cook's got my favorite pastries for dinner, lassie," he told her rapidly retreating form.

Turning his attention toward me once again, he took the stairs with a brisk stride and before I could move, was standing next to me in the hallway. "Now, don't you be getting angry with me before you've heard my plan, Miss Cowper." I heard a tease in his voice, but a friendly one, not mocking or sarcastic. "The lass is unhappy and we did promise her a day to enjoy." He paused, but raised a firm hand at my attempt to speak.

"I know what you're thinking, but I give you my word of honor that I will be a gentleman. I can be when I so choose, you know?" Doubt continued to remain my most prominent emotion, which he registered with another smile. "There's a place I've been wanting you to see anyway, and this picnic would be a good chance to take you there."

"I don't know of any place I could possibly want you to show me, Mr. McCrae," I replied caustically, certain there must be an ulterior motive lurking behind his kindness.

"Well, we'll be seeing about that, won't we, Miss Cowper? But shouldn't we call a truce for the day? Sarah needs an outing; she should get her mind off schoolwork and troubles for a bit. Don't you agree?"

I had to admit he was right, and said so hesitantly, still unwilling to accept his offer. "Where did you have in mind for the trip?" I asked.

"Ah, now that's to be my surprise. To both you and Sarah. We'll need to leave around eight o'clock, though, for it's a fair piece by carriage. We should return before dark." He turned and began to walk away, calling back as he went, "Dress warmly, Miss Cowper. There's a wee nip in the air these days, and I would nae want Lyle to return and find I'd let you become ill again."

I bristled at his interference and cursed myself for getting into this situation. How could I possibly have let him talk me into going God only knows where with him? At least Sarah would be there, and if I knew her, she'd be chattering to Ian the entire day, so perhaps I might enjoy the time without having too much contact with him. Smiling, I began walking toward the kitchen with the hope of finding Sarah and mending fences. She was to have her outing after all.

Saturday dawned a true fall day--clear and bright, with just a touch of crisp in the air. Leaves of gold, red and orange glittered against the morning sky as we set out in one of the carriages. Sarah sat nestled in front with Ian, while Nero and I rode in back, accompanied by a large picnic hamper prepared once again by Mrs. Blum. Nero's wet nose kept straying toward the basket, and I was forced to swat it several times, until finally, swayed, he stretched across the leather seat, head resting on his paws, for a nap.

Sarah hadn't stopped chattering, as I'd suspected she wouldn't, since we'd left the manor. Every now and then, Ian would turn to look at me, a slow smile pulling the corners of his mouth at the earnest conversation of the young girl. I began to wonder if perhaps I'd been wrong to judge him so harshly. Maybe he truly did want to make amends for his earlier behavior. Lyle and Sarah thought so highly of the man--surely he couldn't be all bad.

When at last Sarah paused for breath, he turned and asked what I thought of this part of the country.

"It's lovely," I answered, "there's a smooth beauty here, quite different from the rugged cliffs and moors where I'm from. I love the rolling green hills with their hedgerows and spots of sheep. It's very peaceful."

"Yes, it is. I wish you could see my Scotland, though. Somehow it manages to capture both rough and gentle. Tis a mysterious land, none quite like it."

"In what way?" I asked, interested in the country Ian had called home.

"Oh, well, we have the jagged hills and rough heather moors, but the vales are smooth and green, with crystal ponds, teaming with fish And more than that, the people themselves seem hard and tough on the surface, but deep inside they're a kind and gentle folk, with uncanny intuition and a certain ability to see beyond what's right in front of them."

"What part of Scotland are you from?"

"The highlands, near Deeside, not too far from Devil's Elbow. Tis lovely as a painting there--pine wood forests with floors of soft fern, and purple heather in the fall, and if you've a wee bit of luck, you'll spot a rare sprig of white amongst it."

This reference to the heather brought pictures of other before my eyes, and they brimmed at the memory of peaceful hours spent on the hills near my village.

Sarah, who'd been sitting rather silent through this exchange, broke in abruptly, "What's the castle like, Ian? Tell us about the castle."

"Ah, lassie, tis made of the finest white granite, with four turrets stretching tall against a sky of blue deeper than your eyes, and each of them points in a different direction--north, south, east, and west--so the keep was fortified from all sides. They even say Queen Mary spent the night there once and my grandfather had a scarf with her seal upon it. Tis a place to be proud of indeed."

This description of his homeland surprised me. He seemed to have an intense love for not only the castle, but the land itself; I hadn't believed him capable of such emotion.

Sarah intruded upon my thoughts again. "Where are we going today, Ian? Surely not to Scotland?"

He laughed and I couldn't help but notice what a refreshing laugh he had, deep and resounding, yet filled with soft music. His face, though tanned to a burnished glow from work in the sun, lit up when he smiled, brightening the shadows in his eyes.

"Nae, little lassie, not today. Just 'round this bend and through a grove of trees, you'll see where we're going. It's a favorite spot of mine, and tis hoping I am that you and Anne will like it too."

I smiled at the way he'd slipped into the use of my first name. It had a pleasant sound on his lips, and I savored it for a brief moment, then turned my attention to the road before us.

As we passed through a grove of silvery birch trees, I saw ahead a sight I will never forget. A familiar pang exploded in my heart, yet I was certain I'd never been here before. Across a wide vale and the woods still before us, standing tall and bleak and majestic in the distance was a hill taller than any I'd ever seen. Capping its peak was an awesome crown, my eyes filled with tears at the sight of it. Glastonbury--abbey ruins with the Tor rising high above--I'd seen drawings of it in history books, but those had never affected me as the actual sight did.

It was like going home. I knew the hill, the tower; I'd been to that place before and, as I gazed at it now, I knew I was being drawn, compelled by a force greater than any I'd ever known to climb those beloved paths once more.

Quickly, I drew in my breath and cast a bewildered glance toward Ian, only to find him staring at me with an odd expression, penetrating, as if he were trying to fathom the depths of my being. Then abruptly the expression changed and he understood. The world stopped around us; and although the horses plodded on, the dog whined restlessly and the breeze fluttered the leaves of the autumn trees, we were frozen in time, two strangers who suddenly realized that their world--their lives--had been waiting eternities for this one moment. This wasn't the first time we'd come this way, Ian and I, and in a flash of brilliant illumination I knew that where we'd gone before, today we would go once again.

The moment slipped by, and the day seemed to go on as it had, yet I couldn't put aside the feeling that something important had happened to me-- that I was no longer the person I'd been a few hours earlier. Ian wasn't the same. The world wasn't the same. For some reason, I kept remembering things that Maddie had told me; *Life is a circle. We each have a destiny that keeps repeating itself. A soul is immortal.* Those were all little pieces of her philosophy that I'd never really understood until today.

Glastonbury was surely a charming little village, but I have no memory of it at all; my eyes saw only the rising pentacle; I wanted only to feel its earth beneath my feet. As we sat much later in the shade of the Glastonbury thorns finishing our luncheon, I looked around, and once again had the sensation that at some point, in some unspecified time, this place had been close to my heart.

When Ian had reached the site at last, it wasn't the ruins, which drew me, but rather the grave--King Arthur and Guinevere lying side by side in the shade of the crumbling abbey wall. This was the same King Arthur I'd revered in the book lent by Ian yet the pang of sadness I felt standing there seemed greater, closer, more real than the characters in those pages. Still, as I looked on the spot where Arthur was said to have lain, a part of my grief was for the fact that I knew he wasn't there, had never rested there except as a living, breathing man full of vigor and courage. This wasn't his grave, or hers either. Yet my sadness at his passing was real. Curiously, for her I felt nothing.

Ian had been strangely silent during the meal, and even Sarah remained somewhat withdrawn. After eating, he got up and strode away, leaving me sitting, staring into space, while Sarah and Nero stretched out side by side on the checkered blanket, napping in the warm lull of afternoon. I, too, felt restless and confused by the morning and, rising removed my cloak and bonnet, and pulled the pins from my hair, letting it cascade down my back. Turning, I headed trance-like toward the Tor.

Where had Ian gone? I wondered. I wished we could talk, speak of the strange experience that had passed between us. Still, the monument atop the hill beckoned me. Sarah would be all right alone; the spot was secluded and Nero there to guard. Something compelled me to climb that hill. I must.

Again I had the sensation that time had stopped. The world around me was silent as a tomb, no birds were singing, even the breeze had stilled. At the foot of the hill, I spotted two paths--one moving straight up its side and the other, veering to the right at a more even slope. I moved to the right, sweeping hair away from my face as I went. The way became steeper and a bit rocky--the jagged points of stones cut into my slippers as I went but I didn't stop, the feel of them was good--familiar--and happiness rose in me at the very pressure of them beneath my feet.

The path stretched on and on, curving up and around the hill. Thought my form was in constant motion, time seemed to have stopped. I counted mentally as I moved farther and farther up the trail. At each new circle I offered a prayer of thanksgiving--for the day, for my life, for all things good--it seemed right to do this and I felt more comforted and renewed at each new level. When I'd counted six, I could see I had only a little way more to climb. One more revolution, and I'd be at the top. Excitement nearly burst within me and eagerly I hurried forward. Beaded drops of perspiration had gathered on my forehead and trickled down my face and neck. A wayward strand of hair tickled my cheek and I brushed it back--fatigue and discomfort forgotten in anticipation.

Rounding the last turn of the path, I saw what was left of St. Michael's chapel. The cold and solemn spire where men had martyred themselves towered overhead, leaving me small and insignificant in its wake. The years had seen the blackest tragedy here, and I shivered with an inner chill matched by the sudden bite of the wind. This place had seen evil, I felt instinctively, yet it was also a holy spot, a place that had been stripped of its glory by the violence and power of men. The earth beneath my feet felt solid and constant, but the tower, the tower did not belong and never would. *A blight upon the Mother's breast*, something in my heart said sadly. Yet this was also a spot of worship, a place where spirit had maintained its presence for centuries, and no man could take that blessing away from it. I thanked the heavens for bringing me back--for the timeless, ongoing love that surrounded and enveloped me as I stood where I'd stood before, for letting me return, home, at last.

When my gaze stopped at the darkened, door-less opening of the chapel, a sight came into view that caused my heart to explode with warmth and ecstasy as well as something else-fear perhaps. In the brightness of the autumn sunshine, standing bare-chested with arms outstretched like some primeval god reclaiming his lost lands, was Ian. For a moment I remained transfixed, watching the light stirring of air through his dark curls, the rhythmic rise and fall of his tanned chest. He seemed to be entranced in his own ritual-a male ritual-another god-like attempt to call this place his own. Yet I knew I belonged here, with him in this place and time, as I hadn't in some other.

I had no sense of movement, but I must have gone forward, for suddenly I stood before him, and his outstretched arms came down and around me in a breathtaking embrace. Eyes locked, we slipped to our knees on the timeworn earth, and my own arms encircled his neck and pulled his head to mine. Fire would have felt little more than warm compared to the heat that surrounded he and I as we knelt there at the base of St. Michael's tower. My hands burned as I touched the smooth, hairless skin of his chest and all the while our mouths explored in an eager, familiar way, as if we'd been separated for ages and had just come together again, at last, and wanted to relive the decades apart in this instant.

Then his mouth drew back and his eyes burned flame into mine and suddenly, he ripped my bodice open, mindless of fabric or propriety. Pulling aside the lace of my chemise, his face moved to my breast and he breathed in the scent of me. As his lips touched its crest the flame from his eyes leapt into my chest, and I pressed him to me, wanting the fire to go on and on and on. Ian's tongue traced its way up, to my neck, to my face, finally back to my mouth, but his hand never left my breast, and I felt a forgotten passion creeping down from there, wanting, needing to be quenched.

Then without warning, the spell was shattered. A small, childish cry broke through our fury and brought us into the present. We turned at the same instant to see Sarah, followed closely by her setter, and the look on her face was nothing short of despair. Tears had begun to spill over and follow an uncertain course down her cheeks, but it was the anger in her light eyes that forced me upright and frightened me with its intensity.

"You'll pay for this," she said quietly, but with venom, and her gaze was turned directly at me. "You'll pay." And with that she turned away and began the long journey back down the Tor.

I faced Ian again, still dazed by everything that happened in the past few moments. He rose and drew me up with him. Once on our feet, he closed the fabric of my bodice tightly, then looked at me with sorrow in his eyes. His gaze was long and intense, and spoke more than words, but at length he said simply, "I'll go to her" and grabbing his shirt from the ground nearby, left me standing confused and alone.

Suddenly the world came crashing in on me with a physical pain so violent I almost fell to the hard earth. The autumn chill had turned into the icy claws of winter, the sun hid behind a gray veil: noises of the day pounded into my head, chattering birds, the bleating of sheep somewhere in the distance, the rustle of leaves in the trees. I touched my face and found that my cheeks were wet; at some point I'd begun to cry and hadn't even realized it. God, what had happened here? The question played itself over and over in my mind. A moment ago I'd felt joy--and passion--where had it gone? Or had they ever really been here at all?

This Anne wanted to believe that Ian had forced himself on her, was helpless against his will. Where had that other girl gone--the girl that wanted his caresses to never stop? The girl who wanted him as much as he wanted her? If Sarah hadn't intruded, where might that moment have ended?

I secured my dress as best as I could and began to walk down. This time I took the straight path, which evidently

Sarah had followed also, thus allowing her to reach us as quickly as she did. I prayed the girl would be all right, that Ian would have some plausible explanation for her, that she might in time forgive me.

Upon reaching the picnic spot, I saw that she and Ian were in earnest conversation, so I began gathering up the remains of the picnic and placing them back in the carriage. I repinned my hair, and fastened my cloak securely at the neck, knowing I must look once more like the governess who had begun this day. Inside, however, I was still trembling.

I approached Sarah and Ian hesitantly, but she turned and surprisingly, offered me a shy, slight smile. "Everything's fine, Anne," she said with just a touch too much sweetness. "I understand how these things sometimes happen."

I turned a questioning look toward Ian, but he nodded reassurance. "Do you really, Sarah?" I asked.

"Yes," she said, eyes down, "Ian has explained it all to me."

What had he told her, I wondered. But this wasn't the time or place to ask. I moved to touch the girl, but when I did, she stiffened, so I knew all was not forgiven. "I am truly sorry I hurt you, Sarah." I told her quietly. "I hope you believe that."

Needless to say, the journey home was a quiet one, with none of the cheer and gaiety of the morn. Each of us seemed lost in thoughts of our own. To me, the day was already becoming a hazy, shadowy dream, and I wondered if any of the things I believed to happen had really occurred at all. Ian must have felt the same, for he scarcely gave me a glance the whole trip back.

Once we arrived at the manor, Sarah went off immediately to find Mrs. Blum and have a light supper, but I lingered near the stables, hoping for a moment to speak with Ian about the younger girl. It seemed an eternity before he was finished assisting the groom with the horses, but at last he came out the door to find me standing silently in the deepening darkness of evening.

"I thought you'd gone," he said quietly, and his tone reminded me more the Ian of yesterday than the Ian on the Tor.

"How is Sarah?" I asked, uncertain how to phrase what I really wanted to know.

"You saw her, did you not? She'll be fine by tomorrow."

"I'm not so sure, Ian. Whatever did you tell her?" I gazed at him intently, searching his eyes for the fire I'd seen earlier today.

He looked down, refusing to meet my stare. "I told her I was swept off my feet by you," he said lightly, mocking me again, and then. "I told her some day she'd understand."

A wistful sad tone echoed in his voice, and I reached out a hand to his arm, but he shook it away, apparently wanting no further contact between us.

"Save that for someone who can appreciate it," he said, almost angrily. "It's late you should be inside." And with that, he abruptly turned away from me and toward the gatehouse.

So, it appeared we were to pretend that nothing had happened, that everything was the same as it had been. Well, it wasn't, and as I stood watching Ian stride away, I knew my life would never be the way it was again.

Chapter 13

And even yet, I dare not let it languish,
Dare not indulge in Memory's rapturous pain...
Emily Brontë

News of Sir Roderick's death came the following day. Mrs. Blum entered my bedchamber early, just as I was stirring wearily from a restless night. A nose still red and sniffling and swollen eyes indicated at once that something terrible had happened; my stomach knotted--Sarah must have told her everything.

Then I'd discovered the real reason for her distress, which was shock enough without the coupling yesterday's misfortunes.

"Master Lyle sent a message for the servants, as well," she informed me, "Poor Sir Roderick and the poor children. Losin' their father like that, an' 'im still a man in 'is prime. Couldn't have been past sixty, and 'ere I am nearin' seventy meself. God rest 'is soul." She crossed herself, then placed an envelope on the bedside table next to me. "Tis for you, dear."

I patted her hand, absently. "How is Sarah taking the news?" I asked.

"Rather badly, I fear. She was crying her little heart out and asking for Master Ian when I left to come to you. Nell's with 'er now."

"I'll dress and go to her right away," I said. But would the girl want to see me after our scene the previous afternoon?

When the housekeeper had left the room, I took the envelope from the table. Lyle's note was brief, saying only that his father had never fully regained consciousness, and the funeral would be held in London, with a memorial service at Leighton Hall upon his and Lady Gwendolyn's return at the end of the week. Evidently it had always been a wish of Sir Roderick to be interred near his fellow diplomatic servants, thus his burial in the city rather than on his own estate.

Beyond this, the lack of detail in Lyle's message caused me to wonder what he was holding back, but he must be terribly upset by his father's sudden death, and would probably fill in all the gaps later. He was Sir Lyle now, accountable to no one for his actions, and certainly not to me. Surely this alone would put a great distance between us--but not so great as the distance I had put with my actions at Glastonbury. Things could never be the same as they'd been before. We'd both changed, and those changes would surely be evident the moment we saw each other again.

I dressed quickly and headed for Sarah's room, walking almost in a daze through the long corridors only to find that Ian was already with the girl when I arrived. I couldn't bear to face the two of them together, and was about to turn back, when Nell exited the chamber.

Sadly she told me, "'Es readin' a letter from her mum, Miss. She seems to take great comfort from Master Ian, she does. Thought I'd jus' leave 'em be for a bit."

"I'm sure that's quite all right, Nell. I'll be in the schoolroom, but please tell Sarah that we won't have lessons again until after her mother and brother arrive and things return to normal. And Nell," I touched her arm. "Please tell her I'm here for her if she needs me."

The girl gave me a curious look, but nodded.

I supposed Sarah's letter would be a mother's loving attempt to ease a daughter's grief. How did Ian feel about Sir Roderick's death, I wondered? He'd never mentioned how well he knew the man, or even if he liked him. I knew he grieved for Lyle and Sarah, though. And he would be there for both of them. I fervently wished for some small way to help Sarah myself, to have her turn to me an this sorrowful time but it became apparent during the next few days that a wall had sprung up between us, and I wasn't to be allowed to share her pain.

I knew she felt I'd betrayed her, and the sad part was that I had. Ian was her special person, even if he was years older than she; and I, who supposedly cared for her brother, lost myself in a moment of senseless passion to the man she idolized. I'd not only betrayed her, I'd broken her heart as well. Facing myself in the mirror each day was trial enough, not to mention the torture of facing her. Even Mrs. Blum sensed something awry between us, for she raised a questioning eye to me each afternoon when instead of taking our exercise together as had been our habit, we went separate ways. I couldn't share my guilt even with that sympathetic soul; it was too strong, the wound too raw, and I too close to my own actions that day on the hill.

How I wished to share it with someone though! Why hadn't I written to Maddie sooner, telling her where I was? Now, if I did, it would seem I was only using her to escape my problems: I owed her better than that. I'd let everyone down--Maddie most of all. But why did she seem so far away right now, just when I needed her most? I cried myself to sleep at night, praying for dreams of her, but my rest was untouched by visions or nightmares; I merely tossed and turned, sleepless, shrinking from the black depths of my soul

On the third day after hearing about her father, Sarah, came to the schoolroom as usual. "I want to have lessons," she said rather sharply, as if daring me to question her further. And so, unquestioning, I went about our activities as normal, assuming she needed this to occupy her mind. If teaching was the only way I could help the girl at present, then so be it. She was quieter than before, and watched me warily, but she seemed friendly enough, and I hoped with time and patience our relationship could be mended; that she'd come to grips with what had happened.

Although exactly what had happened I still wasn't sure myself--I hadn't seen Ian since the morning we'd heard the news; apparently he was deliberately avoiding me. Perhaps I was avoiding him as well, for I had no idea what I'd say if I was to meet him by chance. He'd taken to eating his meals elsewhere, and Sarah and I had been having trays in our rooms; neither of us seemed to have much of an appetite these days, so the house held the dismal silence of a tomb.

My mind stayed so wrapped up in its own problems, I scarcely noticed the changed atmosphere. Lyle was coming home, and with him, Lady Gwendolyn. How long until Sarah told them about the picnic? And would that mean the end of my stay at Leighton Hall? I hated the pain Lyle would suffer because of me. He'd taken me in, cared for me--and I'd repaid him with this. Of course he would have to know the truth eventually, but I didn't want it to come on top of this other loss. If only I could convince Sarah to wait and let me tell him the story...but I'd no right to ask anything of her, and even less right to think of making this my home after abusing the love and affection of these good people; there must be an evil side to me after all, such as my dream had portended, and in that case, rather than cause further harm, I should leave.

But even as I reasoned all this, Maddie's words came back haunting. "Your destiny lies here. You cannot leave this place." So it seemed I must remain for a time and face the unhappiness to come. If only she were here to guide me. I'd never felt so lost and alone, even in all the time with Rev. Jaspar; and the one thing I needed most I didn't have--a friend.

***

The day before Lyle was due to return home with his step-mother, the dreary confines of the house at last became all too apparent, and I sought once again the spacious moors. Oddly enough, I was no longer afraid of encountering Martin Rollins, not after the damage I'd done myself in a single afternoon. The real test of my endurance lay in the days ahead, looking at Lyle and not weeping for what might have been, having his Lady Gwendolyn discover the type of person into whose hands she'd put the care of her only child. How could Martin harm me further?

A sharp wind nipped at my face as I crossed the garden--mostly barren now, except for several evergreens and a few late roses clinging tenaciously to their vines, looking as sad and forlorn as I felt. Leaves had begun leaving their pleasant perches weeks ago, the trees reached out like empty, spidery webs waiting for their prey. Even the sky hung dull and gray.

I drew my cloak tighter as I headed up a brown hillside. The flesh seemed tight against my body--I'd lost weight, and a quick glance in the mirror before I'd left this morning had shown sunken eyes and pale skin. *It doesn't matter*, I'd thought. Tomorrow might be the day on which my fate was determined, only the dark hours of the night remained to be survived: then I would know my destiny. So long, yet so soon. The world was repaying me for my foolishness, and I didn't care. Nothing mattered anymore. Bleakness surrounded me. I was abandoned once again. Not even my animal friends came to support me. No one, not even Maddie.

"I'll never be more than a thought away." I heard her voice so clearly I jumped, then, remembering that those were the very words she'd spoken on our last day together, I sank to the ground under a nearby tree, and letting go of my restraint, I wept.

Warmly, clearly, her voice came to me again. 'Trust your feelings, dear. Let the hills speak to you now. Receive your strength from them."

I listened, and indeed, I heard the wind whispering its words across my breast. The earth was warm beneath me and, sitting up, I leaned against the tree, resting against the hard, rough trunk, drawing the power of it into my own body.

My mind drifted back to happier times, walking the sea cliffs with Maddie, talking to my rabbit prince in the forest, riding Charlie across the moors, lying in the heather. Life had been so simple. For all its troubles, it had been easy then. I closed my eyes and drifted into a light sleep.

The sound of footsteps brought me back to the present. I looked up, squinting against the glare of the sun. A dark figure stood before me in a heavy cloak, a tall and foreboding giant; I shaded my brow to better see the face. Ian. He stared at me with silent disapproval.

"You should nae be out alone." He said quietly. "Lyle asked me to keep a watch over you, but how am I to do that if you insist on wandering about by yourself?" The tone was cold, devoid of all emotion, and I winced, trying not to remember the fiery man on the Tor.

I lowered my gaze, brushing aside a stray bit of moisture from my cheek. He knelt easily by my side and remained silent for a long time. I felt rather than saw the slow in and out movement of his breath, and though we were at odds, a strange sense of security surrounded me.

When I spoke my voice sound far away, husky, as if it wasn't mine at all. "What happened to us, Ian? I want to know what happened that day on the Tor? Was it real or just a dream? Tell me...please tell me."

I didn't expect him to respond, and for a long time he didn't speak. When he did at last, his voice was as full as mine had been moments earlier. "I'd like to believe a lot of things about it, lass, that it never happened, or that you were the precocious wench I'm still not sure you aren't." He gave me a long look. "But, I'm afraid it was a real moment. But a moment best forgotten, I think.

"When I was a little boy, my grandmother used to tell me stories about the Glastonbury Tor. She was English, you see, and lived not far from there as a child." He had a sorrowing look as he continued to speak. "She knew it well, she did.

At any rate, she told me it was an ancient, magic place and the veil between the real world and the world of the spirit was very thin there, so sometimes you could slip back and forth between the two. I always thought she was telling me fairy tales, stories invented to brighten a trouble child's mind." A quiet pause followed and he sat, evidently remembering another life as I'd been doing a short while before.

After a bit, he continued. "I don't know if it's really possible Anne, but it seems to me, for just an instant, you and I were caught up in another world, a past where perhaps we knew and loved one another." There was a long pause as he considered his words. "I suppose that could be one explanation for what happened. But we have to remember that the past is over. We live in this life, and we must live it in a different way."

When I remained silent, he turned, staring at me curiously. "Don't you agree?"

"I suppose so."

"What were you thinking?"

"Only that your grandmother reminds me of a friend of mine. Spinning yarns of mystery and magic and leaving me to wonder all the while if she was speaking words of wisdom or simply foolishness."

He laughed that singing pleasant laugh of his. "Aye, that's Gran all right. Yet I miss her very much. I always believed she loved me most in the world."

"Yes, I felt the same about Maddie. Sometimes I think if I could talk with her for just a moment, she would make everything right again."

Silence ensued, stirred only by an occasional rustle of leaves. Magically, the sound of a lark burst forth from the tree above us. Listening to the sorrowful notes, the sadness of Ian's words consumed me. Why could there be no present for us? Being here with him was good; I looked toward him, drinking in the earthiness, the depths. Then suddenly, I thought of Lyle and shivered at what tomorrow might bring.

"We should be getting back,' Ian said. "There's a chill in the air."

Touching his arm timidly, I asked, "What about Lyle?"

"What about him?" he returned, bristling at the mention of his friend's name.

"What will happen if he finds out?"

"Aye, and what if he does? Now that would spoil your pretty plans, would it not?"

My temper flared and I lashed back at him. And it could spoil yours as well, couldn't it?"

Fury burned in his dark eyes. His fingers gripped my arm as he rose, yanking me up with him. Turning me to face him, he glared bitterly into my eyes, but behind his anger was a trace of some emotion I couldn't read. "My plans concern only Lyle's well-being. Nothing more, nothing less." He gave me a shake, then released me so quickly, I almost fell. "So you needn't worry, my dear Miss Cowper. I have no intentions of shattering Lyle's illusions of you."

Cheeks red with both humiliation and anger, if had I been a man, I would have struck him down in that moment. Pure, raw hatred flowed through my veins. Never had I experienced such emotion. "I have no intention of letting you shatter his illusions, sir. I plan to tell him myself."

"And do you plan to tell him how you played the trollop at Ram's Head before you came here?"

I did hit him then. The shock that registered on his face was surprising, but I had no desire to stay and mince further words with him. I turned abruptly toward Leighton Hall, walking rapidly, warmed now by my rage. He was despicable--worse than Martin Rollins. At least Martin was quite visibly a scoundrel; Ian hid behind a mask of kindness and concern. How could I have believed for even one moment that I cared for this man? A thought was too good for him, much less any feelings of affection. I would relish tomorrow, for if indeed the worst did happen, at least Ian McCrae would be out of my life forever.

Chapter 14

My worn heart throbs so wildly
'Twill break for thee...
Emily Brontë

Despite the somber air pervading at Leighton Hall, there was a flurry of activity the following morn. Polished oak banisters shown like glass; in fact, the entire hall sparkled despite the all-too-evident signs of mourning and the sobriety of death which hung about the house. Sir Lyle and Lady Gwendolyn would arrive at any moment; the servants went purposely about preparing the house for a welcome return in spite of the sad circumstances.

The fondness felt by all for Sarah and her brother had never been more apparent than over the last few days. I'd seen heads bent together murmuring about 'poor Master Lyle' or 'poor little Miss Sarah'--I wondered if this sentiment held true for the mistress of the house, for I noticed her name was not mentioned in these circles.

Even Mrs. Blum refused to discuss her return, except to tell me, "There'll be much to prepare before the lady arrives, so I'll not be 'aving too much time for chats, lassie." Everyone seemed aware the mistress' expectations would be high, even in this time of grief.

I had my own dreads about her return, and they were more than just the obvious. I remembered the day in the gallery when I'd looked upon her portrait and felt that sense of suffocation. The thought of Lady Gwendolyn made me afraid, although I didn't know why a stranger should frighten me so.

But no matter, soon enough I would know exactly what type of person she was. All too soon, in fact. Perhaps even on this day, though I hoped not, for surely she and Lyle would have other concerns to deal with at present. Neighbors had been coming and going with food and condolences all week, and I felt sure that would continue at least until after the services.

On this particular morn, I'd risen early, hoping to attend Sarah with her toilet, but upon reaching her quarters, I found Nell already there, so I left them busily primping with her hair and clothing and strolled back down the spotless, somber hallway, seeking a quiet spot where I could prepare myself for the day ahead. Taking my cloak from a peg near the side door, I left the house. The day was brisk but clear, and the solitude of the garden was beckoning. I knew I should stay close to the Hall, for Lyle would be concerned if I wasn't nearby when he arrived.

I sank down on the lonely, abandoned chaise. No one came here these days other than me, and even Sarah kept to the warmer quarters of the house. Today I felt a little less bleak; *que sera, sera* I'd decided and pushing despair aside, glanced about, taking in my surroundings; the setting still beautiful despite the absence of its color. The yews held their sculptured cut and the white bark of birches shined brightly against a cloudless sky. Silence reigned here in this time of year, but I needed that solitude for the quiet gathering of thoughts and feelings. How I wished to see this place in the spring--alive with life, and sound, and hues of every shade!

A wet chill slipped down my face, but I brushed the tear away. *I mustn't be sad when Lyle arrives. I must give him smiles; he mustn't suspect that anything is wrong.* But wouldn't he guess when he saw the pallor of my complexion, the way the garments hung against my thin form? *I'll say I've been feeling ill. That's true enough.*

Feeling something against my leg, I glanced down and saw a book protruding from under the cushion where I sat. Pulling it out, I gave a short, almost desperate little laugh. *Le Morte d'Arthur*--How much had passed since I'd first read those pages! I flipped casually through the book, no longer needing to take in the words. These characters were alive to me--they were more than just fictional beings created to amuse someone's passing moments. Since Glastonbury...

Arthur had become a real king betrayed by a real friend, a real wife. I knew about betrayal. God, how I knew! Where did my sympathies lie now, I wondered. With Arthur, or with Lancelot? Or with Guinevere? Or someone else? Something was missing from the story, but I didn't know what.

"What am I doing," I said aloud, "reflecting on these people as if I knew them personally." And indeed, I'd been so deep into my reverie, I'd failed to hear the sound of horses on the gravel drive announcing an arrival. A gentle touch at my shoulder indicated I was no longer the sole occupant of the garden.

I looked up to find Lyle gazing down at me, eyes overflowing with sadness and love. In an instant, he was on his knees at my side, his mouth finding mine, covering it with wild longing. His long, thin fingers entwined themselves in my hair, pulling loose its comb and gathering up the falling curls. My former fears suddenly turned into a desperate need to be loved and to love in return, and for a moment I clung to him, wanting never to forgo the warmth and protection of his arms.

'My lord,' I thought, and how wonderful the thought, as if I'd been waiting centuries for his return. When at length he drew back to look at me, I noticed for the first time the dark shadows and the pallor of *his* skin.

Forgetting my own problems, I asked, "Has it been horrible for you?"

He nodded a silent reply and a terrible guilt washed over me at the further hurt I would shortly inflict upon him. If only I could have spared him that agony! His hand pushed a stray curl from my brow and traced a gentle path

110

down my cheek. "Knowing you would be here when I returned has made all the difference."

"Oh, Lyle..." I broke off, not knowing how to continue. Too soon. Much too soon to burden him with the truth.

I was saved from further comment by the appearance of Sarah leading a tall, attractive woman by the hand. She was even more beautiful than her portrait had indicated. Her soft auburn hair was swept away from the regal face, drawn up beneath a stylish bonnet. Eyes green as spring foliage gazed at me coolly as she glided across the garden, a black swan--for so rich and dark was her velvet traveling suit, she seemed almost like that medieval bird itself. It was also of the finest cut; she had exquisite taste, and obviously the money with which to satisfy it.

"Here he is. Mummy," Sarah told her, "I knew he'd be with Anne." Then to me, "Anne, this is my mother, Lady Gwendolyn Leighton. And this, dear Mummy, is Anne Cowper, the best governess I've ever had."

The word "best" seemed a little too stressed, and I gazed at her, questioning, but she met my eyes levelly, seemingly sincere.

"Oh, Lyle." Sarah exclaimed, relinquishing her mother's hand only to run to her brother's side, "Anne and I have missed you so much!" She gave me an entreating look around his arms. I suddenly realized she was forging a silent bond between us. I gave her a grateful smile.

Turning back to Lady Gwendolyn, I found her studying me with open curiosity and a trace of something else--hostility perhaps?

I extended a hand when she didn't speak. "How nice to meet you at last," I said. "Your family has been so good to me. I'm just sorry we had to meet at such an unhappy time for you.

For a moment her gaze grew hard, like a steel blade against my flesh. I shivered, but then the look vanished, and having regained her cool composure, she took my outstretched palm. "Yes, it's been very difficult, we must all begin to put our lives back together."

I saw Lyle wince behind her and I wondered at his stepmother continued without pause in a voice deep with hidden tones. "I'm so glad you're here Anne. I hope I may call you Anne. Lyle's told me about you, I feel as if we're old friends already."

She smiled as she spoke, but her eyes still held their icy glint. The hand she'd offered was cold and dry, and she clasped my own almost too tightly. Again I was touched by the feeling that she was a hard, calculating person whose life had never been easy, whose victories had all been won at a high price. And something else about her troubled me. Some flicker of recognition I couldn't quite grasp.

"Well," Lady Gwendolyn took up our silence, "it's getting rather damp here, so I think we should return to the house and have something to eat. By the way, I haven't seen Ian yet. Where is he hiding anyway?"

"I'll look for him, Mummy," Sarah chirped, heading off toward the stables.

"Hurry, dear. I don't want you to catch a cold. Or miss your noonday meal." Turning back to Lyle and me, she went on, "As for you two, after we eat you can visit all you like as I plan to rest from the journey. But just now I want to hear all about my daughter. Come, come," and with that she headed back toward the house, leaving us no choice but to accept her wishes and follow her inside.

***

Immediately after dinner that evening, Lyle drew me aside and asked quietly if we might talk in the library for a few minutes. Lady Gwendolyn had taken the evening meal in her bedchamber and planned to retire early, according to Mrs. Blum, so ours had been a simple affair with only Sarah, Lyle and myself present; Ian was God only knew where. Sarah hadn't located him for lunch, and since then he hadn't bothered to show up at all. But Lyle obviously had other things on his mind and hadn't appeared to notice.

Sarah left us to go upstairs, and I followed her brother, curious, into the dark room filled with books, again quivering at the eerie shadows playing across the walls and curtains. A fire roared angrily in the grate, and the room felt stuffy and confining, but Lyle motioned for me to sit while he poured us both a sherry. A moment later, he approached the chaise on which I sat, sinking wearily down by my side.

"I hope you aren't too tired this evening...there's something I'd really like to discuss with you before my father's memorial service." He sighed, then for a moment his thoughts seemed to turn inward. After a time, he spoke again. "I want you to know that my feelings for you haven't changed in the least, despite my father's death. I've been afraid you might think they would, that I had more important obligations now."

"Lyle..." I began as he paused but he motioned me back to silence.

"No, please, let me finish. You are still very important to me--I want you to know that--but there are, I'm afraid, certain circumstances that are going to render it necessary for me to be away for a short time...and then well, then I don't know exactly what may happen."

I started to speak again, but once more he held up his hand, indicating that I should let him continue. "Anne, my dearest, what I am about to tell you will be in strictest confidence. I don't want Sarah to know about any of this yet, but I have made certain promises to you, and I feel I owe you this explanation."

"You don't owe me anything. Lyle," I said feebly.

"But I do, my dear. You've given me so much already, and

I have so much to give you..." His voice trailed off, then he gave a short laugh. "Unfortunately, I've just discovered I have a prior commitment."

I looked at him, wondering what he meant.

"When my father was ill, he lapsed in and out of consciousness, but all the while I had the oddest feeling that he wanted to tell me something. He struggled and struggled with it, but could never seem to get the words out. Several times, however, I thought I heard him say the word, 'sister' " Lyle laughed again, but there was pain in his eyes. "I thought he wanted me to look after Sarah. How wrong I was!"

He rubbed his temples, then pushed fallen hair back from his drawn face, continuing at last, "Two days before we left London, Father's solicitor came to the house and read his will. I thought I knew my father well Anne. I really believed that. Now I wonder if I knew him at all." He stopped, dropping his face into his hands.

Reaching over, I touched his arm. "What, Lyle?"

"I have another sister, Anne. Besides Sarah. The will said, and I quote, 'I hereby bequeath one-third of my financial wealth to my daughter, Emily Antoinette Morgan Leighton. And may God forgive me.'"

I stared, completely surprised by this announcement. "But who is her mother?" I asked.

"That is a very good question, my dear. He simply didn't say. My stepmother was heartbroken when she heard the news. Evidently Father never indicated to her that he had another daughter and I certainly have no idea who her mother might have been. I can't even speculate as to the age of the child...God, but it hurts me to think he had a child and never told me, never told anyone! I suppose she was some love child he wanted to forget, but never quite could. I'll tell you this, I intend to find the girl. No sister of mine is going to be left lost and abandoned in this world. I'll find her if it's the last thing I do." Then he turned to me, love filling his gaze once more.

"I'm sorry, Anne But surely you of all people understand why I must do this. Do you mind terribly if we put off getting to know each other better for just a while longer? I must go to London and give some papers to the solicitor, then I'll return as soon as possible. After that, I promise you we can spend every free moment with one another. No one wants that more than I."

"No, of course I don't mind. And I do know better than anyone how it feels to be abandoned. Certainly you must find your sister. And she will be all the luckier for having you. If there's anything I can do..."

"Thank you, dear Anne. I know you will do what you can." He leaned close to me and placed a light kiss on my forehead. "For now, I ask only that you be here for me. I seem to draw an unusual amount of strength from that."

***

Rain droned rhythmically against the panes of my window. Today I would go to Sir Roderick's memorial service and give Lyle my strength. At least I could do that. It was little

enough, since I certainly hadn't given him my loyalty. Although his news had come as a surprise, after some reflection I began to hope sincerely that he would find his sister, and find her soon. Perhaps that would lessen some of the grief he might feel at losing me. He was such a decent man. How I regretted that experience with Ian, wished it had never occurred!

But it had, and I couldn't lie to him or myself. Sooner or later the truth must be known, even though its telling would probably destroy any hope we might have of happiness together. What might happen to me then, I didn't know, but I knew I'd always have Maddie and resolved to swallow my pride and write her soon. Surely my destiny had been met, not very well I had to admit, but what further good could come of my staying here now? For the moment Lyle needed me so I'd remain and offer what comfort I could. But time was running out; any day now it would be completely gone, and I must then move on.

Chapter 15

Both they and I shall fall beneath
The fate we cannot flee...
Emily Brontë

"I need you here. Lyle. Whatever papers Mr. Blackstone wants from you, he can come and retrieve himself. I insist." Lady Gwendolyn's words held authority. Two days had passed since Sir Roderick's memorial service, and Lyle had just announced his intention of leaving for London the next. I hated to be party to their conversation, but since Lyle had broached the matter during breakfast, it seemed I had no choice. Sarah hadn't come down yet, so he, Lady Gwendolyn and I had the table to ourselves. Since their return, all meals were taken in the formal dining room, and I missed the comfortable warmth and cheery brightness of the smaller chamber, but Lady Gwendolyn favored propriety, thus our present quarters.

"But Mother," Lyle countered, "you know how strongly I feel about this."

"Of course I do, and believe me, I understand, but you've already been away from the estate for far too long, and I don't see what good can come of your going back to London. Blackstone can handle the situation much more efficiently than you, and I'm sure he'll report to us the moment he has any news. Besides, there's your future to consider." Her look now focused on me, and I felt the blood burning in my cheeks. Dear God, she mustn't use me as a tool against Lyle! I couldn't bear it.

"Anne knows, Mother, and she understands as well."

"I see." Lady Gwendolyn's tone had dropped and held a cold, threatening darkness. "So Anne knows that your father and my husband was a womanizer who left some poor illegitimate bastard child God knows where..."

"Mother, please. You don't want Sarah to walk in on this."

"And why ever not? Why shouldn't Sarah know, especially considering the fact that *Anne* knows? After all, Sarah is a member of this family."

"She's also a child."

"Ha, child indeed. I was a year from marriage when I her age. It's high time you let the girl grow up, Lyle. Anne's not much older, are you, my dear?"

Before I had a chance to respond, Lyle's voice took on a threat of its own. "Anne is a mature young woman whom I intend to know much better in the future. And, God willing, someday she too will be a member of this family."

"Please," I interrupted hoarsely. "I shouldn't be hearing any of this. Your mother is right, Lyle."

Lady Gwendolyn's piercing eyes turned to me and again I shivered with their ice, but it was her words that really startled me, so unexpected were they. "I respect my son's wishes, Anne," she said. "It was just a shock, discovering that he'd told you already. You can imagine the embarrassment I'm suffering over this."

"Of course," I murmured.

"Then you must also understand why I need Lyle here at moment. I need his comfort, his support, his strength. He, dear Anne, whether he knows it or not, needs yours." Why did her eyes seem to be testing, even though she spoke only reassurance? I shuddered inwardly. Lyle, however, interrupted my thoughts and any further comments I might have added.

"All right, all right. I'll send for Blackstone today. Actually, I suppose you re right. I can't be of much help to him in London, and it's true that you and Anne both need me here. God knows I haven't been much good to Ian lately. By the way, has anyone seen Ian?"

Mrs. Blum, who'd just entered the room with another pot of steaming tea, spoke up. "Mr. McCrae's been a wee bit under the weather the past few days. Caught a chill walkin' up from the gatehouse in tha rain, like as not the lad's been trying to ride it out, but when I saw 'im last evening with 'is face flushed and pale, I sent him straight to the gatehouse with a 'ot toddy from my ole Nanna's mix, and a bowl filled with stewed poultry. I 'aven't been to check on 'im today though."

Lady Gwendolyn immediately took charge of the situation. "That won't be necessary. Mrs. Blum," she said, "Anne and I will see to his needs. I want Sarah to have one more day of relaxation before she begins her studies again. She seemed a little worn out after the service. In fact, I'm surprised she hasn't fallen ill herself. Ask Nell to prepare a tray for her and I'll carry it up myself while you're getting a basket ready for us to take to Ian."

"Humph," I heard the housekeeper mutter, but without further comment she left the room to carry out her task. I looked at Lady Gwendolyn dismayed. Why did she need me to go with her to see Ian? Things were uncomfortable enough between us without her presence. I couldn't very well refuse my employer, however.

"It's typical of Ian not to let anyone know he is ill," she continued. "The man is so stubborn. Another reason why you're needed at home, Lyle."

"All right, Mother. You've pled your case and won." Lyle rose and headed toward the door. "I guess I'd better get my note off to Blackstone now. Tell Ian I'll look in on him later. Maybe Anne, you could fix him up one of your remedies?" He gave me a warm smile.

I returned it. "If Cook will let me in her kitchen, I'd be glad to," I replied.

116

"Oh, and do you think we might take a walk this afternoon if you're free?"

"Yes, I'd like that."

"Good. Until later, then."

Nell entered at just that moment with a tray for Sarah. After Lady Gwendolyn had left the room, I set out toward the kitchen to prepare the remedy for Ian, but my mind was so occupied with other matters the entire time. I'm surprised I even managed to remember the ingredients.

What, I wondered, were the motives of Lyle's stepmother? There was something about her I didn't trust, and she always seemed to be watching me. Even at the memorial I had felt her chilly eyes boring into me, looking for what I didn't know, but inquisitive and probing all the same. Was she observing me with the intention of discovering whether or not I was worthy of Lyle's affection? If so, she needn't fear on that count as I'd already decided I wasn't. In fact, I'd already posted my letter to Maddie, telling her I'd be returning to Countisbury soon and would explain everything when I saw her.

But would I have to explain to Maddie? Somehow, I felt certain she knew everything and wouldn't approve of my intentions to leave. "You're running away instead of facing the problem," she'd say, and she was right, but what choice did I have at this point? I had to leave before I did more damage here than I'd done already.

A short while after I'd returned to the dining room, Lady Gwendolyn reentered the room, accompanied by Mrs. Blum. "Yes, I think she's got a temperature too." And seeing me, she asked, "Anne, what do you suggest?"

"A cup of chamomile tea with a dash of mint should relax her, and you might rub a little linseed oil on her chest," was flattered at all this deference to my medical knowledge.

"Excellent." Then to Mrs. Blum, "Please take care of it, and tell her I'll be in to see her later. It's this damp old house--in the winter there's simply no way of keeping the wet drafts out."

"Aye, its a fact, madam," the housekeeper replied, "I'll see to 'er right away." With that she turned and headed down the corridor. Where Sarah was concerned, she gave no hesitation; the girl had a high priority with her.

"Ah, Anne, your presence has certainly been invaluable to us on this day. And now, if you're ready, we should be off to see Ian."

"Are you sure you want me to accompany you, madam?"

"Of course, dear girl. Why shouldn't I--and no more of this 'madam'. Please call me Gwendolyn. You're more than a servant in this house. You know that."

We took our cloaks from the rack and donned them. A brisk autumn wind blew outside, filling the air with a fine mist. An eerie gray twilight cast its shadows across the morning. Our fast pace gave us little chance for further conservation, but all too quickly we arrived at the gatehouse. I'd never see Ian's cottage so close; it looked quaint from a distance, but from this vantage point I could see that although the brownish gray stone matched the manor, the house itself was old and in need of repair. The wood was shredding in places, and the roof looked like it might not hold back the tide of another winter storm. Even the paned windows gazed at us dull and clouded.

Lady Gwendolyn gave a quick rap at the solid oak door. After a moment, when no one had responded, she turned the handle and entered. I followed slowly. The interior of Ian's house was dark, with only small amounts of light filtering in through the mullion glass. I noticed, with much surprise, that he had books--everywhere--on the mantle, face down at the table, scattered across the floor. Other than that, the place appeared neat and clean; a braided rug beckoned warmly from next to the hearth where a fire had almost lost its warmth. The horsehair sofa and chair crowded around the fireplace, dark and earthy colors like Ian himself; and the dining table and chairs were sturdy walnut, built for a man's pleasure.

My companion wrinkled her nose. "The poor man needs a woman's touch," she said. "I'll look in the other room while you build up the fire." Quickly she moved through a door, and a moment later I heard her voice again, this time admonishing Ian. "Why didn't you tell someone you were ill? You know we would have come sooner had we known."

Not waiting to hear his reply, I removed my cloak and busied myself with the fire, taking what logs were left in the bin and using some nearby kindling to replenish its glow. A few minutes later a cackling blaze filled the cavity and I rubbed my hands together, enjoying the heat, letting it thaw my still icy fingers. Settling myself in a nearby chair, I noticed with interest the large volumes scattered about. "Parish Register", one tattered volume read. I reached to open the book, when my eye was drawn toward a smaller book lying nearby. I picked it up and read, "Poetry of Sir Robert Burns".

Turning to a page whose corner was folded down, I was immediately drawn in by the words of the poet-

> How fair the art, my bonnie lass,
> How much in love am I
> And I will love still my dear
>
> Till all the seas gang dry.
> Till all the seas gang dry, my dear,
> And rocks melt in the sun,
> And I will love thee still, my dear,
> While the sands of time shall run.

The verse was simple, but I was surprised to find it one that Ian had marked. Why, I wondered? He didn't appear a particularly romantic person. Whom would he love 'till all the seas gang dry'?

Then I saw another bulge in the book, and turned to something even more astonishing: a piece of torn fabric. I brushed a tear away as I gazed at it. The material was from the dress I'd worn that day on Glastonbury.

So Ian *had* felt something too...

Looking up, I was startled to see Gwendolyn at me. "I called you," she said sharply.

"Oh, I'm sorry. I didn't hear."

She continued looking at me with that calculating gaze. She knows, I thought. She knows. But she didn't speak, except to say, "Ian would like something to read. Since you've obviously found a good book, why don't you take it to him, while I finish straightening in here."

"Yes, yes of course." I jumped from the chair, hurrying out of the room. That woman made me so nervous, I didn't want to be in her presence any longer than necessary. Even Ian was a relief.

In only a moment I took in the heavy, mahogany wardrobe, a window, curtains drawn to let in what small amount of light that the day offered, an oversized bed, with Ian, propped up between two fluffy, cloud-like pillows. Only a moment, before all I could see was him, dark circles shadowing bloodshot eyes, his pale face, and the smile that drew up the corners of his mouth at my entrance.

"Lady Gwendolyn told me to bring you this," I said, and his smile disappeared.

"Duty call, I see," he said sarcastically.

Why did it always have to be like this between us? I tried again. "I'm sorry you're ill."

"Why?" he asked quietly, "afraid I might slip into delirium and give your little secret away?"

"I don't have any secrets."

"Ah, but don't you, my dear Anne?"

"Ian," I moved close and lay the book beside him. "Why do you have a piece of material from my dress in here?"

His face turned whiter than the pillow pressed against his head. He didn't speak and our eyes locked, and for another instant we were the same two people we'd been on the Tor, wanting, needing, loving, knowing. Then the spell was shattered by a voice. For one brief second I recognized that voice from another time, another place, and I knew then that although I didn't understand all of what was happening, we were caught up in a drama from long ago that would not be denied and must be played to its end.

***

The way back to the manor was stone-cold, worse than it had been earlier in the day. Strangely, however, Gwendolyn wanted to walk slowly and talk.

"So what do you think of Ian?" she asked, studying me intently.

Non-committingly, I replied, "He seems to be a hard worker. And he cares a lot for Lyle and Sarah."

"Yes, he does." I heard a hint of slyness in her voice. "And does he care for you as well?"

"Why should he?" I asked through chattering teeth.

"I don't know why he should, but I know why he shouldn't, as does he."

I stopped and stared at her, curious. "What do you mean?"

"My dear Anne, didn't Sarah or Mrs. Blum tell you? There's madness in Ian's family. His father committed suicide. And his grandmother, well, she ran off with the family fortune, leaving them all starving half to death in that dreary old castle."

So that was the horrible death Mrs. Blum had hinted at! How sad for Ian. I wondered how it had happened.

"His father shot himself," Gwendolyn supplied. "It's all too distasteful to discuss, but Ian knows he can never marry. He might pass the seed of insanity on to his own children."

"But I thought..." I broke off, not knowing how to continue.

"You thought Sarah might one day marry him?" She had an uncanny ability to read my mind. "Sarah would like to believe that, I'm afraid. Of course she doesn't know the complete story of Ian's past. Some day, when she's older, I plan to tell her about it. For now, why not let her have her fantasy?"

I could think of many reasons, but said nothing further. We were in the garden now, and it lay still and dead around us; even the evergreens seemed to droop today. So Ian could never marry. Was that why he'd pushed me aside, told me there was no future for us? What future did I have now, then?

Gwendolyn put a gloved hand on my arm, but I could feel its frost even through the fabric. "I would not have the man here at all, but Lyle says he owes him an old debt from their college days and so he stays. Still Anne. Lyle is the better man. Oh, I know, he doesn't have the mystique of Ian, or the dark, smoldering good looks, but he would care for you, and love you forever."

"But-"

"Not now, Anne. Take some time to think about it very carefully. And don't worry about what may or may not have happened while Lyle was away. What he doesn't know won't harm him."

I stared at her, stunned. How could she know? And what was she suggesting?

Once more she read my thoughts.

"Just take some time to think about it. All I ask is that you give him a chance."

"I could never mislead Lyle," I said quietly.

When she spoke again, I heard that frightening note of authority in her voice. "I'm not asking you to mislead him, Anne. Just don't tell him things that might hurt him."

The rest of our way passed in silence. I had no desire to speak further, so bewildered was I by this development. But by the time we'd reached the Hall, not only did I feel a physical chill, the cold hand of fear had a paralyzing grip around my heart.

Chapter 16

False she was, and unrelenting...
Emily Brontë

Having thrust me at first unwillingly into Ian's company, Gwendolyn now seemed just as determined to keep us apart. She insisted without explanation to Mrs. Blum that "in the future, Mr. McCrae will be taking all his meals at the gatehouse," and asked Lyle to please conduct his business with Ian in the estate office, as she didn't want Sarah exposed to further illness of any sort.

"Tis no concern of mine," said the housekeeper when she told me these events later, "But Mr. Ian's a good man, and a friend of Sir Lyle's, and tis a shame, if you ask me, for him to be treated like a common servant."

I nodded in agreement, for indeed I too thought Lady Gwendolyn's treatment of Ian rather shameful, but as Mrs. Blum had said, it was no concern of mine. Besides, I wasn't any too unhappy about being given the opportunity to remain at Leighton Hall without having to answer for my actions with Ian.

The place was becoming more and more important to me; I felt obsessed by it, enthralled with the thought that I might one day be its mistress. Hadn't Gwendolyn as much as given me permission? After all, I had no future with Ian, and it was easy to understand how a man such as himself might be carried away by passion, especially considering he could have no future with any woman. I forgave him--and myself. It was nothing; it was over. My fear faded into the distance.

Once again, my mornings were consumed by lessons with Sarah; but now, during the afternoons, instead of taking exercise as I had in the past, Gwendolyn insisted that both her daughter and I accompany her on the many rounds of visits to the neighboring estates--repayment for their generous concern at the time of Sir Roderick's death. Apparently she had no intentions of returning to London in the near future. But her mourning took on a frivolous note--she had a new wardrobe of black gowns made up--so that when we went calling she was always at the height of fashion.

This, as well as acceptance by the society in which she moved, seemed very important to Gwendolyn. I, on the other hand, dreaded the idea of meeting strangers, especially people whose social class was so far above my own. Sensing this, Gwendolyn assured me that I was to be the 'niece of an earl," and while I allowed her to do this, I had no real belief that anyone would ever believe I truly was such.

Before these excursions began, she took Sarah and me to Langport on a shopping expedition, buying me dresses and bonnets in such an assortment of shapes and sizes that I'd thought my head would spin right off. Upon first approaching the town from which I'd fled some weeks before, I'd felt a little faint. I found my gaze darting to and fro, searching the faces, looking for signs of Martin Rollins. Why would he be here, though? Since he hadn't found me, there would be no reason for him to remain in this spot.

Soon, however, I began to relax and truly enjoy the place; we'd crossed a large, arched stone bridge when we first arrived--Great Bow Bridge, Sarah told me, and later we would see the Little Bow Bridge. Many stalls and burbage tenements clustered about the market area from which I'd made my escape, and nearby Lady Gwendolyn pointed out the tower of Huish Episcopi, one of the most splendid in Somerset, she said. Attractively poised above an old gateway at the riverside district was the *hanging chapel* where a school was currently lodged, and Georgian houses lined the street, many of which had been constructed from Ham stone that was quarried nearby, according to my guides. Langport had a character and charm all its own, and except for one unfortunate yet curious incident. I was able to enjoy our tour.

As the day wore on I got more and more caught up in the excitement of making purchases, of being treated like someone's daughter, I forgot to be wary and were it not for a stroke of luck, would have been caught in a somewhat embarrassing situation.

Sarah and I had just returned to the carriage; as it was a cold day, we were just about to close the door when I saw Lady Gwendolyn leaving the establishment from which we had just embarked. From out of nowhere, a large woman came into view, and as I watched her, I drew in a quick breath, causing Sarah to give me an inquisitive stare.

Following my line of vision, she asked, "Do you know that woman, Anne?"

By this time, I was certain it was Dottie from Ram's Head. What was she doing here in Langport? I wondered. The sight of her brought back all kinds of unpleasant memories of mistreatment, abandonment and fear of that place. But somehow, here today in this daylight, I wasn't frightened of her. More than anything, I felt embarrassed of my past. Almost as if what Ian had believed of me then was true. But it wasn't... Dottie had been my jailer, nothing more.

Then suddenly, as I watched, she collided full-force with Gwendolyn on the walkway. Both looked shocked to have encountered the other, but what shocked me was simply seeing that recognition on their faces.

"Anne?" Sarah questioned again.

"Uh, no, not really, Sarah."

At that point, we both turned our sights back to the scene, where, oddly, Gwendolyn was seriously conversing with the woman.

"I wonder if Mummy knows her," Sarah said. "It looks as if she does, doesn't it?"

And indeed it did at that. I saw Gwendolyn utter what looked to be a stinging retort at something the woman said, then she opened her reticule and took something from it, which she handed to the other party. After this, she headed toward the carriage and us.

As she climbed inside, Sarah queried, "Who was that large woman, Mummy?"

Gwendolyn had a pinched look, but she seemed to bite back angry words to reply, "Some poor thing begging for pennies."

"But what did you say to her, Mummy?" Sarah continued. "Did you tell her she could work at Leighton Hall?"

"Goodness no." Gwendolyn retorted, "She has no place at a manor house. She asked about employment, of course, but I told her we had nothing available." She threw me a look I couldn't fathom, but I remained silent.

Perhaps Lyle had told her about my experience at Ram's Head, but I had no wish to admit I knew the other woman at all, or to discuss that whole experience in front of Sarah. Still, I didn't believe for one moment that Gwendolyn was telling the truth. She and Dottie were acquainted. How, I didn't know, but they were. And Dottie had told her something she didn't like at all, for I could see that she was restraining her anger even now.

We drove home mostly in silence, although I said my thanks at one point to Gwendolyn--who had insisted on paying for everything that day, and wouldn't hear of my contributing even a small amount.

"If you're to accompany me about the countryside, I shall dress you. Besides, I want my future daughter-in-law to look exquisite, radiant, in fact-- right now, your colors are all wrong. That pale skin of yours needs a brighter shade next to it, and really, dear Anne, we must get some weight on your bones." She laughed, deep and throaty, and I wondered once more if her motives were true, but ignoring my uncertainties, I put aside the strange meeting between her and Dottie, forgot my distrust, Martin Rollins, all the unpleasant things in my past--and did as she said.

I ate; I bloomed; I met the neighbors, and although I didn't realize at the time, I became more and more vain, reveling in my new-found status. Not only did I learn much about social etiquette from those visits with the gentry, I also discovered quite a lot about Lady Gwendolyn. Chats over afternoon tea could be quite informative. While she was discussing this and that with the lady of the house and Sarah played elsewhere with the younger children, usually one of the daughters or *nieces* and I had time for our own conversation. Apparently, while Lyle's mother was accepted in the community, she was not well-liked; the respect of the neighbors had been primarily for Sir Roderick, and perhaps Lyle as well.

"'Twas quite a scandal when he re-married," Lady Isobel from Fairfield Manor told me. "His wife had been dead for less than three months, and no one really knows where he met *her*. He just appeared from London one day with *her* one his arm, and that was that."

"Lyle seems to think quite well of Lady Gwendolyn," I responded.

"Oh, yes, well, she coddled and cooed over him, and as his mother had only just died, he needed someone to show him special attention. She didn't spend half as much time with Sarah, poor thing. And the child would do anything to impress her mother. It's quite a pity actually."

I had to agree inwardly that it was. As Gwendolyn was my employer, I kept my comments on these remarks to a minimum, but I wondered about them all the same. Where had Sir Roderick met her? What was her background? I came to wish I'd pursued the answers to those questions, but at the time more interesting things were taking place in my life, and my mistress' past was no concern of mine.

I enjoyed my outings tremendously. Having never had friends before, meeting young women my own age appealed to me--still I was somewhat shy and kept most of my thoughts to myself, letting others do most of the talking. At times it crossed my mind that the young ladies I met spoke mostly of trivial matters--the latest party, the newest fashion, the handsomest young man (of which Lyle was definitely a contender according to my new-found friends). But I, too, soon became caught up in these things, swept away on an ocean of self-interest.

I rarely thought of Ian. I knew he was up and about, for I'd seen him riding across the fields on his black stallion, but he was occupied with his own work. Lyle and I spent every free moment together, leaving little time for anything, or anyone, else. We took long walks in the afternoon when the weather was fine; on rainy, cold days, we stayed in the drawing room playing cards or chess (Lyle was teaching me this most interesting game) or reading to one another.

We found we had much in common and could discuss anything from history, to geography, even politics, and rarely did we disagree. A comfortable companionship permeated our togetherness, and if it didn't feel quite like love or passion, well, I ignored this, tempted by the future which lay in his hands; thoughts of a home and family in a grand house, cared for by a kind man, with everything I'd ever wanted at my fingertips.

One day during a walk about the estate while Lyle was pointing out various improvements he someday hoped to make, I asked him about his plans for himself. Would he return to London to take up his father's diplomatic career or remain in the country?

"It's odd you should ask," he replied. "Father always intended for me to follow in his footsteps. We almost came to blows over my decision to attend Cambridge rather than accept a commission in the military But now that he'd gone, and please don't misunderstand, I'd bring him back if I could, but well, now that he's gone, it's almost as if I've been freed--now I can follow my own desires."

"Which are?"

"To make Leighton a profitable estate, I suppose. As I told you once before, agriculture had always been a passion of mine. My mother's grandfather, my real mother, Caroline, was a country squire who had a farm not far from her. Before he died, I used to spend every free moment there, learning about the land, and crops, and farm machinery.

"I'd like to be able to fill a need in this county--produce grown and sold at the markets, the finest wool from our sheep, milk from our dairy cattle. The land here is prime for farming, and with hard work and patience, I know we could make a success of it. We've made a start, Ian and I, but there's a long way to go."

"And does Ian share your dream?" I asked, curious as to how Lyle perceived his friend.

"Ian feels he owes me, which is ridiculous. If anyone owes, tis I. At Cambridge, some of the fellows questioned my masculinity from time to time, and Ian always put things right for me, if you know what I mean. But he believes that because I've taken him in and given him work, he owes it to me to stay and run the place.

"Someday though, he'll have enough saved to go back to Scotland and refurbish his castle. I'd like to believe he cares about Leighton Hall as well though."

"I'm sure he does," came my reply, yet I wondered.

"And what about you, my dear? Do you care about the estate?"

"Very much, Lyle. It's a wonderful place and I'm glad you're going to have the opportunity to pursue your dreams for it."

"And will you be here to pursue them with me?" he asked, reaching for my hand and gazing long into my eyes.

"That's up to you. I suppose."

"No, Anne, it's for both of us to decide. I'm very liberated, you see. Any future of ours will be with the understanding that we are equals."

I smiled and our walk resumed, as did our days. When Lyle and I were together I felt safe and protected, as if I were a princess in a glass case and no harm could ever touch me there. But when I was apart from him, I questioned my happiness. What right did I have to all this, to his love? I could never be his equal socially. Why did I selfishly allow myself to believe it was so, when at any moment I might be snatched away by my other life, returned to my guardian or his cousin in London?

But no word had come from him as of yet, although some time had passed since I'd written. Perhaps it was because Maddie had been right about my destiny... I belonged here and was simply being given my second chance.

***

"It's your move, Anne." Lyle's words brought me to the moment.

"So it is," I responded, basking in the warm glow of firelight, wishing our evening might never end. Lady Gwendolyn and Sarah sat near us and, their needlework laid aside, were whispering intently. Smiling to myself, I wondered what mischief they were planning now. I felt gloriously happy in the knowledge that they both seemed to want Lyle and I to marry, especially Sarah, whom I'd thought lost to me forever.

"Anne," Lyle said again. "Shall we stop playing now?"

"Oh, Lyle, I'm sorry. I've just been daydreaming."

"About what, my dear?"

"Oh, nothing in particular."

He laughed. "Well, I hope that's a good sign." He reached across the chessboard and squeezed my hand. "I also hope I know what you were thinking about."

My cheeks felt hot, but I smiled.

"Lyle," Gwendolyn broke in, "there's a lovely view of the moon tonight from the gallery. Why don't you take Anne for a stroll?"

Why did her eyes seem so menacing? At odd moments like this, I felt threatened when she pushed us together.

"Would you like that, Anne?" he asked.

"I'm afraid I'm really rather tired, Lyle. Why don't you just walk me to my room instead?"

His stepmother and Sarah looked mildly disappointed but turning back to their conversation. Lyle and I rose, and wishing them both goodnight, left the room.

The Great Hall was dark and chilly as we crossed it, but streams of moonlight cast odd shadows across the tile.

The house had an unusual stillness that I'd noticed frequently of late, and I wondered the servants hadn't bothered to light the lamps.

In response to my question, Lyle replied, "They bother Mother's eyes, so she asked them only to light a few. But you needn't be afraid when you're with me, you know?"

"I'm not afraid. I've just had the oddest sensation of being watched the past few days. I don't know... it's difficult to explain."

This was the first time I'd admitted this, even to myself. I'd been so intent on my happiness, I hadn't wanted anything to shatter it.

"You're not still worrying about Martin Rollins are you?"

"I don't think so. I guess he's given up trying to find me. Still, I would have thought he'd have reported to my guardian by now and we'd have some word. It seems rather strange that Rev. Jaspar hasn't written."

"My darling Anne," Lyle turned to me and took my shoulders, "someday I'll take you back to Countisbury and then you can find out what's happened to that foolish old man. And you can show him what a good life you're made for yourself without his help."

I had to smile at his intensity, but changing the subject, I asked, "What do you hear from you solicitor?"

He shrugged as we resumed walking. "Nothing, I'm afraid. His courier came for my father's papers, but the last note I had from him said he hadn't made any progress. We don't even know how long ago all this may have occurred."

"I'm sorry," I said quietly, "I didn't mean to bring up a subject which distresses you.

Lyle's eyes brightened as he looked at me. "Oh, Anne, how I love you! I believe I love you more with every day that passes." We'd reached the door to my room at last, and he took me tenderly into his arms. He bent his head to mine and I drew my arms up and around his tall form.

"Please don't ever leave me, darling," he said, "I believe I'd die if you did."

"Oh, Lyle...

Our lips met, his devouring mine; mine making motions, searching for passion, finding only friendship. *I'll love him in time*, I thought, *it comes with being together, having a life*. But even as the thought occurred, darkness rose up in me, triumphant; it seemed to pervade my being and take form, and the form was a face with dark eyes and hair. I should have known in that instant I was holding back the truth, from Lyle, from myself But instead I refused to acknowledge it, until the moment came at last when it was too late.

Chapter 17

The holly is dark when the rose-briar blooms...
Emily Brontë

Thus my emotional swings continued; soaring high in the air one minute, near to touching the treetops, the sun glowing against my face, lighting my days, glorifying my every thought. But in the next instant, low to the ground, feet dragging the earth, depressed, afraid of my very shadow. My feelings of being watched intensified during these moments--a click of a door behind me in a dark corridor, the movement of a curtain at the window when I gazed up from outdoors, the sense of eyes on me; I couldn't shake these sensations. And the dreams returned... I was often awakened during the night by the sound of movement in a room above my own, footsteps, or a strange rocking motion, yet I knew those chambers to be unoccupied, so what could I be hearing? It must be the dreams...

What I remembered of them specifically was once again the voices; arguing, angry: two women bitterly at odds with one another--where had the other woman come from? Two men, both hurting, in pain, hearts breaking, and what, a third man with a voice I knew, a mocking voice, the voice of Martin Rollins! These characters haunted my dreams, but refused to show their faces. How I longed to understand their meaning! Knowledge seemed so close, if only I could open my eyes, I thought, I would see it, comprehend it, but all that remained were the sounds, no words, no faces, nothing else.

No news came from Rev. Jaspar, no word for Lyle about his sister. Rev. Liddell came to review my progress with Sarah and said she was moving along admirably, but when I was alone in the schoolroom with her, I noticed that she, like her mother, seemed to be constantly watching me, waiting, but for what? What were they looking for? What did they want?

One evening when Lyle still hadn't come in from the estate, Gwendolyn and I sat before a blazing fire, she with her sewing and I reading a new novel by Mr. Charles Dickens that I'd discovered in the library. After a time, I looked up to find Gwendolyn staring, seemingly intrigued by my presence; I had the distinct feeling she wanted to ask me something, but didn't know how to broach the subject. Finally, she spoke to me abruptly, "Was he never good to you?"

"Who?" I asked uncertainly.

"Your guardian, of course."

"Oh. Well, I suppose he is a good man, but I don't think he really knew how to relate to children. I never felt he cared for me, but at the same time, I can't really say he was cruel."

"You appear to have turned out well enough. He can't have been too bad a guardian.

I looked at her cautiously. "He taught me to have high morals, and I have a friend who helped me learn to believe in myself, so I guess my life in Countisbury wasn't as bad as I thought at the time."

"I would imagine you miss your friends," she went on, still pressing.

"One in particular, yes, but most of all I miss the cliffs and the ruggedness of the moors and the taste of salt mist in the air."

"Yes, the ocean is especially lovely there," she mused inwardly.

"You've been there, then?"

She looked up quickly, taken by surprise at my question. "Yes," she answered reluctantly, "a long time ago."

Then she fell silent once again intent on her stitchery, an indication that our conversation was over. I had the awkward sensation that I'd missed something in our exchange, that she was trying to find out something specific, but I had no idea whether she'd learned what she wanted or not. I certainly was no closer to an understanding of her, so at a loss for further words, I returned to my reading.

The months slipped by and before I knew it, Christmas was nearly upon us. And what a Christmas it was! Never had I experienced a holiday such as that! Leighton Hall was decked out in festivity--the servants hung bright green wreaths of fir tied with big white bows in the foyer and along the polished oak banisters of the stairways. Garlands of mistletoe danced gaily about every door, and the tables boasted candle-lit arrangements of holly with shiny red berries. Mrs. Blum went about humming carols, and from time to time the servants would join her in a burst of singing. During those days, the Hall was a happy, joyous place to be, and my fears of being watched vanished with the gaiety of it all.

Gwendolyn left us for a few days, "I must go to London she exclaimed. "The shops in Langport simply aren't adequate for my shopping needs. Besides, there are some matters concerning the house there that I had better look into." And so she went and perhaps this accounted for some of the lightness, as if a dark shadow had been lifted from over us all.

Sarah and I spent our afternoons indoors working on our own gifts. She embroidered handkerchiefs for her mother and Lyle. I knew she was making a special gift for Ian, but this she chose not to share with me so I suspected that a portion of her distrust remained even after all this time. I copied verse into a special book I was making for Lyle. For Gwendolyn, I'd sewn a lavender sachet of smooth white satin tied with pink ribbons. On the fabric, I'd embroidered a small black swan that reminded me of the first time I'd seen her--a black swan gliding across the winter garden. Sarah's gift was to be a small picture of a castle I had begun to paint from a drawing in *Le Morte D'Arthur*.

While I knew it wouldn't be appropriate for me to give Ian a personal gift, I did manage to make up several little tins of herbal tea from a special recipe of Maddie's. Jamie, the gardener, had helped me find all the right ingredients. "Her Ladyship the first 'ad an herb garden, she did. An 'ah 'elped 'er plant it," he told me proudly. "'Ah've kept it up in her memory, God rest 'er soul. She'd be glad to 'ave someone put 'er plants to use."

So my tea would be made and since I planned to give Mrs. Blum and Nell and Cook each one, I thought perhaps it wouldn't be too obvious for me to make an extra for Ian. The time I spent preparing them in the large airy kitchen was wonderful. The heat from the big black ovens gave the room a warm glow, and Cook gave me a small corner in which to work. Although she was grudging as usual, it was the season of giving, and even Cook was not above remembering this. She soon began to cheer up when I commented on the fabulous smells filling the air--cakes, pies and pastries, sauces sweet and savory, fresh baked bread! The aromas were heavenly!

Finally Lady Gwendolyn returned, spirits high, wearing a new outfit of black satin brocade, laden with trunks and packages from the town. "I'm having a dinner party on Christmas Eve," she announced, her vivid green eyes flashing. "We'll invite about thirty guests, and after the meal Rev. Liddell will conduct a midnight service in the chapel

Lyle stared at her. "Don't you think it's a little too soon after Father's death to be entertaining, Mother?"

"Nonsense," she told him flatly, "You know we always have services here, and the neighbors have been so kind to us during this time of trouble. I want to do something in return. At any rate, the staff will expect to have their usual celebrations and I don't see why we shouldn't do likewise."

"I think perhaps they'd understand considering the circumstances."

"Life goes on, Lyle," she said, "I miss your father too. But we have your future to consider." She looked toward the chair in which I was sitting with a book, trying to ignore their conversation. "You wouldn't want Anne to think we don't celebrate Christmas at Leighton Hall, now would you?"

Lyle's gaze turned to me and his face brightened. "Very well, Mother, once again you have won your case." So the dinner party was set for Christmas Eve and our days became a flurry of activity and planning.

I never realized so much was involved in the undertaking of a simply dinner party. Gwendolyn insisted that I have an active hand in the event--she showed me lists of people to be invited and together we selected those whom *she* felt were most appropriate; menus were gone over carefully choosing something to suit the taste of each guest, music for the service was arranged, and on and on and on.

I wondered what I should wear for such an occasion, and had just about decided on a gray silk when

Gwendolyn informed me that she had made arrangements for both Sarah and me in London. She pulled out two large boxes while the girl and I stood, dumbfounded and curious, two excited children instead of only one. A dress of dark green velvet with a high collar trimmed in Belgian lace had been purchased for her daughter.

"None of this mourning for you, Anne," she said, "You didn't even know Roderick, so you have a light, cheerful dress." The dress she laid before me was ivory satin, and its rows and rows of fabric fell from a tiny gathered waist, beaded with seed pearls. The neckline was so low that when I first tried it on, I blushed and insisted I'd need a shawl for the evening.

"Ridiculous," Gwendolyn insisted, "A woman's bosom was made to be shown. Lyle will love the gown." So even in this she had her way, for didn't I want more than anything to be loved and admired? But her eyes betrayed envy, and I shivered against their glitter. I knew why I was doing this, but why was she? I felt no real affection from her, so why bother? Why?

I wondered if Ian was to be invited to this affair, for his name hadn't come up when we spoke of invitations. Sarah must have been of the same mind for one morning, in my presence, she asked her mother about it. Lady Gwendolyn wrinkled her nose distastefully and tilted up her chin.

"Of course not, Sarah. I know you are very fond of Ian, and he is Lyle's friend, but you must remember that he is employed by us. The staff do not, by habit, attend our social functions."

Sarah's face dropped and I could see she was close to tears, but her mother continued without notice. "Ian has informed Lyle that he will be spending the holidays with his aunt in Scotland. In fact, I do believe he's leaving tomorrow."

"But Mother, what about my gift?" Sarah cried, really upset by now. "I've made a special present for him!"

I, too, was feeling oddly disappointed that Ian would not be staying at Leighton Hall over the holidays. "Perhaps Mr. McCrae might join us for dinner this evening," I suggested hesitantly, "and Sarah could give him her gift then."

"I think not," the older woman shot me an angry glance. "As I said, socializing with an employee is not acceptable." Then turning back to her daughter, "You'd better grow accustomed to that fact, Sarah."

I wanted to ask why, then, was it acceptable to socialize with me, but held my tongue. After Gwendolyn had left the room, I turned to the girl. "Sarah," I said slowly, "Would you like me to take your gift to Ian?"

She looked doubtful and I knew she mistrusted my motives, but apparently her desire for Ian to have the present on which she'd worked so hard won out. "Will you promise to come back straightaway and tell me what he said?" she asked eagerly.

"I promise," I replied, squeezing her hand, "Straightaway."

As I headed toward the gatehouse a few minutes later, I began to have serious reservations about my errand. Did I have some other reason for wanting to see Ian? I'd stopped by the kitchen just long enough to pick up one of my tins of tea. *It's the season of giving* I thought, *that is the only reason I'm going.*

Ian looked surprised when he opened the door. After inviting me in, he addressed me slowly. "So how are you?"

"I'm well," I replied, taking the chair he offered, "And you?"

"Well enough. Just getting some things together for my trip to Scotland."

"How long will you be gone?"

"No more than a week. I'm just staying over the holiday."

"I see."

Neither of us spoke for several moments. "Will you visit your estate while you're there?" I asked finally.

A sad expression crossed his face. "Yes," he said softly, "There's a caretaker there, Old Ben. He's been with the family for years, and he looks after the place for me. I'll check in with him to be sure there've been no vandals or poachers about."

"You must miss your home quite a lot."

"I miss the place it could have been if my mother hadn't died and Gran hadn't left, and my father, well my father is another matter."

"How long has he been dead?" I asked as tenderly as I could.

"Five years. Five long years since he shot himself and left me with nothing--nothing to see to the needs of Castle Crac. I guess I should thank God I've been able to keep that. But there's so much to be done there, and every time I return it seems to have fallen into worse disrepair. I don't know if I'll ever have enough to make it the place it was."

"I'm sorry."

He gave me a long look. "No, I'm sorry," he said at last "I don't think you came to hear about my problems."

"Actually, I came to bring you a gift from Sarah." He took it and stared at the wrapping for a time.

Finally he tore open the string and drew out a knitted scarf. "My family colors..." he said, fingering gently the red and blue design. "I showed them to Sarah once and she remembered. Please give her my thanks. Tell her I'll treasure it always."

"I've brought you a tin of tea," I said. "It isn't much, but it's a special herbal recipe. I hope you'll enjoy it."

"Gran used to make herbal tea. I've missed the taste of it over the years." He stood then, placing both the scarf and the container on the table. "I have a gift for Sarah, too," he handed me a small packet which he retrieved from the mantle, then he put something wrapped in a soft piece of cloth in my other hand. "And this is for you. I was going to leave then with Mrs. Blum, but since you're here, I'd like for you to open it now."

"You shouldn't have, Ian," I said softly.

"No, Anne, I've been unkind to you and this is my way of saying I'm sorry. I hope we can at least try to be friends in the future."

"I'd like that."

The fabric held a tiny oval locket, and I drew in my breath. On the front, engraved in the gold, was the image of a swan. "It's lovely, Ian, but I really shouldn't take it. This should be for your wife." I wanted to bite back the words the instant I'd said them, for I suddenly recalled Gwendolyn's story about how he could never marry. But Ian didn't appear to notice.

"I want you to have it. It was Gran's and she'd be proud to think that a lovely young English girl is wearing it. Look, it opens."

He unfastened the hidden clasp and a picture of a handsome man that looked a little like Ian himself gazed out me. "He's my grandfather. You can put another picture there though, if you like."

"I'd love to have it there," I told him, "I will treasure this always." I gave him a warm smile and turned to go.

He followed me to the door, then without warning, bent his lips to my forehead. "Merry Christmas, Anne."

The encounter stayed with me. I couldn't seem to shake my feeling of surprise at his kindness. He'd sent Sarah a pretty copper pin fashioned to look like her dog, Nero, and she was overjoyed and wore it every day.

But though I loved the locket, I kept it hidden beneath my bodice, for I had a strange notion that both Sarah and her mother would be distressed should I tell them from whom it had come. And Lyle, of course, would be hurt. But why shouldn't Ian give it to me, I asked myself, if he could never marry, who else would he give it to? My delusions led me away from the truth once again.

Chapter 18

Or is the heart thou dost adore,
A faithless heart to thee?
Emily Brontë

The long-awaited Christmas Eve dinner party arrived at last! The village had buzzed with the news of it from the moment invitations went out-- Gwendolyn was well-known for her gala affairs, and despite Sir Roderick's death, this one promised to be as grand as any.

And indeed the formal dining room glistened with light and laughter. Its marble columns were draped with colorful ribbons and the cherubs painted on the vaulted ceilings smiled down on us cheerily. Gwendolyn sat resplendent at the head of the long table flanked by an admiring squire on one side and Rev. Liddell on the other. Her deep laughter echoed across the room, her bosom heaving seductively with each throaty movement. The red lights of her auburn hair sparkled in the candlelight and contrasted nicely against the dress of black velvet--her emblem of mourning. At her neck was an ornamental gold chain from which hung an unusual black swan.

My own locket had been placed aside for the evening, for it should have been too obvious with the low-cut neckline of my gown. Gwendolyn herself had loaned me a fabulous diamond pendant, and while the jewel sparkled against my pale throat, my skin felt bare without the locket.

I was curious as to where she'd come by her swan. Something about it had always seemed familiar, but I supposed I was simply confusing it with the one on the locket Ian had given me.

Shrugging the thought aside I proceeded to concentrate on the plentiful meal before me. Four courses in all, Cook had truly outdone herself. The table overflowed with her culinary delights--fricasseed fowl, roast haunch of venison, ham and peas, julienne soup, fresh perch--the list went on and on. I found it difficult to remember that I was now a lady, and "ladies should always eat like a bird at social gatherings" as Gwendolyn had told me.

Lyle, seated across from me, rarely took his eyes from my face during the entire evening. I saw many a young woman cast an envious glance my way, including my friend Lady Isobel, but he never noticed; his gaze was for me alone.

How proudly I held my head! The gown I wore was like that of a queen and I couldn't fail to see that it aroused not only Lyle's interest, but quite a few other gentlemen's as well. I saw many of the young ladies' mothers staring with disapproval in my direction, evidently displeased that a newcomer was taking attention away from their own marriageable girls. But none of the young men present came anywhere close to Lyle's good looks or even Ian's for that matter. How was Ian enjoying his holiday with his aunt, I wondered? I bet many a girl would have swooned over him this night. And yet, it was I to whom they both had been drawn--I, lonely Anne from Countisbury had the hearts of two men at her feet. How strangely elated that made me feel! My dreams had almost all come true!

Toward the end of the meal, however, the spell was shattered. As we all sat, enjoying iced pudding, rich pastries with cream fillings, damson tarts and trifles, Lady Gwendolyn stood and began tapping her spoon delicately against a crystal goblet.

"I have an important announcement to make," she said, a secretive smile teasing at the corners of her mouth. Whispers went round, but soon silence fell once more.

"You have all been so kind to and supportive during the sad untimely death of my husband and now I know you're all aware that my stepson, Sir Lyle, will be presiding over Leighton Hall henceforth." Nodding heads could be seen as she went one, "So, of course, it's only natural that he should seek a wife."

I felt the blood begin to leave my face; my skin became clammy and moist. What was she up to now?

"It is my extreme pleasure to present to you at this time my future daughter-in-law, Miss Anne Cowper."

I must have gasped aloud, for all eyes turned toward me like spectators on the winning horse. A flurry of sound fluttered through the air. My friend Lady Isobel raised a questioning eyebrow, probably surprised that I hadn't given a hint of any such development. *I mustn't faint*, I thought,

I mustn't act startled.

Across the table, I saw such a look of utter astonishment on Lyle's face that I knew he'd had no knowledge of her plan. Even Sarah appeared ignorant of her mother's intentions. But Lyle, of course, took action like the true gentleman he was.

Rising, he came around the table to stand beside my chair, placing an arm lovingly around my shoulders. "A toast for my darling Anne," he said aloud, and stooping to place a tender kiss on my forehead, he whispered, "Don't worry, my dear, everything will be fine."

But it wasn't fine. How could she do such a thing? My heart thumped unnaturally throughout the remainder of the meal, and later in the salon, amid the many congratulations of the ladies. They were happy I wouldn't be available now, this would mean their own daughters were back in the running. But I, I was stunned at the announcement. I'd had no further chance to speak to Lyle, for the gentlemen had retired to brandy and cigars, and Gwendolyn avoided me completely, except to cast me a mocking wink as I stood surrounded by well-wishers. Anger rose up within me. How dare she presume in such a manner? How dare she?

All through the service I considered the situation; I didn't know what she wanted, but I was not someone to be used. While Rev. Liddell's droning voice read the Christmas story from the Book of Luke, I tried to decide how to best handle the matter. Lyle and I had been set up and Gwendolyn knew it; if he didn't propose to me now, we'd both be humiliated. And I wouldn't stand for her forcing his hand. I simply would not! I tried to join in with the singing of holiday carols, but the spirit of the season had been spoiled for me. I wanted this day to be over. At last, I decided I must speak my mind as soon as possible.

After we'd bid the last visitors good night and wished each of them a Merry Christmas, I turned to Lady Gwendolyn angrily. "How could you," I gasped as much from anger as dismay, "embarrass Lyle and me that way?"

She eyed me like a cat with a small insect. Lyle, who'd been seeing a last guest out, moved toward us. "I wasn't aware that what I said was cause for embarrassment, I thought *you*, for one, would be delighted."

"Lyle had never discussed marriage with me."

"Perhaps he's only shy," his stepmother said coyly.

"He is not shy. Did it ever occur to you that perhaps he doesn't wish to marry me?"

"Is that true, Lyle?" She turned to him. "Do you not want to marry Anne?"

"That's not the point, Mother, and well you know it. That decision should be between Anne and I, and no one else."

"Well, my dear boy," her eyes held a cold threat directed at me, though she spoke to her stepson, "it might be wise for you and her to discuss that very important issue before someone else steps in and does it first."

A shiver crossed my body. Was she going to bring up the subject of Ian now? Why was she trying to force this upon us?

The matter was dropped then, but not before Lyle was able to send me a curious look. Surely he wondered "who" might step in and ask for my hand before him.

I passed a restless night, and the next day even the rounds of gift-giving under the present-laden tree didn't brighten my spirits. Christmas suddenly lacked the luster that the previous weeks had possessed. Lyle's present to me was a small cameo ivory-carved with a dark tortoise shell background. "The girl reminded me of you," he told me, but something in his words held distance.

Later that afternoon he asked if we might take a stroll in the garden.

"Lyle," I began slowly as we walked among the trees and bushes, "About last night...I feel terribly about what your stepmother did."

He stopped and turned my face to his. "There's absolutely no reason for you to feel bad, Anne."

"I know but..."

"No, please let me finish. I've thought a great deal about it, and Mother's right. I should have asked you long before now. I suppose I was afraid you'd say no."

"If you ask me now, I must say no," I told him with force.

"But why?"

"Because I would always believe you stepmother forced your hand. I don't want to begin a marriage that way."

"But surely you know..."

"I know you care for me and that perhaps someday you might want a future with me. But when the time is right, if you want me for your wife, you'll be the one to ask."

His arms folded around me and his mouth met mine, his tongue probing gently. Deftly, he pulled at the buttons of my bodice and finding flesh beneath, roamed my bare skin with feather-like movements. I could feel my body begin to respond. Then his mouth moved lower and found the beginning of a breast beneath my dress, heaving deeply as the warmth began to spread. A fire burned within me, a force rose up and began to lay claim on me.

All I want...all I want...all I want, I can have. The words repeated themselves like a chant, threatening to choke and destroy me if I let them.

Then abruptly I remembered the day on the Tor, with Ian. Suddenly Lyle's touch burned, hot as a flame and painful, and I pulled back, out of the embrace.

"No!" I said, gulping the air, "No!"

Confused and ever the gentleman, Lyle stepped away. "I'm so sorry. I didn't mean to take advantage of you. Please forgive me."

I was at once contrite. I'd overreacted; he hadn't meant to frighten me.

"It's late," I said for lack of a better response, "I must go in now."

And with that our Christmas ended. What had begun as a happy, special holiday for me, ended on a sour note. Perhaps now I'd lost Lyle forever-- Leighton Hall would never be mine. I'd refused his proposal, scorned his embraces. Would he forgive me? Did I want him to?

***

I dreamt of Lyle that night, and yet with the strangest feeling he wasn't Lyle at all. The man whose visage crossed my sleep was dark, and spoke with a strange accent, but something in his gaze told me it was Lyle all the same. We walked beside a clear, blue stream; how odd, I thought, this place reminds me of Glastonbury, and indeed when I looked up, I saw the Tor looming ahead.

The man was my dear friend; perhaps, I reasoned, if *he* loved me, I could forget the other... let go of my obsession, have a serene life. Then, anger swelled within my breast, but no, he too, loves her. They both love her-and I have no one, no one left who loves only me. Pain arched across my heart.

But then came another thought. No one indeed; and what about the child stirring within my womb? He would be mine. Surely she would not deny me that. His love would be mine alone, and through him I would reach the father; our souls might touch again, as they touched once before in that instant before we knew our love was forbidden...

Chapter 19

An undefined, an awful dream.
A dream of what had gone before...
Emily Brontë

February came and with it the heart of winter, and we were mostly indoors except for some sunny afternoons when Lyle would come for me after lunch and we'd go riding across the barren field. The evening in the garden was not mentioned again except for a short note from Lyle the next day that said, "Dearest Anne, what a cad I was. Dare I hope for your forgiveness?"

I sent it back with an affirmative response and that was the end of the matter. Neither was his proposal brought up--and oddly enough, I felt a strange sense of relief at that. I wanted Lyle and all he had to offer, but I hadn't been ready to say "yes."

We still don't know each other well enough, I told myself. But was this the real reason? What of the dream I'd had about him? What did it mean? Who was the woman who had the love of them both? I wished I knew if that dream was somehow connected to be *voices*. I had the strangest feeling that it was, but I couldn't quite grasp how. If only Maddie were here to explain them to me. I must write to Maddie. I'd put if off for too long. I'd promised, and I had neglected that promise. But I promised myself and my friend I'd set it right soon enough. How I needed her wisdom now!

Sarah and I continued with our studies, never discussing my future as a member of her family. She acted quite unusual these days, continually staring at me when she thought I wasn't looking, watching my every move from under veiled gazes.

Early one bright morning we were in the schoolroom when, without warning, Ian entered. So startled was I by his unexpected appearance that I jumped.

Sarah hopped up and ran over, hugging him. "Ian, I've missed you horribly. Where on earth have you been?"

While they talked, I had a chance to study him closely. His face had a pallor about it; I wondered if he'd been ill again. We hadn't seen each other this close since my visit to the gatehouse at Christmas. He and Lyle had both been busy, snow and ice played havoc on plants and animals, as well as the tenants, and even Lyle's days had sometimes been too full for visits. Suddenly I realized how much I'd missed seeing Ian.

"I've been busy, little lass," I heard him telling Sarah. "Estates don't run by themselves, you know; the poor sheep have to be kept safe and warm this time of year, and someone's always got a leaky roof or some other problem. How've you been, then?"

"Oh, pretty well," she answered." So what brings you doing here today?"

"I've come with a message for Anne from Lyle." He turned to me, refusing to meet my gaze directly. "He's to go to Langport for the afternoon and says he can't meet you for a ride today."

"Oh," I said. "Thank you for going to the trouble of delivering it."

"It was no trouble, lass." He raised his gaze to mine them. "I enjoyed the tea. It reminded me very much of Gran's. Thank you."

Some strong emotion tugged at my heart. "You're welcome. I hope you haven't been ill again."

"No I've been well indeed," but his voice didn't ring true and I wondered what was troubling him.

"I'd best be going now. Goodbye, and to you, Sarah." He turned and strode from the room, leaving us both in silence.

The rest of our morning passed without event and after luncheon I decided I needed some fresh air and would take my ride without Lyle. Sarah was visiting with her mother, so I donned my warmest cloak and headed for the stables. I was a well-dressed young woman now, thanks to Gwendolyn. I had gloves of the softest leather and a fur-lined bonnet, even a riding habit of deep jade velvet. I no longer had need of those meager items I'd lost when coming to Leighton Hall.

I'd forgiven her for the Christmas Eve announcement, but I still didn't trust her. Since that day she'd been rather withdrawn from me, but continued to look for any chance to push Lyle and me together. We ignored her as much as possible.

Nero ran from behind a wooden door as I approached the horses' stalls, leaping at me and barking, obviously too cooped up lately and wanting a romp. I stood playing with him while one of the grooms readied the horse.

"All right, boy, you can come with me. But you'd better stay out from beneath Mrs. Merriweather's feet." He licked the hand I offered eagerly, and I laughed.

A short while later dog, horse, and I were racing across the bleak hills, wind biting sharply into my cheeks, gloved- hands frozen to the horse's reins. The moors, like the garden, offered me solace even in the midst of their grayest hour. I enjoyed the rides with Lyle but little had I realized how I missed this solitude! Slowing the horse to a walk, I took in the silvery shimmer of winter--it had snowed recently and a fine powder still covered the ground, sparkling in the sunlight. Tiny diamond-bright droplets nestled among the branches of the trees and every now and again one or two would slide to the ground, creating a quiet little serenade of magical music. A lone thrush's song rang out sadly, as if it had lost its way and its loved ones, and was all alone in the world. I had felt that way once... Happiness swelled in me now at the thought that I was no longer alone.

But why then, why, did I feel this unease, stirring of restlessness, uncertainty?

I wished I could stay out forever, but the day began to darken; dinner would be served soon and I'd better return in time to dress. Nero had wandered off somewhere, and after searching for him for some time, I finally concluded he could find his own way back to the Hall and turned Mrs. Merriweather in that direction.

Suddenly, from out of nowhere, a shot rang out.

Startled, the horse whinnied and pawed the air as I fought to gain control. After several moments, I managed to get her quieted down without being unseated.

But where had the shot come from, I wondered? And who had fired it? No one was within sight, although I couldn't see far into the grove of trees just to my left. I knew I should tell Lyle about this as soon as he returned. If it were poachers, he would want to know right away.

The horse cantered on, still skittish, but I handled her without further problems. I had an uneasy qualm once again, however, and suddenly I felt tired, drained, wanting only to find and bed and sleep. Sleep. I wished I could sleep forever.

***

A solitary figure rode bareback across the moon-dark moor, long black hair flowing out behind her. I watched her. No, I was her-no, I only watched. It made no sense.

Abruptly she reined the animal toward a tall hill. A castle loomed in the distance. The girl laughed. She was thinking about living in that castle, being its mistress, ruling its lands and people.

"No, child. That is not for you." A voice filled up the blackness of the night.

The girl laughed again. "What right have you to say? You, who have abandoned your children, allowed false gods to come before them-you have no right to order me about." The sky lit brilliantly for a moment, then a loud clap of thunder rang out, causing the girl to shiver.

"Do not attempt to control your own destiny, child" the voice threatened. "I warn you it will not serve you well."

The girl remained silent this time, and the vibrations of sound appeared to fade away. Finally, the girl motioned the horse forward once more, toward the castle.

"This must be," she said quietly. "This must be."

"Anne! Anne, wake up!" Someone was shaking me, but I didn't want to come back. I'd been about to discover something important. I knew it. I must stay. I'd seen the faces.

"Anne, please wake up. Please!" Sarah's voice broke through the mist, and I forced my eyes open at last. "Oh, Anne, please, please hurry and wake up! I need you!" The girl was sobbing, great wet tears rolled down her cheeks, making her distress all-too-obvious at last. I struggled into a sitting position.

"What is it, Sarah? What's the matter?"

"It's, it's Nero," she cried, "he's run away and he hasn't come home."

Remembering when I'd last seen the dog, I tried to soothe the girl. "He's wandering about somewhere, I'm sure. He'll be back by morning."

"But he never stays out at night. He always comes to the house to eat, then he sleeps in my room. And it's snowing, Anne. He could freeze to death!"

I studied her for a long moment, streaked face, damp hair. Poor child, I thought, she doesn't ask that much from me these days. Surely I can find the dog for her. But what if the mysterious person with the gun should return? I couldn't worry about that now though. Surely I'd be safe enough if I hurried.

"All right," I said, "I'll go out and look for him. Tell your mother I may be late for dinner and I'll have something later."

"Oh, thank you, Anne! Thank you so much!" She hugged me tightly and I felt satisfied with myself--her affection was important to me and perhaps I was beginning to win it back.

I retrieved my cloak from a chair where I'd laid it after returning from my earlier ride and headed toward one of the east doors. No doubt Nero had gone snooping around the old shepherd's hut near the spot I'd been riding. He was probably there sleeping right now.

Not wanting to disturb the groom for a second time that day, I headed for a foot-path near the edge of the lawn. Bitter cold gripped me at once and indeed, a light snow had begun to fall. The daylight had almost disappeared and I hoped I would be back at the Hall before complete darkness fell. The sky had turned gray and a silver moon was just barely peering through on the horizon, giving the evening an eerie glow, and I hurried along the path trying not to dwell on my fears of being followed. I called out to Nero as I went, but my own voice was the only sound I heard, echoing back hauntingly through the trees.

Everything was still and so quiet, even the air seemed to hang listlessly around me. The only sound I heard, other than my own voice, was the occasional flutter of a solitary leaf as it left its perch, eager to join its companions already sleeping on the earth far below. I must have looked behind me at least fifty times, checking the way I'd come, but each time I saw nothing more than my own footprints on the snow-covered path and the gently falling flakes lighting atop the hedgerows and covering them with a speckled coat.

I drew my cloak tighter against the chill and hurried on. Finally, after what seemed an eternity, I came to a fork in the trail that led to the old shepherd's hut. Still I'd seen no sign of Nero. Unfortunately I would have to leave the path to reach the dwelling. When I did so it was with the utmost reluctance, for the woods were dark and frightening, and my mind was brought back to the night I'd fled Martin Rollins. These trees loomed above even more menacingly, but I tried to turn my thoughts away from their threat and toward the task at hand.

"Nero," I called, "here boy. Where are you, Nero?" Pushing through a grove of firs, I saw the back of the hut. What few strands of moonlight there were gave it a frightening appearance and I dreaded going closer. The snow was falling more steadily now, and I could feel the damp of it beginning to seep through my cloak. *At least I'll be dry in there,* I thought and went ahead as bravely as I could.

I walked around to the front of the place, then stopped in surprise. A light was coming from inside the cottage! The door stood open just a few inches and a dim glow spilled into the darkness. A knot began to form inside me. Who could be here--Lyle had always said no one lived in this old place. Cautious and silent, I went closer until at last I was able to see into the room. It looked empty. Forgetful of Nero, I pushed the heavy door to and moved hesitantly inside.

A half-burned candle sat in the middle of a shaky- looking table, casting long dancing trails across the walls. The place had a lived-in look about it: odd, since supposedly it was uninhabited. Yet now, a candle stood burning, a blanket was spread across an old wooden bed, and the remains of a fire smoldered in the grate. And the smell...there was a distinct, musty odor in the air. Who could have been here? Was it someone from the Hall perhaps, or an intruder? Whoever it was, it appeared they planned on returning soon, so I had best be on my way before they did.

As I turned to go, a book lying on the bed caught my eye. Thinking it might give a clue as to the inhabitant's identity I went and picked it up. Uninterested in the title, I turned at once to the frontispiece, hoping to find a clue there. Suddenly, the room began to spin, and I sank to the bed in horror. Martin Rollins Martin Rollins Martin Rollins

The name pounded through my head until I thought it would literally beat me to the ground. I covered my ears trying to drive out the sound, but it only got louder and louder till I felt I'd scream if it didn't stop.

Then, it ceased. And was replaced by another noise. This time it was the sound of a door. Slamming. Shut. I looked up quickly and saw that it was indeed closed tight. The wind hadn't blown it thus. The wind wasn't blowing. I felt almost overpowered with my own fear, but I managed to rise and go to the door. It was bolted from the outside!

My God! I thought frantically. *Someone's locked me in here! I can't get out!* I banged against the wood, calling out, hoping against hope it was an accident, that whoever it was would return and set me free, but then abruptly, I fell silent. What if Martin Rollins had locked me in here? The book on the bed was his...who else would be coming to this place?

The candle was beginning to sputter and wave. And the cold of my damp clothes and this fireless room was beginning to make my whole body feel numb. My eyes searched the fading light. No windows, no other door. I was trapped here until someone chose to come and let me out And if it was indeed Martin who came back...my fear began to close in on me then and I backed slowly into a corner, never taking my eyes from the candle's dying flame.

When I could go no further. I slipped to the floor, shivering inside and out. The black was becoming as suffocating as a tomb, and it crept in upon me, closer and closer, shutting out not only the light, but the air as well. When at last the candle's dim glow fluttered away completely, my horror took control, and I entered into an oblivion of my own.

Chapter 20

...my sad soul forget its pride,
And longed for one to love me here...
Emily Brontë

I have no idea how long I remained unconscious on that cold wooden floor. When I awoke, my body was stiff and ached all over. Darkness black as pitch enveloped me, but little by little my eyes adjusted and I made out dimly outlined shapes of furniture. My head throbbed, but finding myself alone relieved some of the pressure. Maybe Martin wouldn't return here at all tonight. Surely someone from the Hall would come to look for me soon. Sarah knew where I was and was bound to alert the servants when I didn't return.

Pulling my cloak tighter, I rose from the corner, thinking to feel my way about in the dark and perhaps find some more matches and another candle. All at once, I heard something from outside the hut. Footsteps. Someone was moving toward the door. Martin had returned after all! What was I going to do? No way out, nowhere to hide. "Dear God, protect me," I prayed.

The outside handle made a grating sound as it turned, but I scarcely heard it over the pounding of my heart. Trembling like a frightened rabbit, I moved back to the shelter of my corner. The door was sliding open. Streaks of shadowed moonlight poured into the room. My legs gave way beneath me and once more I slipped to the floor. I sat, shaking with nauseating fear.

A man's silhouette was outlined in the dim glow of light that now rushed in through the open door. He moved inside, closer and closer to the spot where I hid. His face was invisible, shadowed in darkness, like my dreams, I thought irrationally. Then suddenly, I knew he was looking directly at me. I'd been discovered. I began to scream and scream, my cries flying out into the night, then striking back at me in terror. Mercifully at last, my world again went black.

***

A fierce swirling mist gathered round me, rising from it the Tor, magnificent and undaunted. Sprawled across a heavy mound of dark earth I lay, blood from the kill still warm on my nude body, running in red rivulets down my skin to mingle with dirt and the dark flow of my hair. *He* loomed above, sunlight highlighting the golden glow of his firm masculinity. The horned mask he wore foretold of his purpose and rank--the stag-hunt, he, my king. My own face was covered by a veil of thin blue gauze, the headdress of a virgin priestess,

147

and as such I must do my duty, to this man and no other. Yet, I felt no fear, only pride, for the Goddess had deemed it to be *so*.

And when he knelt at my side, quickly drawing me near, I swelled with the power of my position, yet even so, wondered if this moment would be enough? The smell of him, sweat, mixed with the dead animal's blood, consumed me. His touch caressed, and hands of steel sent shivers of delight over me, washing my quivering youth with the water of life; his soul seemed to reach in and stroke my own. Night pressed down upon us...we were one, and our oneness stretched on into eternity.

Oh, to be with him forever, my king and lover...oh, but what he could give me! More riches than I'd ever dreamed possible, security in a world of uncertainty a kingdom to rule. And his body...his lovemaking...never in my wildest imaginings would I have suspected passion to be thus. How could I spend the rest of my life serving only the Mother? What kind of life would that be--after this?

When at last we parted, I breathed a ragged sigh, feeling complete and filled for the first time ever. Who had given such pleasure? I must see the face of this newly-sworn king. As I reached up to untie the mask shielding his face, he pushed aside the cloth covering my own. As it slid down, his eyes, clearer than blue ice, met mine.

He recoiled, horrified at what he saw, and I too, felt initial shock at first recognition. I knew him; I had played childish games with him, sung lullabies in the even, run along the shores of a pebbled beach. My heart screamed out in horror--how could you, Great Mother; of all things, how could this happen? Tears of anguish burned hot against my cheeks.

But little by little the pain ebbed; my mind adjusted to the idea, and I contemplated its uses. The stag hunt slipped into a memory, as did my promise to the Goddess; everything was forgotten--except my own desires. *And so I will have all I want,* I thought. *And I will have you again my love. Indeed, I will. Even if you are my brother.*

***

Arms entangled me. I fought for control of myself, of my senses. Who held me? What had happened just now? A dream, or reality?

As my vision began to clear, I saw who held me bound. Lyle--safe, reliable, Lyle. But my mind kept screaming out, *My brother! My brother! He's my brother!* I felt shaken, confused, lost in a cloud I struggled, even against Lyle.

"Shh, Anne, it's all right," he said. "Everything is all right. I'm here. It's Lyle."

The dark shadows enveloped us like a web, so tightly I could scarcely make out our faces--which kept fading in and out of the others I'd seen, leaving me to wonder who was who.

"Anne," Lyle whispered, "what's happened here? Why didn't you wait for me if you needed to go out? Anne my precious Anne. Don't you know how much I love you? Agony bled in his voice, but I was lost in agonies of my own.

I wanted to be pulled in, to cling him as I'd done so ago. But I couldn't...I couldn't. I mustn't forget what had happened.

I managed at last to push his hold away. "No!" I screamed at him. "No! Never, not for anything!" And I jumped from the floor, filled with a power that came from I knew not where.

He backed from me somewhat with a shocked look on his face. "Anne?" he asked almost feebly, seeming to question my very existence.

I headed blindly toward the door, yanked it open, then with a quick thought that he might attempt to follow me, slammed it shut and bolted it. I must get away from this place, from him, from myself, before all this threatened to destroy me.

Now I had no fear of the woods or the trees. I ran, paying no heed to the darkness. I ran, until I could run no more. Then I slowed my pace somewhat, but only to catch my breath.

What had I done back there? Had I given myself to Lyle or had that happened been only in my mind? If only I knew the truth.

And if something had happened, why hadn't I stopped it? Could I have stopped it? Was I using this as a way to bind him to me permanently? Was I trying, once more, to force destiny's hand?

The stables were in sight now, and I felt a pang of guilt at having left Lyle locked inside the hut. But they would discover him soon enough, and I wanted time to leave this place. I knew now that I must return to Maddie, for I had questions that only she could answer, and it was time I had those answers.

I stumbled in the darkness and looked down to the furry object at my feet. Nero!

Was he dead? I reached down and felt for a heartbeat. No, he was alive, but appeared to be in a very deep sleep. He could be ill, I thought. Or drugged...

The corridors lay in dark shadows as I entered the hall. So who had wanted me to go out alone bad enough to do something to the dog? Martin Rollins? If so, how did Sarah fit into all this? Or did she?

I would have to slip a quick note under Mrs. Blum's door before I left, because I didn't want anything to happen to Sarah's dog. Or Lyle.

Looking up, I realized my lack of attention had led me up one stairway more than was necessary. I started to turn back when I saw a faint light coming from under one of the doors. Who could be there? These chambers were unoccupied.

For the second time that evening, I moved uncertainly toward a lighted doorway. So numb was I with all that had already occurred today, I scarcely knew what I was doing. Approaching slowly, I peered into the partially opened crevice. Firelight dimly lit the room, but little by little, I made out a large bed, and in the center, what appeared to be a single body lying upon it. I felt the blood rushing to my face. There must be two bodies there, for their movements indicated they were in the throes of passion.

A moment passed while I stood, unable to move from the spot. All the earlier memories of the blood, the sweat, the passion came flooding back upon me. These two moved with that same rhythmic movement, slow and with fluid motion. The woman's hands pressed the man's buttocks tightly to her. His head was bent to one breast and he fondled the other gently as he slipped in and out of her body.

Embarrassed, I started to turn away and return the lovers to their privacy when my attention became focused on the woman's cascading auburn curls. Only one person at Leighton Hall had hair that particular shade, and it wasn't one of the servants! Gwendolyn! Squinting against the shadows, I saw that it was indeed she who lay there. Fully nude, her body glistened with drops of jewel-like sweat against white skin, and occasionally a cry of pleasure escaped her throat. No trace of the grieving widow here! She was obviously enjoying the encounter.

But who was the man? I knew of no suitors or male acquaintances who had ever called before. Was this secret tryst something recent, or had she been meeting someone even before Sir Roderick's death?

My head was pounding with these and a hundred other questions, but then my attention was suddenly drawn back to them as their passion became more intense even as I willed my gaze away. All at once, the man's back arched and he raised his body for one final thrust. In that instant I saw his face and recoiled, grabbing the wall in horror. It was Martin Rollins!

Chapter 21

...turn away from passion's call,
And curb my own wild will...
Emily Brontë

Somehow I made it back to my room without collapsing. This last was too much, my body had become like water, fluid and with no form of its own. Once in my own chamber, I sank down upon the bed. I couldn't believe what I'd just seen! The person who'd tried to attack me at Ram's Head, whom I feared and thought to have escaped, was in this very house! And even worse, he was Gwendolyn's lover! How on earth had she allowed herself to become involved with such a man? Surely she couldn't be aware of his true character; she must have been beguiled by his charms. I remembered the suave voice and slick appearance I'd first seen in the parlor at the rectory. And yet, there'd always been something about her that troubled me. Had my intuition been right after all?

Poor Lyle! Searching so diligently for the illegitimate child of his father, while here in his own home, his stepmother conducted her own illicit love affair. His family honor appeared to be threatened at every turn. And *why* did the people he loved continually let him down--myself included? What was I to do now? What? I knew I didn't love Lyle; I wanted all he had to offer, but I didn't truly love him the way a woman is supposed to love a man. With the passion and fire and intensity I felt for another.

I closed my eyes against a fresh onslaught of tears. I knew I must leave immediately, but having shut my eyes, sleep must have claimed me for a few moments, for suddenly I was in another room, a cold room, a room that frightened me. I recognized it almost at once--the library! Firelight flickered across the floor and I widened my gaze in an attempt to take in more of the scene before me. The heaviness of the velvet drapes and dark paneling were suffocating, the air tight and thin.

Then abruptly, I saw a large huddled shape lying nearby. I pulled my mind back but, refusing to be diverted, it carried me onward to the still mass. A body. Covered with blood and immobile in death. Fear rose in me, but I strained my eyes to see who they were. Fingers drenched in red clutched the rug in a frozen grip. On one hand, I saw a signet ring with a family crest I'd seen before. In the Great Hall.

Lyle's.

A cold sweat jolted me into wakefulness. The scene had been so vivid, so real. My body shook with the horror of it. This had been no vision from the past. Lyle had been lying there. It must have been Lyle! Dear God, I couldn't let this happen! I had to find a way to stop it!

I rose from the bed and went to the pitcher sitting on my bureau. I splashed the icy water across my face several times, and finally, certain I was wide awake, went to the window and gazed across the lawn. The moon had come out and hung high overhead. Near midnight, I thought. Breathing deeply, I willed Maddie to come, to guide me, to tell me what to do. I couldn't stay here any longer--I wouldn't be a danger to Lyle, and I had no right to a future with him, knowing as I did that any relationship would be largely based on my materialistic needs, not love. But I couldn't leave without Maddie's consent; she'd told me my destiny lie behind these walls, that I mustn't run away from it. But surely now, the time had come for me to go. With every ounce of being my soul possessed, I summoned her presence to me now. For a while all remained as it was, then after a few moments, the quiet stillness passed, and I heard her.

"You can leave now, my dearest. Come home to Maddie. I have your answers. It's time now. I'm here. I'm here."

My body suddenly relaxed; I took a deep breath and sighed. I could leave. I was free. Her glow still tingled around me and despite the chill, I felt warmth I hadn't experienced for ages. "Thank you. Maddie," I breathed aloud, "Thank you."

And so without another moment's hesitation, I went to the wardrobe, removed a few necessities, and packed them in my valise. I penned a quick note to Mrs. Blum, asking that she see to Lyle and Nero. Maddie would help me now. She knew everything, and she would advise me as to the course I should take. While I was with her, I'd pay a visit to my guardian; it was time he told me the truth about the mysterious Martin Rollins!

So I left Leighton Hall--in the middle of the night, frightened, friendless, and alone, filled with doubt and uncertainty about myself and my future. Langport was a five-mile walk, but I knew I could catch the train there at dawn and be on my way before Lyle discovered me missing. Probably before he himself was discovered in the old abandoned hut.

I knew I could never stay in this place and make a wise decision about my future. I was too pulled by the attractions of all it had to offer. Something told me I had made the wrong choice once before and I must not make it again. Besides, after the dreams and visions I'd experienced this night, I didn't trust myself to remain. What if I had an evil side and that nature was beginning to take over? Was I losing my mind completely? Who was I? Who was the dark-haired girl? Who killed the person in the library? Were they all me? *Please, no*, my heart cried. *I don't want to be a calculating, depraved person, using others to achieve my own ends. Please let distance and my friend's wisdom help me put it all in perspective.*

Silence covered the night like a shroud as I made my way across the grounds toward the nearest road. For some reason the darkness didn't bother me--it was far less a danger than the black unknown of my soul. What will Maddie have to tell me, I wondered. What does she know? I firmly believed my friend did indeed have the answers I sought. But could she help me save Lyle from whatever disaster lay ahead. Especially if I was the cause of that disaster. She must. She must.

All at once, a horse sprang from a wooded grove beside the road! He whinnied loudly and I jumped back with a shriek.

An angry voice spoke from inside a dark, hooded cape. "And just where do you think you're going in the middle of the night, might I ask?"

Ian. Good Lord, what am I to tell him? And what on earth was he doing out at this hour?

"I couldn't sleep," he said, reading my thoughts. "So I decided to take a midnight ride. Then who should I see leaving the Hall, but none other than yourself, my dear Miss Cowper. Well?"

I continued to stare at him blankly, trembling against more than the cold.

"Well?" he thundered.

"I'm leaving," I said.

"I gathered as much. But why? And what are you leaving with?" He pointed toward my valise.

I felt my anger rising, but held it in check. He had every right to be suspicious. My behavior was odd to say the least.

"I really can't explain it now, Ian. But you may check my things if you like. I'm not taking anything except some clothes. Something's happened. I must go. I have to see my friend Maddie."

His look softened and I wondered if he was remembering our conversation that day on the moors. "So were you planning on walking the entire way to Langport on this cold, winter night?"

"Yes," I replied simply.

"Aye, and tis frozen you'd be when you arrived. If you arrived at all...

"I have no choice. I don't want anyone to know I've left."

He seemed undecided as to what he should do, but suddenly, he reached down. "Up with you then," he said, "I'll take you there myself."

And before I knew what had happened, I was deposited in front of him on the black horse Titan. I remembered the last time they'd come to my rescue. How angry he'd been that day! But now he seemed content to let me relax my tired and cold body against his, soaking up the heat of his flesh, snuggling deep into the woolen cape.

He didn't speak for some time, but at last he did, in a soft caressing tone unlike the one he normally employed when speaking to me. "Can I help, lass?"

I was uncertain. Could I trust him? Did he really want to help? I wasn't at all sure. "I can only tell you that I'm having second thoughts," I answered, "about myself. I need the answers to some questions."

You seemed frightened a moment ago."

"I, I saw something that made me afraid tonight."

"Do you want to talk about it?"

I hesitated. "I saw someone with Lady Gwendolyn whom I have reason to fear."

I could feel Ian's gaze boring into the back of my head. "Is that all?" he asked.

I jerked around, trying to see his face. "What do you mean?"

"I mean, is that the only thing you're running away from?"

"Isn't that enough?"

We both fell silent for a time, then he spoke again. "Who did you see her with?" he asked.

"Martin Rollins," I said slowly.

"The man who was taking you away from your guardian?" Ian didn't sound surprised.

"Yes."

"And where were they when you saw them?"

I felt the blood rush to my face. "I can't tell you that."

He laughed. "I guess that fairly well tells me. You saw then in a rather embarrassing situation, I take it."

I nodded.

Ian continued in the same gentle vein. "I've suspected for some time that *Lady* Gwendolyn wasn't as faithful as she pretended." He stroked a strand of hair that had slipped from my hood before he went on. "But I suspect you saw her with someone who resembled Martin Rollins. I doubt it could have been the same man. Besides lass, you haven't seen him for months."

"But it *was* him, Ian. It was. And I'm worried about Lyle."

I felt his body stiffen behind me. But surprisingly, he didn't sound angry when he next spoke. "Is that why you're leaving?" he asked, "To see if you can find out anything from your guardian?"

"Partly."

"I see. I knew there was more. Anne..." his voice sounded wistful and sad.

"What?" I asked softly.

"I wish I could tell you. But I can't...I can't." He broke off and I heard a crack in his tone.

"Why can't you just admit you care for me?" I asked. "Is it so difficult?"

He gave a weak laugh. "There are so many reasons I can't admit that. So many reasons."

"Lady Gwendolyn told me about the madness in your family," I said abruptly.

I heard his sharp intake of breath and for some moments he didn't speak. "Is that what you thought, then?"

"Isn't it true?"

"Perhaps so, but not in the way you might think."

He said no more, and quiet fell around us; only a few seconds later we reached the station. I hadn't even noticed we'd entered the town, so absorbed was I by his presence, his words. But now the fact that I must leave him me with a heavy heart, and I felt weak and defenseless again.

"Wait here," Ian said, sliding from the horse's back. Several minutes later he returned, and after helping me to the ground, he placed something in my hand. "A ticket to Mineshead...that should be near enough to your village that you could hire a carriage to take you the rest of the trip. The Barnstaple train doesn't come til midday, and I didn't feel you'd be wanting to wait that long. This one leaves at dawn."

"I don't know how to thank you," I said, touched by his surprising concern for my well-being.

"Do you need money for the carriage?" he continued.

"No, I...I have enough, I think."

"Then I'll leave you here."

"Ian," I hesitated, then proceeded slowly. "You know the old shepherd's hut in the woods?"

"Of course, it's been abandoned for ages now."

"When you get back, I think you should check it for poachers."

He gave me a curious look. "Why?"

"Just please go there. All right?"

He nodded and then moved toward his horse, but he must have sensed my distress for he stopped and turned to me again. Without warning he took me by the shoulders and bent to place the tenderest of kisses upon my forehead. The spot tingled at his touch and I felt a strange tug within my breast.

"Don't forget me," he said. "I'll be here should you ever need a friend. And don't worry about Lyle. I'll keep a watch on him."

Then he mounted his horse, and turning him away, faded into the night.

***

My first trip on board the black iron beast that men called a train was not such as I would have expected. Thank God Ian had purchased my ticket, for I wasn't sure I could have figured out the maze of schedules and timetables in time to catch the morning train. The noise in my coach was hideous, the seats hard, and the countryside flew by so fast it made my head swim.

After a few minutes of nauseated perusal, I closed my eyes against the scenery, wanting only to sleep. I was exhausted after the night's experiences. Unfortunately that blessed commodity was not so easily attained--my rest was tormented by the old dreams, but this time the voices had the faces of Lyle and Ian and Martin Rollins. This time when Lyle's face faded into a mist, I welcomed Ian's dark smoldering eyes.

Finally I decided it would be wiser to stay awake the final distance and try to occupy my mind with some task of my own choosing rather than be haunted by visions I could not control. I pulled a book from my valise and spent the remainder of the journey reading a book about the lives of the saints. The book had been destined for return to Rev. Liddell and I felt guilty about having it, but I promised myself I'd post it to him as soon as possible. At least it gave me something to do, and indeed I needed to read about the lives of those holy ones for I had certainly proved myself to be among the worse of sinners! Or had I? I still wasn't sure exactly what had happened with Lyle but regardless of that, at some point, in some time other than my own, I had been a terrible person. My visions had shown me that!

Somehow, as the trip progressed, the weight began to lift from me a little and I felt stronger than I would ever have suspected possible. Maybe all that had happened had helped give me the strength to face myself as a woman and a person. With each passing moment, it was becoming more and more important for me to know the truth about who I was, whereas in the past, I'd always more or less accepted my fate not to know. I couldn't help but feel a little glad that I'd broken away once and for all from that helpless girl and was finally finding that I had it in my power to stand on my own.

When at last the train pulled in to Mineshead, I'd recovered tremendously and proceeded immediately to try and find a way to get to Countisbury. Remembering my wagon ride with the old man in Somerset, I asked a red-cheeked porter to point me in the direction of the town market. Surely someone would be going in my direction, if not now, then later in the day.

Upon finding the place, I moved amidst the hustling throng, questioning vendors as to their day-end destinations. Unfortunately, most of the people lived in the area of Mineshead, and I could find none who planned to journey as far as Lynton at the end of the day. Then, I remembered the mail coach--the drivers I'd listened to with such interest what seemed like centuries ago! Perhaps if I hurried I might get lucky and be able to ride with him!

A bleary-eyed old fisherwoman pointed me in the direction of the post office and I rushed off hoping I wouldn't be too late, for the position of the sun indicated it would soon be midday, and if memory served me well, the post had always arrived shortly after the noon meal. This time I was in luck!

"'Ad some trouble wi' the coach today, did I, miss, so 'ah'm late startin' out. Hope ye won't be afeared 'o a fast trip down the 'ills."

Assuring him I would not, I climbed up, assisted by the firm grip he offered, and almost at once we were on our way toward the coastal road.

"Some bread and cheese for yer lunch, miss?" he asked as we rode along high atop the rig. Tom Kebby's stocky middle-aged form boasted a sandy thatch of blondish hair and a friendly grin.

"Thank you, Tom," I replied. How hard it was to believe I'd been away for eight long months. It seemed like only yesterday. Tom's cheery whistle reminded me of many a village lad's, and I realized with amazement that I'd missed the simplicity of my life at Countisbury. Just as I'd missed the ocean salt in the air and the sea breeze against my cheeks. In that instant, I felt uncontrollably happy. The warm sun on my face reminded me that spring was on the way. Soon I'd be with my dearest friend, and all would be well.

"Tis a lovely day, ain't it miss?" Tom asked.

I smiled at him. "Yes," I said sincerely, "It is."

"Have ye lived in Countisbury long?"

"Seventeen years."

"Ye're a native then, air ye?"

"Yes, I suppose I am at that."

"So where kin I be leavin' ye, miss? The village is across yon hill, and ah'll be stoppin' at the Blue Ball. You can get out there, unless you need to go a pace or so further."

Past experience told me that Tom and the innkeeper at the Blue Ball would be exchanging discussions for some time, so I decided I would walk the remainder of the distance to Maddie's hut.

"I want to visit a friend first," I told him, "so if you don't mind, I'll get out at the road leading to Lynton."

"Know somebody in Lynton, do ye?"

"Not exactly," I laughed, "actually, I can't say as I know anyone there. My friend lives in the Valley."

The man looked at me a little oddly and shook his head. "Can't says I 'eard a anyone livin' in the Valley."

"Well, my friend's a little shy," I said, smiling.

When at last he let me off, I gave him some coins for his trouble and he beamed at me merrily, then whistling, wished me a fair day and drove on to his stop. As I headed across the moors toward Maddie's, I wondered at what task I'd find her today. I had to see her before I went to the rectory, and I prayed a silent prayer that I'd find her. Still, I wasn't sure what to say when I did. How could I tell her all that had happened to me over the past few months? And would I have to? How many times it had seemed she was there beside me, taking the same steps as I, listening to the words as I spoke them. Then at other times, she seemed to abandon me completely.

I gazed across my moors as I walked--they were sleeping now and I let them rest, hoping I would be here in the spring to gently awaken them from their slumbers. As I approached the ocean wall, I stared into the glare of the sun against the waves, shading my eyes against the brightness. Squinting, I looked toward the rocks of Satan's Leap and saw her there, standing on the cliff's edge just as I'd seen her that first day, wind in her arms, cape swirling around the tall majestic form. For a moment I was frozen yet again, but before I could draw my next breath, she turned toward me and I screamed in both agony and joy, "Maddie!" and my voice echoed out across the water.

I never seemed to move, but in the next instant we were clinging to one another, our bodies melting into one--mine renewed in her glowing presence. Tears ran down our cheeks and flowed into a single river as we stood, locked in a timeless eternity. At last we separated, two beings once more, and began to walk slowly away from the sea, toward the moors, the trees, and home.

***

"It hasn't been easy for you, has it, my dear?" Maddie asked as she made me a cup of chamomile tea from the special herbs that grew in her garden.

"No," I answered softly.

"You've done well, child. You've met your destiny and now your future is in the hands of the gods. That's as it must be."

"Oh, Maddie," I said, beginning to sob, "I've done wrong. I've done so much wrong."

"No, RoseAnne, this time you've done what's right. Sometimes we are placed in situations over which we have no control, and we must live through those times as best we can. You've done well, my dear, and you haven't tried to use the circumstances to control your own fate. You've come face to face with false, self-serving love, and you're learned that the call of the heart is more important."

"But I wanted to control my destiny, Maddie. I wanted to. I tried to. A part of me still wants that."

She patted my hand. "Of course it does. But you're here, aren't you? You didn't take that course this time. You've left the decisions to the immortals, whose wisdom far exceeds your own, and who always have your best interests at heart. You couldn't have chosen a wiser path."

I looked at her curiously, wondering, yet feeling I understood her better than ever in the past. "How is it that you're always here for me, Maddie? Every time I needed you, really needed you, you've been here. And now, I need you not just for myself, but for someone else too. I need you to help us both."

She laughed. "I know that, my dear. And so I shall help you. And so I shall. But we'll talk more of this later. For now, you must live this life and not become too wrapped up in your yesterdays. I want you to have a good night's rest here, then tomorrow, you must do your duty."

"My duty?"

"Rev. Jaspar is ill. You must care for him now as he cared for you when you were a child. Also, I know you have questions to ask him before he dies."

Shock hit me. "He's dying?"

"Yes, he is, RoseAnne. The gods have decided he's done his penance and may return to them. But first he must answer your questions. And, he needs you, child."

"Needs me?" I laughed a little sarcastically. "I imagine I'm the last person he needs right now."

"Ah, RoseAnne, you mustn't be bitter. Jaspar had choices to make too. Still, he has a love for you he could never admit. I think you'll find him a changed man." She smiled at me warmly and gave my arm another pat. "Now let's tuck you in for a good rest, and in the morning you'll be ready for the task at hand. After that, you and I will have a good, long talk."

"Yes, Maddie," I answered meekly, still wishing fervently that I needn't wait for my talk with her.

"You must have your answers from the Rev, first, love," she said, reading my thoughts. "Mine have kept for centuries. A few more days won't make a difference."

Chapter 22

...Earth's the same, but oh to see
How wildly Time has altered me-
Emily Brontë

Dread hung heavy upon me as I headed toward the rectory early the next morning. Maddie has sent me off with a hot cup of herbal tea and large fluffy biscuits and jam in my belly. But although my hunger was satisfied, my nerves and curiosity were not. Thus far my mission appeared to be a failure, for not only had Maddie refused to give me any hint of the answers I needed for my emotional well-being but now it seemed Rev. Jaspar would not be able to shed any light onto the details of my past. What exactly was his ailment? I wondered. Hopefully, he would recover--I couldn't have traveled so far for naught. But Maddie didn't believe this to be so, and Maddie was usually right.

At least I'd had the joy of seeing my dear friend again, and of being here back in this spot I loved so well. Looking around at the early morning splendor of these moors, it occurred to me that they and Maddie had a lot in common. Always they were there for me, strong and safe, carrying a timeless grace that would never fade or alter. Even in the winter's bleakness she had a cheery smile, just as these earthy folds hid their warmth beneath the gray sky. I wished all relationships could be as simple as the one I had with Maddie. She was my friend, simply and completely. She wanted nothing more than my love, just as I wanted nothing more from her.

I was home. The words felt so good. So right. But even as I thought them, I felt a strange tug within my breast. The Tor had felt this way too. Would anywhere ever feel completely like home to me after my experience there? Even Leighton Hall paled in comparison to that tall, imposing hill with its morning mists, silent sunsets, the thorns of spring in full bloom. I knew all that, I knew it, even though I'd only been there once in early fall. Why then had I thought the Hall to be so important? Worth giving up everything for? What had happened to me--the girl who loved the moors, and combes, and forests? Where had *I* been these past few months?

I saw my life with such a clarity that it startled me--the selfishness, the vanity, the hunger for passion and love. Anyone's love--no matter what the cost to that person--or myself! I couldn't believe the lack of feeling I'd shown toward others, despite all my pretenses of caring for those around me. Ian had been more right about me than he'd known. And what about Ian? What were the secrets he held back? Why couldn't he admit he cared for me?

A terrible thought struck me out of the blues Could Ian somehow be involved with Martin Rollins? Was that why he'd failed to show surprise when I mentioned that I'd seen Martin with Gwendolyn? *Dear Heaven, don't let it be so!* I prayed. Don't let him be part of that! It didn't matter about the madness in his family, or his refusal to acknowledge me, or that Sarah had a schoolgirl crush on him--I cared for Ian. The only thing that mattered was my heart, telling me I loved him, that he was special, and that the warmth of his arms along could provide the shelter I craved in this life.

The prick of tears was close but I choked them back seeing that at last the gray stone of the rectory was upon me. I gazed at the small square building and saw it as I never really had before. No dainty curtains graced its bare-paned windows, no cheerful flowers smiled from the bed; the slate roof shone dully against a cloudy sky. There were so many years of heartache here in this dreary setting, wasted years. I opened the old wooden gate and approached the door with mounting alarm. Would I be strong enough to face the house's occupants? To take their hard cold attitudes and still stand strong? *I don't know!* My brain screamed, *I don't know!* All the years of loneliness and pain hit me once again, and it took every ounce of courage I possessed to raise my hand and knock.

A moment passed before Mrs. Rickett appeared. "Lands sakes and Lord have mercy on our souls--If it t'isn't Anne! What on earth are you doing 'ere, girlie? Though Lord knows you couldn't 'ave come at a better time. I need your 'elp somethin' awful. Rev.'s been ill...we'd both given up on you since we've neer 'eard a word in these months past. Near broke 'is 'eart, you did, missie. And after all 'e did for you. You should be ashamed of yerself." She clucked her tongue in disgust. "So 'ow'd you come to be 'ere now? I see no carriage waitin. Don't suppose you walked all the way from London, did you now?"

I stared at her, surprised that she didn't know I hadn't been in London at all. She peered around me at the road in front of the house and I took advantage of the pause to insert a few words of my own.

"It's a long story, Mrs. Rickett, and one I'd rather save for later. I'd like to see Rev. Jaspar now if I may."

She pulled herself up haughtily at my authoritative tone. "So, London's made you high and mighty, 'as it now? Well, young lady, ah'll not be putting up with your airs around 'ere. I raised you from a naked babe, and you'd best be treatin' me with some respect. Now hang up your cloak and bonnet and I'll find you an apron in the kitchen. When the Rev.'s awake uh'll be soon enough for you to see 'im." With that she bustled off into the other room leaving me gazing after her in dismay.

Obviously, little had changed in the time I'd been away from Mrs. Rickett and she still expected me to do her bidding as if I was a child. Not wanting to get into an argument in my first few minutes back, I smiled at her large disappearing form and proceeded to do as I was told When I entered the kitchen a few moments later she handed me an apron that reminded me all too quickly of the drab garb I had worn before I left this place. Glancing down at my soft floral gown, I remembered the day Mrs. Blum had helped me cut the pattern. How proud I had been of this, one of my first dresses purchased with my wages as a governess! Of course it wasn't as fancy as the ones Gwendolyn had bought, but this one was mine--all mine--and nothing could compare with that sense of satisfaction.

Still, my present appearance was probably distressing to Mrs. Rickett, who had always insisted on keeping me clothed in the most dreary of colors. Oh well, I thought, I'm a different person now, and like it or not, she's going to have to accept that fact. Donning the apron indifferently, I hastened after her down the long dark hall that led to my guardian's room.

"Since you're so bound on seeing 'im, you can just sit 'ere for a spell. His fever's up a bit today, and 'e needs spongin' with a damp cloth on and off. I've got more than enough work to keep me busy elsewhere."

Before we reached the room I asked her who was taking services during the Rev.'s infirmary. "The vicar over at Lynton is sending his curate over on Sunday's for worship. But the Rev.'s presence is sorely missed in the village. No one sees to the needs of the sick and the poor these days. His shoes will be hard to fill, I fear." She sniffled a little and I realized with amazement that she must truly care for him. He'd never treated her much better than he had me, but she seemed sorry he was dying.

Could she have loved him? I wondered. I couldn't imagine anyone being in love with Rev. Jasper, but perhaps, in her own way, she had been. After she'd gone, I looked toward the bed and was startled by the sight that met my eyes. Was this wasted figure the same man I'd left only a few months ago? He'd always been thin but with features of iron, whereas now, he looked little more than a corpse. Flesh hung loosely from his frame and his gray hair had a dull lifeless tint to it. Rasping, shallow breaths emitted from his throat, but from the look of him, I was amazed he was breathing at all.

I moved to the bed and hesitantly picked up a damp cloth, placing it gently to the feverish brow. "Oh, God," I prayed aloud, "Please don't let him die. Not yet. Please." I felt a sense of anger rising within me.

As if one or both of them heard me, his eyelids fluttered open and he looked at me without surprise. "Anne," he said hoarsely, and struggled to take my hand. "Forgive..." and then once more in lapsed into unconsciousness. I wept tears of frustration that I'd come all this way only to find him like this. Once again he'd let me down.

"Curse you," I said bitterly, then felt ashamed of my uncharitable thoughts. His life was almost over, and apparently he knew he'd done me wrong or he wouldn't have asked for my forgiveness. I must find it within me to give it, but all the same, I would pray that before he died, he would live to give me the answers I so desperately sought.

The next few days I spent almost entirely in the room of the dying man. I nursed him with a loving care I never knew I could feel for him, applying my earlier training from Maddie to ensure that his days and nights were as comfortable as possible. My anger seemed to have faded into its own recesses. Left in its place was a powerful desire to make his last days peaceful.

He lapsed in and out of consciousness but rarely did he have the strength to speak, so I spent most his waking hours reading aloud from the Bible. This seemed to relax him and from time to time he'd smile at me weakly. How strange, I thought, that smile did look on his normally stern face. I tried to remember if ever, during my childhood, I'd seen him laugh or smile, but I was hard-pressed to think of even one time.

"Gaiety is the devil's play," he told me once when he found me singing cheerily as I polished the oaken rails in the church. "God expects only piety in His house."

"But sir," I'd asked meekly, and in the innocence of childhood, "Why is it that God doesn't like us to smile in His house?"

"There is a time and a place, girl," he thundered, "God's house is for solemn worship. Naught more. And," he added, giving me one of his blackest looks, "I'll thank you not to question my rules in the future."

I had learned quickly that Rev. Jaspar hated to be contradicted in any manner. To avoid conflict, I'd simply accepted this quirk of his nature and went about my tasks, pushing my own ideas into the dark recesses of my being. But when I was alone on the moors, I'd pull out those thoughts and examine them, and my young heart had rebelled. I promised myself that some day I would find a world of my own and fill it to overflowing with laughter and gaiety. So for a time I had found it, yet even that world had its own sadness and sobriety.

What could have made my guardian so hard, I wondered. On my fourth day back at the rectory, I discovered the answer. Not only did what I found shock me, but it also helped me to understand a little of his bitterness.

Rev. Jaspar was sleeping and I'd gone to his study to do some dusting, when I accidentally knocked a small old Bible on a top shelf to the floor. Picking it up, I absentmindedly turned its pages and stopped at the register of marriages and deaths in the center of the book. Several of my guardian's kinsmen were listed, but what caught my eye was an astonishing entry under marriages:

Jaspar Fitzgerald Cowper to Glenda Anne Ridgeley June 5, 1839

Could it be that the "Cousin Glenda' in London was in reality Rev. Jaspar's wife? But no, apparently not, for an entry on the next page read thus:

Glenda Anne Cowper - died May 14, 1840

She died the same year I was born, and they hadn't even been married a year. No wonder he was resentful of an abandoned child, when his own wife had been taken before she could give him one of his own. Poor man! For the first time I understood his harshness. He had lost a young wife, and who knows, she might even have died in childbirth. That would make it a double tragedy.

Closing the Bible, I carried it with me as I walked the long corridor to the kitchen. Mrs. Rickett, her back to me, was busily kneading bread at the large table in the center of the room.

"How did Rev. Jaspar's wife die, Mrs. Rickett?" I asked her abruptly as I entered.

"Lord have mercy!" she said, jumping around clumsily, sending flour flying into the air, "you frightened me 'alf to death, girlie! Don't you know you're supposed to announce yourself when comm' into a room?"

"I'm sorry I frightened you," I said impatiently. "But I just discovered that Rev. Jaspar was married at one time, and I thought perhaps you might know how his wife died?"

"Well, miss, she went to 'er sister's in Mineshead to 'er with pneumonia, an' caught it herself. Just as well, if you ask me." She shook her head disapprovingly.

"But why was I never told he was married?"

"'E hated people to talk about it and forbid me to even mention one word to you. Besides, it was a long time ago. She was very young and irresponsible. 'E's been better off without 'er and 'e knows it well." She blushed as she spoke the words and pushed a stray wisp of gray hair from her face with a floury finger.

"What was she like?" I inquired, still curious and shocked at this new information.

"I never knew the girl meself. But she 'ad a reputation, she did. And ah'll never understand why 'e married 'er." She shook her head again, then appearing embarrassed at having said too much, went on hastily, "You'd best be gettin' back to your patient missy, and quit diggin' around in 'is personal belongings. He's not dead yet, and you won't be findin' anything of value in there, if that's why you're thinkin'. Now get on with you--I've got me work to do!"

I gave her a rather pointed look but took the Bible nonetheless and returned to my guardian's bedside. I noted with surprise that he seemed to be resting a little easier today, and indeed, he opened his eyes and spoke shortly after I sat down.

"Anne," he said in his raspy voice, holding out a frail hand to me, "Come a little closer. Please."

I moved to the bed and clasped his hand tightly. "How are you feeling, sir?"

"Better, much better," then noticing the Bible that I still held, he asked, "Are you going to read to me?"

"Rev. Jaspar." I began hesitantly, unsure if this was the right time to broach such a sensitive subject, "Why didn't you want me to know you were married once? And that your wife died? I'm so sorry."

A sad look crossed his pale face and I feared I shouldn't have brought the topic up. Then surprisingly, a tear rolled down his wrinkled cheek. At last he gave me a slow sad smile, then he squeezed my hand with what little strength he had left.

"She didn't die, my dear. She's still alive."

Now it was my turn to look confused. "But this Bible shows her death recorded."

"Yes I wanted her to be dead, so when she left, I convinced myself it was so, and even went so far as to place the date in that Bible. It was a terrible sin to desecrate the Holy Book with such a lie, but I had done worse, and I wanted it so desperately to be true, I came to believe it was."

He paused as I continued to stare at him in confusion. "But if she is still alive, where is she?" Then with sudden realization, "Is *she* 'Cousin Glenda' in London?"

He nodded sadly. "Yes, Anne, she is. And I'm afraid there's more." Something in his eyes told me he'd been carrying this burden for a long time, and that I should prepare myself for the worst. I'd wanted the truth and now I must steel myself to its blow.

"She's your mother, Anne," he said slowly with emphasis on every word, "She's your mother."

The words I'd waited so long to hear didn't seem to mean anything to me now. The woman who was my mother hadn't even allowed me to come to London to meet her. She didn't want me and never had. And if she was my mother, then all this time Rev. Jaspar had really been my father. And he hadn't even loved me enough to tell me. Why? I wanted to scream. Why?

He must have read my thoughts for he went on before I could speak. "She was my wife, Anne, and God forgive me for my lust in taking her. I couldn't live without her, I thought. Of course, I had no choice after what happened..."

There was a long pause here and his face was contorted with pain and anguish. Whatever it was, the memory was a horrible one for him.

At last he continued, "I found her in the church, God's holy sanctuary, fornicating with some filthy village boy. I pulled him off her like a madman and cast him aside. Then, I, I His voice was choked with sobs and for a moment I feared he would slip away from me once again. But finally he went on in a hoarse whisper. "I was overcome with passion, and I took her, Anne. And may God curse me for it. I was mad, I couldn't stop myself...but somehow, as terrible as I was, I believe she wanted it.

"I'm sorry you have to hear this, child, but the truth must be told before I die. You must hear it all."

I wondered that there could be more to this awful story, for obviously he had married her and attempted to rectify any wrong he had done. But I remained silent and he went on, "Afterwards, Anne, when I was able to see clearly and rationally again, I discovered the deed I had done. The unforgivable deed what she had held over me all these years.

"When I cast the boy aside, he must have struck his head on the hard pew, because when we next looked at him, he was dead."

I must have gasped aloud, for he shook his head and said, "Yes, yes, I know. I, a man of the cloth, had murdered. Murdered in God's holiest sanctuary... I will never forgive myself, even if God should ever so deem to forgive me. Never."

"But what did you do?" I managed to ask at last.

"Anne, you must understand, my vocation was, is, everything to me. I know it was wrong, but I believed at the time I was a good preacher, that I was destined to help others. Even, that I could take the life of this young girl, and mold her into one of God's creatures. I could not let my destiny slip away because of one accident. For it truly was an accident. I never meant to kill the boy. Only to frighten him away.

"So we buried him in a recently dug grave in the cemetery. And I took Glenda in. I loved her..." he sobbed and I felt genuine pity for him. "She thought I'd give her all the things she didn't have when we met, money, position, a home. But my life as a clergyman wasn't good enough. She soon discovered that I wanted nothing more than to serve God, while she wanted wealth, jewels, beautiful clothes, all things my meager wages would never provide." He stopped for a moment, reliving a past, which must be all too real for him in this instant.

"She told me one day she was going to London to 'seek her fortune'. I had to concoct some story, so I said she'd gone to visit a sick relative. Eventually, when she didn't return, I told people she had caught the sickness herself and died.

"Later she came back her by night, pregnant by some rich lord who was already married, and told me she was going back to him after the birth. That *I* was to keep the child for her." He gave me an imploring look, but I could only return it blankly, unable to comprehend the harsh reality of my dreams.

"She told me if I didn't provide for her until the baby came, she'd reveal the truth about the boy's body in the cemetery and destroy my life." Wiping a tear from his eyes, he told me in a pleading voice, "I had no choice, don't you see? I had to set her up in a flat in Mineshead, and then, I had to take you, you...my wife's own bastard! The very thought of you made me sick with disgust. Every time I looked at you, I remembered her unfaithfulness. I steeled myself against loving you because in you I was constantly reminded of her and him."

"Who is he?" I asked softly, afraid to breathe.

He laughed a short hoarse cackle, then burst into a fit of coughing. When it subsided, he looked at me and shook his head. "The amazing part is, I never found out. She wouldn't tell me at the time, protecting his reputation, she said, and when she sent her lackey here for you, he didn't say either. I'm not sure how much he knew, even. Wanted to bring you out, she told me. Give you a home and family at last. Humph, had some use for you, most likely. Glenda never wanted to give anyone anything."

"She never planned for me to come to London," I said quietly.

"What?"

"Martin Rollins was taking me to a finishing school. But on the way we stopped at an inn, and he left me there for a time. Then he came back and tried to attack me, and I ran away. I've been staying with the family who took me in."

"Dear God forgive me. What you must have gone through because of me! How can I ever repair the damage I've done to you?"

I shook my head, for truly I didn't know. My mind was stunned at his story and my emotions ranged from fury at him to confusion as to how a mother could do such horrible things--to her child and to others. And somewhere between the two was pity for myself. When I found my voice at last, my question was intended only to tear my thoughts away from the battle within.

"Who exactly is this Martin Rollins anyway?"

Again came the sarcastic laugh. "Alas, I must disappoint you again, my dear. I tried to track him down after you'd gone, but I don't have many contacts in London and no one I knew had ever heard of him. He's probably some cad Glenda picked up to help her keep her youthful image. That type of thing was always very important to her.

"I don't even know where she is, Anne. If I had any idea, believe me I'd tell you. But she's always been very adamant about keeping her new identity a secret. I couldn't trace her if I wanted to."

"But why did you let me go with him, if you didn't know anything about the man?"

"I thought you'd be alright, child. That you'd be happier with your mother. I knew you'd never been content here with me and I hoped she'd decided to acknowledge you at last. I should have known I was wrong. When you didn't write I assumed that either you were very happy or that she'd destroyed your letters because she still didn't want me to find her. I had no idea you were in trouble."

"But I did write to you! I wanted you to know where I was, at least."

"Perhaps Rollins somehow kept your letters from me. Or Gwen." His face was filled with anguish. "I'm so very, very sorry, my dear child. Can you ever forgive me?"

Bitterness washed over me like a gigantic wave, but as I gazed at him, I saw only that he was dying and needed my forgiveness. Again, I couldn't find it in my heart to curse him. "Yes," I said without feeling "I forgive you."

"Thank God," he said, bringing my hand to his dry lips. "Thank God." Exhausted from his confession, his head sank into the pillow and he closed his tear-filled eyes. I stood numbly beside the bed for a long moment, then walked slowly from the room. Removing my cloak and bonnet from the rack, I silently fled the house that had been my prison for so long. Even then, delivered of its secrets, I still wasn't free of the bonds. But I must escape for a time; I needed the serenity of my moors, the crushing waves of the sea in which to drown my grief. After that, I knew I would seek the comfort of Maddie's arms. Then perhaps, and only then, would I find the strength to return.

Chapter 23

Does memory sleep in Lethan rest?
Or wakes its whisper in thy breast?
Emily Brontë

The moors sagged with a late afternoon fog as I made my way across them. The heavy grayness of the sky once again accurately defined my own feelings. I had much to consider. I'd wanted answers: now I had them. But what had I to be happy about? My mother was no better than the guardian I'd always believed cold and heartless. At least he had reason to be that way. How could a mother not want her own child? What excuse did she have? Selfishness? Greed? Vanity?

I must have spent hours walking the distance that normally Charlie and I would have sped across. Where was my beloved horse, I wondered? Why hadn't he been to see me since I'd returned? Had he grown tired of coming day after day never to find me there? Somehow I'd always had the feeling that he knew I'd gone and when I'd come back. Just like Maddie.

I bit back a sob. Why couldn't *she* have been my mother? I loved her so. This would have been such a happy moment had that been the case. Instead, a day that should have been dancing with joyful light had turned into my darkest. What had I done to deserve such a fate? I shivered unreasonably at this thought, feeling a ripple of some unknown emotion cross my body. What, my mind cried. What?

My tears had been exhausted by the time I reached my friend's abode. The sun had fallen low in the sky, but time no longer held meaning for me. I must see Maddie before I returned to the pain of the rectory.

I drew my cloak tightly about me, wanting not only to keep out the winter wet, but to alleviate the aching chill that clutched at my heart as well. Maddie's wooden gate beckoned and I wondered what words of wisdom she could offer me today: this day when my suffering seemed black and as impenetrable as tar. But in every crisis of my life she'd been there, offering comfort and support, always finding a way to reach out to me. If anyone had a guardian angel, I certainly did in Maddie.

Light glittered gaily from her window as I walked up to oh-so-familiar path. Before I could even raise my hand to knock, the door was opened and without preamble I was in her safe, sheltering arms. "Oh, Maddie," I cried, "Oh, Maddie!"

After a moment she led me inside and sat me in a chair beside the warm crackling fire, then placed a cup of hot tea in my hands. Maddie had a recipe for every ailment it seemed.

"So you've had your answers at last, and they weren't what you'd hoped for, were they my dear?"

"No," I replied simply, no longer surprised at her ability to read me so easily.

"Life often turns out that way, love." Pulling up a chair beside me. She took one of my icy hands in her own. "I can't make the hurt any less, RoseAnne, but I can predict that your future will be brighter than your past."

I looked at her through tears and returned the squeeze of her hand. "There's so much about myself I don't understand, Maddie. Why have I had to suffer so? There's so much confusion in my life. What terrible thing have I done to be so blighted?" Weeping openly now, my eyes pleaded, desperately begging for answers.

She sighed. "Do you really want to know the reasons, my child?"

"Yes, Maddie. Yes, I do. If there is an answer to that question, I want to know what it is. I want to understand, and if it's not too late, maybe I can make it right."

"I think you've begun to make it right already, my dear. You did that when you gave up Leighton Hall and returned here."

Confused, I searched her eyes, waiting for explanations. As usual she gave her light little laugh before going on. "Dearest child, there is an intensity about you which has changed very little throughout all these years. It's quite remarkable really." Pausing, she squeezed my hand again. "Do you remember when you were younger, and I told you about the circle of life, about the souls reincarnated to suffer for past sins?"

I thought back, and there came to my mind a day, standing beside her as she worked at the table, listening to her answer a question I had asked about death. "Yes," I whispered, "I remember," and for a brief instant I also remembered my fear; her words had gone against everything my guardian had drilled into my head and while I found hope in them, it was difficult to toss aside a lifetime of instruction.

Maddie laughed again. "I see you haven't forgotten your confusion either."

"Yes. I remember it all. You said that often our present lives provide an opportunity to correct mistakes made in former ones. I wasn't really sure that was possible. I'm still not sure it is."

"Ah, but my dear girl, there are many people who disbelieve. People like your Rev. Jaspar, I'm afraid. But I know that this is true, and I think RoseAnne, that in your heart, you know it as well." A moment of silence followed as she drew her chair even closer, then clasped my other hand. "All your life you have been haunted by dreams you didn't understand. Some of the dreams were about your future, but many of them were about your past. A past of long, long ago. A life you lived before this life."

Flashes of the nightmares passed before my eyes. The girl riding her horse, the young child she'd led by the hand, the two men who loved and hated. Two men who'd once been the best of friends. And the woman...the woman who wanted to destroy them all. Yes, I knew the visions, but I'd never known what they meant.

"The girl promised to serve her Goddess," Maddie went on. "She took an oath of chastity. Hundreds of years ago, at a place called Avalon. You know it today as Glastonbury." I looked up, shocked at her statement. Then a sense of almost relief hit. So I *had* been there before; I did know the place.

"The girl turned her back on the Goddess she had sworn to obey. She did so in order to plot her own destiny in the world. She thought she knew better than the Mother. She loved where it was forbidden, and bore an illegitimate son who came in time to destroy a kingdom. When a soul causes such destruction in one life, it must pay for it in another."

So there had been a child! I'd seen the boy in one of my dreams. "Are you saying I was the priestess?" I asked, quietly fearful.

Maddie patted my arm gently. "I am only showing you how it is possible that you might have come to your present circumstances, RoseAnne. If you turned your back on the Mother in one lifetime, then wouldn't the Mother perhaps turn her back on you in another?"

I shivered. And yet, her words made sense. If indeed I had forsaken a goddess I swore to always obey, couldn't this be her way of getting vengeance? And this would fit with my dreams--the passion, and the evil behind it. But when would my suffering be over? How long must I pay? I didn't want to be a selfish, willful creature, out to take what I could from the world. I wanted forgiveness. Reading my mind once more, Maddie pushed a stray curl from my forehead.

"You have not attempted to use those around you this time, dearest, so you may yet be redeemed and bound for happiness." Her smile caressed my fears.

"And Glastonbury, Maddie? Did I feel so strange when I was there because I'd been there before, in another life?"

"The veil is very thin there, RoseAnne. For a moment you touched a time when a forbidden ecstasy was shared. That love was impossible, but in this life, you may have another chance."

Her words sounded familiar, but try as I might, I couldn't recall where I'd heard them before. I prodded her for more "Why was the love forbidden? Simply because the girl was sworn to a vow of chastity?" Stillness fell over us, broken only by the spitting of the fire.

"Because the man was her brother."

The room began to spin and the vividness of my vision in the old hut came back with all-too-much clarity. The blood and sweat, the passion, the feel of his hands across my naked skin.

But denying it, I spoke out harshly, "That's impossible. I could never have been that girl. I wouldn't do such a thing. Even in another lifetime."

"Ah, but my dear, what if you didn't know the man was your brother?"

A shiver ran over me and I pulled my chair nearer to the fire, away from my friend's probing eyes. The flickering light lent a dull glow to the room and for just a moment, we seemed to be stung before a campfire, crickets chirping around us in some ancient, medieval forest. A misty fog floated through the still night air, gathering in the quiet world. Maddie was there, offering me her guidance as always, but her features were different, harder and more masculine. With shock, I realized it was a man who sat and told me of the future, a wise man of the past, a man who would protect me from myself, but again I chose to shut out the words, insistent on choosing my own destiny. I was startled into the present my Maddie's warm touch on my brow.

"I see you know me," she said softly.

"Yes," my voice shook, "I remember some of it now."

"That's as it should be then. Your knowledge comes only as a warning. That life has no place in this one. Once you've accepted it, you can begin to move ahead. To put the dreams and visions behind you as they should be. Hopefully, understanding will make your way a little easier."

"But I seemed so horrible, Maddie. So self-serving. I loved him, but I used him too. How could he want me still? How could he?" My anguish echoed across the silent room, but my friend merely stroked my arm for a time.

"Love is like that, my darling. It forgives and it follows."

Still trembling. I turned to face her. "Is there more?

You mentioned a warning?" I grabbed her hand tightly. "I'm worried about Lyle, Maddie. I don't understand these messages from the past. Maddie? Who is the man I wronged in this life?"

"Ah, but you must discover *that* for yourself, RoseAnne. A difficult time lies yet ahead, and I cannot take away the pain you must suffer. I wish I could, but I haven't that kind of power."

"But you'll be here with me, won't you Maddie? You won't leave me?"

A pleasant laugh dispelled the somber atmosphere and she reached to touch my cheek. "I must leave you for a couple of weeks, dear one. There's illness in Parracombe and I'm needed there. But I'll return shortly. You'll be fine until then."

I wished I had her confidence. At this moment I felt it would be years, if ever, before I would completely understand the events of this day. To discover my guardian a murderer, to learn of my mother's abandonment, my past lives, vows of chastity. Had it all really happened? What more was to come? Still, it suddenly seemed that the last piece of the puzzle had slipped into place. I remembered the dark-haired girl's pain, coupled with her grim determination. Her first love had been innocent but she had sought to use it for her own ends. Luckily I had stopped myself from making that same mistake.

A sense of peace settled over me and looking toward the window, I saw again the darkness. Reluctantly, I rose from my chair. "I should be getting back now. Mrs. Rickett will be furious with me. We can speak of this again?"

"Perhaps, my dear, but remember what I said. The past is behind you. You must move ahead. And you must have faith, RoseAnne." I kissed her velvety cheek and hurried to don my cloak, but she softly reached for my arm and spoke again. "You've no need to hurry, lass; he's got no use for you any longer."

Her announcement didn't surprise me--what could surprise me after this day? Now the only thought that occurred to me was that my guardian's fate had overtaken him at last.

Chapter 24

If I have sinned, long, long ago
That sin was purified by woe--
I've suffered on through day and night;
I've trod a dark and frightful way.
Emily Brontë

The hour was late when I approached the path leading to the rectory door. A carriage stood in front of the house--the doctors no doubt, and at this time of night that could only mean one thing. Maddie had been right--my guardian was dead. An odd twinge of remorse struck me at the wasted experience of our lives together. We might have given on another comfort; instead we only caused each other heartbreak.

The doctor was still seeing to arrangements concerning the dead man when I entered the house, so Mrs. Rickett took advantage of the opportunity to chastise me through bellowing sobs.

"How could you leave the poor man, foolish girl? Him bein' ill as 'e was. Left 'im alone to die, you did, and after all 'ed done for you." She blew her nose loudly into a damp handkerchief. "You're inhuman, that's what you are. A cruel selfish child."

I flinched at her words, but drew myself up proudly and went into my guardian's room to discuss arrangements with the doctor. I felt numb, unable to believe that the person who'd controlled so much of my life was gone forever. He may not have treated me well, but in his own way, Rev. Jaspar had looked after me--now I was truly on my own.

"Heart and lungs simply gave out," the doctor responded when I asked a few moments later; then he went on to say he would send for the vicar in Lynton if I wanted to hold services tomorrow afternoon. "Did the Rev, have any other family?" he asked finally.

Pausing for an instant, I recalled our earlier conversation. "No," I said at last, shaking my head, "not that I know of."

***

Of course the following day was rainy. Had I ever been to a funeral where rain hadn't fallen? All morning Mrs. Rickett and I had stood in the cold church and greeted villagers who'd come to pay their last respects to my guardian. I wasn't surprised by this, for the parish church had always been full and I knew that many of these simple people would miss the Rev.'s kindness to them. He'd always been faithful in his duties, however negligent he was in his love.

At one point my eye was caught by the pew bench embellishing the image of the chained swan. I thought back to the night I'd sat there feeling myself a prisoner in this place, and remembered the weeping man I'd seen a few moments later. His chains were broken now, but were mine? Would I ever really be free from the chains of my past? Both in this life and any others I'd led? *What will it take,* my heart cried, *what will it take?*

Later in the day as we gazed into the open grave and listened to the words being spoken by Rev. Mann, the vicar from Lynton, I experienced more of the sadness I'd felt the previous evening. As the coffin was lowered into the frozen ground, I brushed from my cheek a wetness more than the rain. My guardian hadn't really been a bad man. His vocation had been everything to him; losing it would have meant total devastation. Perhaps he might even have loved me a little--if he hadn't known that I was his wife's illegitimate child. What a burden that must have been! That, and the murder he'd committed in an act of rage. I wondered what crimes of the past he'd been paying for. As I cast my clump of damp earth onto his final resting spot I said a silent prayer that wherever he was now, he would be happy, and if he should someday return to this earth, his life might be easier.

After the crowd dispersed, Mrs. Rickett and I turned toward the house.

Looking at the cold gray stone of the rectory, I wondered where I would go. Rev. Mann's curate would be coming in a soon to take over services until a permanent replacement could be found. Although Mrs. Rickett had family who might be willing to take her in, I had no one except Maddie. *Oh well,* I thought, *time enough to worry about that. Today I must write to Lyle and let him know I'm alright.*

But at the image of Lyle, I once again began to wonder about our last evening together. What had happened, and how angry was he with me for running away? I felt certain that Ian must have persuaded him to give me some time alone, and thus his not contacting me.

Approaching the house a moment later, I was astonished to see a strange carriage parked in front. "Now who on earth could that be?" Mrs. Rickett asked, weariness plain in her voice. "I thought everyone had gone."

We walked in the door, only to be greeted by even greater shock. Ian stepped out from the parlor!

"Who's this?" the housekeeper exclaimed.

I, for one, was too dumbfounded to answer her question.

"Ian McCrae, ma'am, and I'm sorry to have to intrude at a time like this, but it's urgent. One of the villagers told me what happened and since everyone seemed to be at the funeral, we made ourselves at home. I didn't want the lass to catch a chill, you see?"

"Lass?" I said, finding my voice as it became Mrs. Rickett's turn to be dumbfounded and silent.

"It's Sarah, Anne. I took her upstairs and put her in an empty bed. She's exhausted from the trip and well, other things. I must talk to you at once."

"What exactly is going on, Ian?"

Nodding toward Mrs. Rickett, he said quietly, "Could I nae speak with you alone?"

"Yes, of course," I answered, bidding him back into the parlor, then turning to the housekeeper. "Mrs. Rickett, would you mind looking in on Sarah to see if there's anything she needs? She's the daughter of the family I was staying with. I promise I'll explain everything later."

For once, she obeyed without retort. I followed Ian into the room with mounting apprehension. "What is it?" I asked tersely.

He collapsed into a nearby chair, a movement so unusual for Ian that I felt a pain begin to grow within me. His gaze met mine with despair. "I don't know where to begin," he said at last, "so much has happened since you left. I'll tell you what I know, and then I've a letter for you from Lyle with the rest."

I waited with dread for him to continue. "I think Lyle may have gone mad, Anne." At my terrified look, he immediately inserted, "Now don't start blaming yourself, because he was fine when I let him out of that old hut."

He laughed a little at that. "Poacher, huh? Well, he did seem a little confused about what had happened, but he was quite sure that *you'd* done the right thing by leaving him there. He seemed rather contrite actually. But later, when I told him about Gwen and Martin, well that's another story.

"He must have confronted her--with I don't know what, because they had a row and she stormed out yesterday afternoon. Last night when he brought me this letter for you, he insisted I take Sarah and leave immediately...that we come to you. He seemed to feel you were both in great danger of some sort. So I took the girl and we stayed overnight in an inn, then came here today. But he acted like a madman, insane with anger--totally unlike himself."

"But what had upset him so?" I asked, unable to imagine an angry Lyle.

"I don't know. Maybe this letter will clear the matter up somewhat. Sarah is worried sick about him and wants me to go back to Leighton Hall. She keeps mumbling something about what her mother did."

He handed me a long envelope, and my hand trembled as I took it. "But how could Sarah be involved in all this? I don't understand." Yet a part of me wondered, remembering the dog and how I'd been led to go to the woods that night.

He touched my arm gently. "Neither do I. But she knows who Martin Rollins is, because she asked me if I knew him. I couldn't get her to tell me any more than that though."

"Oh God..." I broke off at a loss for further words.

Ian took me in his arms and held me silently for a long time. "You must read the letter now, love, and perhaps it will help us both to understand."

I nodded and Ian backed out the door without speaking, leaving me alone in the room, suddenly cold and empty of his warming presence. Had I known what news it would bring, perhaps I would never have broken its seal. Indeed, I found before me all the truth I'd ever wanted to know.

My Dearest Anne,

I begin this letter by sending you my love, for wherever I am at this moment, you must know I will always treasure the thought of you. I realized, somewhat belatedly perhaps, that what I wanted between us could never be, and not just in light of what I've discovered. Your heart belongs to another, I think, and if it's who I believe it is, I wish only the best for you both.

As for me, well, our future could never have been regardless. A letter came from my solicitor in London with news at last of my sister. God curse the day I decided to search for her. It seems my father was worse than I thought, love, for he married the girl's mother and still refused to acknowledge the child. My stepmother lied to me, Anne; she knew where my sister was from the beginning. She was her mother.

You see, my darling, my father left a letter for me, hidden in a safe place and only just discovered. It told me he had sired a child by his mistress long before my mother died. They farmed her away to a parsonage to be raised, then after he married that same mistress and made her Lady Gwendolyn, he tried to bring the daughter to London, but his wife kept finding reasons against it, until finally it was too late.

And now it's too late for us, my dear, for the place they sent her was a village called Countisbury, and a man named Rev. Jaspar Cowper. The girl, my love, my sister, is you.

But have no fear, Anne, she'll pay for her cruelty and neglect. She'll pay if it's the last thing I do.

Please don't ever forget I love you.

Your brother,

Lyle

The paper fluttered to the floor and I sat for a long time in stunned silence. Eventually I rose, an empty corpse, and turned toward the window. Ian was standing outside by

But how could I ever face him with the knowledge of my parentage? And perhaps, with the knowledge that I had slept with my own brother. Had I? Lyle hadn't mentioned it. But would he? What had Ian said, that he seemed *contrite*?

The horror of all that had happened was suddenly too much. My mother, my father, my guardian-betrayed by all. I needed space-to breathe, to think, to decide. And what would I decide? What should I do?

Slipping out the back way, I began to run across the moor, drawn by the dangerous cliffs of Foreland Point and the smothering embrace of the sea.

Chapter 25

My spirit drank a mingled tone
Of seraph's song and demons groan--
What thy soul bore thy soul alone
Within itself may tell.
Emily Brontë

'How wrong Maddie had been-' was my irrational thought as I ran blindly across the moor. I hadn't been forgiven for my past sins--I was never to be forgiven. My life hadn't changed at all-Lyle was my brother! The words burned through like a fiery sun. My brother! And I had most probably lain with him again! Again. Oh, perhaps it had been done in innocence, but hadn't that priestess been innocent too? Evidently I was doomed to spend eternity repeating the same fate. Well, not if I could help it! There must be some way to correct the wrong I'd done. Then and only then would I be released from this hell!

I stumbled over a root in the dense fog of the morning and was flung roughly to the ground. Harsh bitter sobs racked my body as I lay where I'd fallen, cursing whatever gods or goddesses had brought me to this point. I didn't want this destiny. Hadn't I paid enough for my past sins? If only I could free myself from their bonds. I must be free. I would be free if it was the last thing I did. And, finally, I knew how I would do it.

Mindful now of a purpose. I rose from the frozen earth and hastened on toward the cliffs. The mist was so thick I could scarcely see the hand in front of my face. I knew by the downward sloping of the landscape and the beginnings of protruding rock beneath my slippers that I was getting close to the edge of the moors. I tried to determine the direction of Satan's Leap, the spot where Maddie so often went to send her own offerings to the heavens.

At last I reached a tall craggy form, and I knew I'd found the place I sought. Silently I stood for a long moment, breathing the deep, salty scent of the sea, solemnly praying for strength and guidance for my task.

"Great Goddess," I called out into the swirling white clouds around me, "Hear me now, I beg you!" I listened for an instant as my voice echoed back across the hidden waves. "I cannot bear to live forever with my past and present sins controlling my life. Please--grant me your forgiveness, and accept the soul I offer you now in retribution. May it rest henceforth in peace."

Remarkably, the fog lifted a little, and I was able to see the jagged edge of rock on the cliffs below me. I swallowed, fighting back the fear rising within me, and prepared to lean forward.

Flashes of my life swept before my eyes; years with Rev. Jaspar, the moors and Maddie, Martin Rollins, Ram's Head with Dottie and Tom, life at Leighton Hall. And then, I saw the old hut...myself and Lyle, alone there. Him comforting me, a blank look on my face as I stared at some undetermined scene.

Suddenly I screamed at him and ran from the room, locking the door after my exit. Nothing more had happened-nothing! I breathed a sigh of relief, and then, I saw *her.*

Gleaming magnificently through a slender break in the puffy clouds, shining and beautiful, she was a vision of womanhood more splendid than any I'd ever seen in my life. I couldn't turn my face away from her light. Waves of billowing luminescence washed over me, permeating my whole being with a cocoon of warmth, wrapping me close in protective arms--I felt marvelously, gloriously happy.

I felt forgiveness.

Then before one breath could follow another, she was gone, leaving me to wonder had she ever been, or had I merely imagined her? But my skin still tingled with the presence, and I knew suddenly I must live. I must live, and live, and live.

But abruptly, from out of nowhere, a hand yanked me away from the cliff's edge. I was thrown in a heap to the ground, and then I heard it. The laughter. The mocking, all-too- familiar laughter.

"Let's not be too hasty about jumping, my dear Anne." Martin Rollins said, sneering at me as he spoke. "First, I should give you a few more reasons. You wouldn't want to die without knowing the whole truth, now would you, dear girl?"

I looked at him blankly, still stunned from my previous encounter. His words made no sense and when I spoke at last the voice seemed not to be my own. "What t-truth?"

His evil laugh hit me once again, and I shivered when he knelt beside me. The wind had resumed its force and his features appeared grotesque as I stared at him through hair whipping about my face. Pushing the strands back, he brought his mouth close, as if he were afraid I might miss some of the words.

"The truth about your mother and I, of course. Oh, yes, dearest, when you've heard it all, you'll want to jump even worse than you did a few moments ago. But first, I'll need you to sign this little confession I've prepared for you. I have it just here," he indicated a pocket inside his tweed jacket. "Then, my pretty one, I'll be completely vindicated from your death and the other as well."

Sanity was slowly returning to my numbed mind and I felt a sudden spurt of anger towards the sinister figure at my side. His continual interference in my life sickened me and, summoning all my courage, I raised my hand to strike him. He merely brushed it away, as he might a distracting insect.

"Aren't you the little vixen, now?" he said in an amused tone as he yanked my head roughly back by the hair then pressed a wet hard kiss on my neck. "You're almost as beautiful as your mother. I could easily postpone your death for a bit longer. Just long enough to taste you sweetness, of course."

I struggled in his arms but he only seemed to enjoy it, and pulled me closer. His head went to my breast, biting it painfully through the fabric of my bodice. "Let me go," I screamed. "You're revolting!"

His head came up, passion quenched, and he gave me a furious scowl. "Oh, so I revolt you, do I? Your dear sweet mother certainly doesn't share your sentiments."

I stared, wondering what on earth he was talking about?

"Yes, your mother and I have been lovers for years. Didn't you notice my initials on her painting in the gallery? We first met then, just after her marriage to Sir Roderick. We've been together without his knowledge for ever so long," he laughed his ugly laugh. "He never even knew that Sarah is my daughter, not his. Gwen made sure of that, just like she made sure everything would work out with her plan. Until you nearly ruined her whole scheme by running away..." He gave me another hateful glare. "But didn't you just happen to wind up at Leighton Hall and fall in love with your own brother!"

"But we didn't know," I sobbed, "We didn't know."

"Of course you didn't know. That's why you believed you could marry him and then kill Lady Gwendolyn and have Sir Roderick's fortune all to yourself. Lyle would have to be gotten rid of eventually so that you could share the money with your accomplice, Ian McCrae."

"What are you talking about? You're insane." The mention of Ian's name had brought me to life as nothing else, and I refused to let this scoundrel drag him into the situation.

My anger only roused his laughter once more. "That may be, my darling, but if I am insane, then your mother was even more so. Surely you don't think I planned all this. Gwen has wanted Leighton Hall since the beginning. That's why she stayed married to the old man for as long as she did. Fate played a cruel trick on her and me, sending you to the very place we were trying to keep you from."

"But why? Why did she want to keep me away from my family?"

"I can see you never knew your mother. She wanted everything for herself. Roderick would have claimed you years ago but she kept finding reasons to wait, putting him off, until at last he threatened to go for you himself. He didn't know where you were at the time, and she had such a hold over him, the spineless fool, that he would never go against her wishes. Still, she felt she was losing him, and that she must isolate you even further, thus my little trip to take you to boarding school."

"But you never took me to the school."

"No, Gwen doesn't know all my little secrets. Ram's Head is just one of them. He gave me a nasty little smile, and I remembered the conversation I'd overheard between he and Dottie. And, that night he tried to attack me.

Trying to bide my time, I said, "But my father must have discovered where I was. He left a note."

"That's why I was taking you away. Besides which, Gwen had come up with a more permanent solution for her husband."

I gasped. "Are you suggesting that *she* killed him?" I stared at him in disbelief, shuddering against both my shock and the suddenly cold wind.

"Actually she just helped his already weak condition along. Poor man had a bad heart anyway. Gwen was going to marry me, and she'd have the title and the money."

"You're a liar," I shot out, unable to believe the horror of what he'd said.

"Oh, poor girl, surely you don't really believe that. Why else would I have come to Countisbury eight months ago to escort you to a finishing school if your own mother hadn't sent me? But you ran away, didn't you?" He glared at me angrily. Then abruptly, he laughed.

"But Gwen solved that as she does everything. When I followed you and discovered where you'd been taken, she was furious at first, but when Lyle came to London and told her how he felt about you, well, she was delighted. 'Well, Martin,' ' she said to me, 'they couldn't have made it easier for us.' ' Her plan, you see, was to make you and your half- brother fall in love then when you discovered your relation, you would both commit suicide, with her help of course. She's brilliant, your mother. Simply brilliant."

Nausea rose in me at the idea that my own mother had schemed to do away with me. I couldn't believe she had plotted all this for money.

"What about Sarah?" I asked, "She would have been heir to the fortune as well. And she's *your* daughter."

"Tut, tut, what's a daughter to me except a way to the fortune? And Gwen alone can give me that." He stopped for a moment, considering. "Still, though your mother delights me, I'm not sure I can count on her to take care of me forever. She's also a dangerous woman, your mother."

I was crying a little for myself but Martin didn't care; he proceeded with his torment.

"But we were speaking of Sarah. Dear little Sarah... Actually she has been somewhat useful to us. She lured you out to that old hut with the dog story. Of course she thought you were crazy and needed to be locked away. I shot at you earlier that day to frighten you." He stroked my breast and laughed. "What exactly did happen in that room, Annie dearest? Were you and brother naughty children?"

I flailed out at him, hitting, hating, wishing I had enough strength to kill him myself.

"Now, now, dear girl, you've hurt me enough already. Running away like that--from your lover, no less. You just keep spoiling things for us. But now, I

180

have you right where I want you, and before you vault over that cliff, I'm going to take what *I* want."

He ripped open my dress, pressing his foul mouth to my bare skin and I dug my nails into his flesh trying to push him back. Mist swirled around us so thickly I could not even see his face, but I fought all the same, determined he would not bring about my end.

His teeth tore into my nipple and I screamed out with pain, but he pushed me to the hard ground and forced his knee between my legs.

Suddenly, an explosion filled the air, and Martin moved no more.

I breathed a sigh of relief. Thank God, I was saved! Still trembling and with great effort, I rolled his motionless body off mine, then looking into the fog to see who my rescuer was. I stared into the face of my mother.

"Good riddance," Gwen said calmly, her gun now directed towards me. "He was right. I *am* a dangerous woman. ." She gave me a slow smile "Besides, I was hoping to end him thus, but I am sorry that you had to be part of it, my dear. The things a man will stoop to."

Gazing at her for the first time as my mother, I was speechless. Her dark hair, loosened by the wind, streamed across her face like the snakes of Medusa, and that combined with the slant of her glaring eyes, made it seem as if she had just stepped from the pages of a Greek tragedy. The clothes she wore were wrinkled, as if she'd been traveling a long time. Irrationally, I wondered how she'd gotten to this place. Or had she known about it from the years she lived in Countisbury? No matter, she stood before me now--my mother. My mother.

This woman's whole existence had consisted of blackmail, murder, abandonment, and lust. I expected to be filled with rage and hatred but instead I pitied her. And that pity exerted in me a calm I could never have felt otherwise. I knew she meant to kill me, but the thought only made me sad for her, nothing else.

"What are you staring at?" she asked, appearing almost as calm as I felt.

"Nothing," I replied. "At my mother, I suppose."

"So he told you before he died, did he?"

For the first time tendrils of shock began to creep in. "Before who died," my voice trembled. "Martin?"

She laughed. "Oh, so you don't know *that*. She paused a moment as if debating, then continued, "No, not Martin. Lyle, of course. I handled my part of the plan. I shot and killed Lyle, with his own gun of course, so it would appear to be a suicide. But when I come here to see if Martin has carried out his instructions, what do I find, he's trying to seduce my own daughter. It was definitely time for him to go."

"Y-you killed Lyle?" I said, not wanting to believe it could be true.

She laughed again. "Yes, daughter. Your lover-brother is gone. I left him lying in a pool of blood. And it's just as well for Martin to die too, because now *he* can be your accomplice in this crime. The two of you, knowing you were discovered, made a suicide pact. It's still a perfect plan."

My calm was replaced suddenly by the rage I hadn't felt a moment earlier. How could she be so callous about killing Lyle? Kind generous Lyle, who loved her like his own mother. And then, she would link Ian's name to this vile man. She, who had destroyed my past, would now destroy my future as well.

"I made no plan with Martin," I said to her, my voice full of ice. "And I will not take responsibility for his death."

A throaty laugh filled the air, and she swept back a handful of hair. "Oh, dear Anne, I know you're not really responsible. Only Martin can take credit for that. If he hadn't been such a womanizer. I couldn't continue to pay blackmail money forever for his behavior. That horrid woman at Ram's Head knew about our relationship. If we'd married, there would have been no end to her demands. Now, it's a clean break." She moved closer to me, the gun in her hand never wavering. "I'm just sorry that you have to go as well. I've never really had a chance to know you as my daughter."

Angry tears pricked my eyes. "Why?" I screamed out at her "Why couldn't you have loved me?"

A bitter look crossed her face, but she held her weapon higher "Love? What exactly is love, my dear? I could have had it all were it not for you. First you were born and I had to return to this dreadful place for nine months. Oh, but Roderick insisted I have the baby. And then, all those years he wanted you back. He wanted his *other* daughter. Humph, his *only* daughter, always you've been a thorn in my side." Her eyes froze me like ice. "Anyway until one has enough money and power to feel secure and safe, how can one ever know love?"

I knew then all Martin had said was true. She was the worst...the true villain, the schemer. I knew as well that she'd led a troubled lonely life and would never be able to give anything to anyone. She may have given me birth, but she had nothing else, and whatever it had been, my life had been better off without her. For the first time ever, even in that moment of complete certainty that my end was imminent and would be brought about by her, my own mother, I felt satisfied with my life. And I felt something even greater, and even more surprising--I felt forgiveness. I understood exactly what the vision in the clouds had granted me.

"Ah, well, dear, enough of this. I'll make this quick so you won't have to suffer, and then I must write your confession and see to Sarah. She will have to be party to this, as she knows about Martin and I, but I'll sure it shouldn't be difficult to convince that girl. And if so, I'll simply have her committed somewhere."

Suddenly filled with a power such as I'd never known, I lunged at her, hoping to throw her off balance and grab the gun. The Goddess rose up inside me and with her the sense I would save myself after all. But as I moved forward, something moved in front of me, and startled, I tripped and fell, hitting my head against a stone jutting from ground. Dazed, I looked up and for a split second saw the billowing dark cloak of a hooded figure.

In the next instant, with a graceful fluid movement, they both plummeted over the edge of Satan's Leap.

***

Gentle kisses caressed my cheeks when my eyes next fluttered open. Ian's warm arms held me and I saw concern and love in his gaze. This was my reason for living. To see this look of love in his eyes forevermore.

"My darling, darling Anne," he said when I reached up to touch his face, "you frightened me to death. When I saw you'd gone I thought I'd lost you forever. God, if I lost you..." he broke off, tears rising in his voice.

I wanted to stay there, safe for eternity, doing nothing more than returning the delicious kisses he was bestowing upon me, but all at once I remembered the sickening reality of what had just occurred.

"Maddie!" I screamed with terrifying certainty and tore myself away from him. I rushed to the cliff's edge. "Maddie!" I screamed again, looking down.

Angry waves crashed against the rocks below, sending a spray of watery mist high into the air. The spray fell silently upon the stone where lay the body of Gwendolyn, battered and twisted grotesquely in death. Beside it lay the dark cloak, its empty folds billowing in the breeze. Maddie was nowhere in sight.

Chapter 26

And another March has woven
Garlands for another May.
Emily Brontë

Oh how long and cold was our return across those much- loved moors that day! As we traversed the familiar hills and vales I pieced the story together for him in which Martin and my mother had finally shattered the remaining remnants of my hopes and dreams. And yet, I still had one left, the one I saw in this dark silent man at my side.

Ian had come upon me only after my mother and the hooded figure I felt certain was Maddie had plunged over the wall of rock into the ocean below. As I recounted my tale, his face registered shock, then anger, and finally pain.

"Lyle..." he said and broke off, his eyes brimming. And then, "I should never have left you alone, lass. I did nae realize until too late that you might have been in real danger." Then, gazing at me with eyes full of love, "You might have died because of me."

"It's over now," I told him quietly, "it's finished." Tears pricked my eyes and I shivered in the chilly air as I thought of both Lyle and Maddie. Ian suspected that her body had fallen beyond the rocks and into the ocean below, but for some reason, I couldn't accept the idea that she was dead, Maybe it was because Maddie was such a vital, alive person, and I knew that no matter where I was, or what I did, a part of her would always be with me. But it was more than that.

Yet, if it was Maddie, had she come to rescue me so that I need not carry the burden of killing my own mother? Hadn't I turned my back on my Mother of the past? Even if this one were wicked, could I live with that guilt again?

Of course, I'd never actually seen the face in the depths of that cloak, so there was no way to be sure it was really her at all. Despite my uncertainty, I felt that she was indeed gone from me, and in this life, it was not likely I would see her again.

How ironic that in finding one love, I must surrender another. It would take years to sort out all that I had learned in the past few days, and I knew that before I did, there would be much grief and suffering. But my life had passed into a new phase now, and I remembered the Goddess I'd seen earlier in the day. Words came to my mind, unbidden.

"Be joyful--live this life in continuing love." Was it Her, or Maddie? No matter, I knew what they meant.

I looked at Ian and knew beyond any shadow of a doubt, that he was my love. His eyes glowed with it as he returned my gaze and my heart filled with joy. The gently arm encircling my waist conveyed to me the side of him I loved best--the kind, affectionate man who had in his own way, suffered as much as I.

Gone was all the anger, the suspicion that had swept through our lives like vicious waves on a stormy lake--replaced with happiness and trust in another. I reveled and gleamed in the sunlight that was suddenly lighting up my life.

Upon returning to the rectory, Ian immediately summoned a doctor from Lynton, the same doctor who'd attended my guardian a few days before. Although he said my cuts and bruises were minor and that I should be fine after a nights' rest. Ian wanted me to go straight to bed.

"But we must tell Sarah *first,*" I said, "especially about Lyle." We agreed we would tell her only as much as needed now, and give her the rest of the story as she grew stronger.

Entering her room, Ian and I found Mrs. Rickett with her, coddling the girl in a tender manner that both surprised and amused me. For the first time, it occurred to me that perhaps if I had been a little plainer instead of the bright rosy child I was, Mrs. Rickett might have taken to me as well.

Sarah clung to me a long time after she'd heard the news, begging my forgiveness for all she'd done to try and hurt me. "I sent you to the forest, Anne. They told me you were a bad person and needed to be taken away. That you would hurt Lyle if you didn't go. Mother said that Mr. Martin had come from a special place you'd run away from, and he must take you back. I didn't know he was a bad man, Anne, I promise I didn't. She said I mustn't tell Lyle because he would be too upset. Oh Anne," she cried into my breast. "Lyle is dead because of me. I can't bear it. I loved him so much and it's my fault. It's all my fault. I'm so very sorry." She fell onto the bed, weeping, and I pressed my body over hers and held her tightly for a long time while Ian and Mrs. Rickett stood by in silence.

Sarah had indeed hurt me but I felt no anger. I remembered the day on the Tor when I'd so desperately hurt her, and I understood. I understood, but her grief for Lyle I couldn't address. I too, felt responsible to his death. If only I'd never come into his life...

Finally I spoke with a calm I didn't feel. "Sarah, it wasn't your fault. That's all nonsense. Martin Rollins was a very bad man, and he fooled a lot of people. He could be quite persuasive. I'm sure you mother didn't really know the kind of person he was. Now I want you to try and not worry. Everything will be fine. But these things take time...and we must all grieve."

Her sobbing slowed a little, and I rose from the bed, leaving her in the capable hands of Mrs. Rickett as Ian and I turned to leave the room. I was at the point of retiring to my own chamber when we were both startled by a knock at the door.

"It may be the sheriff," Ian said. "The doctor was going to send for him. I'll take care of it." And he moved down the hallway while I turned back toward my room.

In the next instant I heard an exclamation that filled my heart with joy for the second time that day. "Anne," Ian called out, "Anne, it's Lyle!"

***

What a joyful reunion we had that night! We shared tears of joy and tears of sorrow: spoke of love lost and love found. Sarah wept in Lyle's arms, begging forgiveness of the three of us while we told her there was nothing to forgive and we must all put the past behind us. Lyle claimed me as his sister, which he assured me with a wistful loving smile was the next best thing to being a wife. I knew we all had our own grieving to do but as time passed must do it in our own way.

Over the next few hours, the three of us, with some help from Sarah, pieced the entire story together. The news from Sir Roderick's solicitor had only confirmed Lyle's suspicions after Ian had told him about my seeing Gwendolyn and Martin together. When he had confronted her the first time she'd stormed angrily from the house, thus giving him time to write the letter to me and send Ian to Countisbury with Sarah.

"I knew he'd take care of the both of you," Lyle told us. "And since I didn't know exactly *where* Martin Rollins was, I wanted someone with you two."

But then Gwendolyn had returned to Leighton Hall, with a pistol and a plan to kill Lyle. She'd told him almost the same story as I'd heard, so he knew of her scheming. Evidently her patience was wearing thin due to the blackmailing by Dottie at Ram's Head and she was ready to be done not only with Lyle and me, but Martin as well.

Luckily for Lyle, her bullet caused a lot of bloodshed, thus making his injury look worse than it actually was. Believing him dead, she left a suicide note and must have headed immediately for Countisbury where she'd discovered Martin with me. Lyle had followed, and though weak from his blood loss, would recover completely from his wound.

"I'm so relieved you're all right, Anne," Lyle told me while stroking Sarah's hair (the girl hadn't moved from his side since he'd arrived). He looked from Ian to me and then back again. "I know," he said quietly, "and I'm happy for you both."

We didn't discuss it further that night, but during the next few days while I grew more and more secure in Ian's love, Lyle, after hearing the balance of the story from us, stayed closer to Sarah and seemed almost to see the girl in a new light. We knew when the time was right, he would gently tell her the rest of the tale.

In her absence we discussed Lady Gwendolyn and Martin's actions at length, and decided that Martin must have followed me to Leighton Hall immediately after I'd left Langport. Perhaps he'd even witnessed Ian's discovering me in the forest glade. Now that we knew he and Gwendolyn had been lovers, it stood to reason that he'd had his own access to the Hall, probably a key to one of the back doors--I remembered the day Lyle had looked so curiously at the cloak I'd taken from a peg near one of those entrances-- allowing him to come and go as we pleased. Hadn't I thought I heard footsteps in the corridor and was being observed from inside the house? It had been Martin, no doubt.

"I knew that one would bring trouble," Ian said of Gwendolyn, "part of the reason she wanted to keep you and me apart was because once, she tried to have her way with me, but I would have none of it. Lyle is my friend, and I'd not intentionally betray him with anyone. Gwendolyn never forgave me."

He looked at Lyle almost guiltily, "I couldn't help loving Anne, Lyle. I'm sorry if I betrayed you in that."

But Lyle simply shrugged "It wasn't meant to be Ian." And looking at me, "I'll have you forever as my sister, and I thank God for that." He paused and continued slowly, "And that nothing ever happened between us that we need regret."

He watched me for a moment, as if debating whether or not to go on. At last he did. "I don't know exactly what you saw that night in the shepherd's hut, Anne. But somehow, even then, before I knew the truth, I accepted the fact that you were not meant for me. And though it saddened me, in another way I was relieved. Do you understand?"

I nodded, knowing exactly what he meant. We did not speak of it again after that.

Sarah appeared to have closed her mind to the all thoughts of the subject much as mine did to thoughts of my parents when I was a child. I have come to believe that our body protects us in that way, when it knows we cannot handle further distress. Most of her days were spent either reading to Lyle, or helping Mrs. Rickett in the kitchen, and surprisingly, she seemed content in these duties. Sarah had always been so pampered that being given useful work seemed to agree with her, and both Mrs. Rickett and Lyle took the girl under a protective wing that I would not have suspected either one of them to possess.

Ian dealt deftly with the constable's questions concerning Martin's death, and when that same official came to talk to me, it was merely a matter of routine. Since the local authorities in Somerset had already been forewarned by Lyle, the incident was closed without further investigation.

One thing I questioned Ian about was the conversation I'd overhead in the library. "I'm afraid that was me, my bonnie. I was trying to convince Lyle he should stay away from you. For my own selfish interests, I might add." With that he kissed my hand, and smiled at me lovingly with his dark-lashed eyes.

As I regained my strength, along with it came a vitality for life I found almost impossible to believe I possessed. I wanted to be well so that Ian and I could begin our life together. Even though he had yet to speak of it, I felt sure we would return, at least for a time, to Leighton Hall. Although I knew that the estate was partly my own, that fact meant nothing to me; as far as I was concerned, it was Lyle's and Sarah's to do with as they would.

I wanted only to be with Ian, to share forever with him, wherever that might lead us. Hopefully, someday we'd return to his castle in Scotland, for he'd told me much about it during our talks. He wanted more than anything to return there and make it a happy place, as it never had been when he was young. Our unhappy childhoods drew us even closer together, for he had felt as unloved and unwanted by his parents who were always there as I had by mine who never were. At least he'd had his grandmother and I'd had Maddie, so we were blessed in that respect. But we both, and Lyle as well, wanted Sarah to know that we cared for her, and we hoped that in time she would recover from her own wounds.

As spring began to unfold its flowery breath, we took long walks across the moor during which I showed Ian all my favorite places, growing happier and happier as the days went by. One sadness was the day Lyle took Sarah and they returned to Leighton Hall to deal with their grief privately, but they promised to return for regular visits with Mrs. Rickett and we promised to join them there in time.

Beyond that, my days were completely content. Even Charlie came back into my life, and he followed up about like a puppy, eager and anxious to please. I was thrilled to see my old friend again, and naturally he and Ian took to one another right away.

"Did you miss me, dearest?" I'd asked him, rubbing his soft nose, then pulling a sugar cube which I always carried, *just in case,* from my pocket.

Of course he nodded his affirmative reply, and Ian and I both laughed, for I had told him all about Charlie's way of communicating.

Our walks never took us along the path toward Maddie's cob hut, whereas once it would have been the first place I went. Whenever I thought of her, I remembered the day the constable had come and we'd told him our suspicions that she had died trying to save me from my mother.

"Ol' woman named Maddie, you say miss? Can't says I ever heard o' her. Not likely some ol' dame coulda pulled a strong young one off you. Mores likely that she slipped and fell," and with that he'd chuckled a little, no doubt considering the feeble-minded condition of women. "At any rate," he'd gone on, "there uz no cloak on the ledge with Lady Gwendolyn. I'll ask if anyone's seen your friend in the village." And he'd shrugged and gone his way. At the time, it hadn't occurred to me to give him Maddie's full name, and anyway, I wanted to believe he was correct, that it hadn't been her after all. Still, my loss felt close and I hadn't gotten up the courage to go to her home, for if she wasn't there, I would know for certain she was gone forever.

Ian seemed to sense my sadness on these walks, and often he tried to distract my thoughts with talk of other things. We discovered more about each other in just a few days time than we had in all those months at Leighton Hall. I was amazed to think there had been a time when I detested him; now we were so close, so much alike, it was almost as if we were the same person. One minute we would talk, about anything and everything, then the next fall silent, and the quiet would settle around us like a warm comfortable glove. And though the early spring air was still cold around us, we could only bask in each other's warmth.

I marveled that a soul's love could last an eternity, but I knew now that ours had done just that. And yet, we never spoke of our bond from the past--I sensed Ian wasn't ready to accept it fully, and I respected this and held my silence. But in our hearts we both knew.

At last I believed Maddie's story completely, but I also understood that finally I was free from the past. The swan's chains were broken, the imprisoned bird could fly-whoever Ian and I had been in that long ago life, in this life he was the man I loved. My affection for Lyle had been a test, and thank heavens I had passed it. Still, it pained me to believe he had only been a pawn and thus had been hurt himself. I could only pray he would, in time, find his own heart's love.

One day in late March, when the hills were just beginning to sprout with the blooms of primroses and violets, Devon myrtle and brooms, I broached the subject of our future with Ian. He'd not yet spoken of it and I was becoming impatient to know what he planned after our return to Leighton Hall. His face turned to me slowly and in the dark eyes I saw such a look of abject despair that I wanted nothing more than to draw back my question and make everything between us as it had been only seconds before.

The silence between us seemed to span centuries. When he spoke, the words were so terrible, so filled with pain, that I will never in all my life be able to forget them.

"There can be no *future* between us, lass. 'Tis why I'll cherish these past few days so much. I've been able to at least have this time with you."

Stunned, I could do nothing more than stare at him. "What do you mean?" I managed to gasp finally. "We love each other!"

"Aye, lassie, that we do. But you have a fortune now, for Sir Roderick left you well provided for, even if he did naught for you when he lived. You need a better man than I in your life. I couldn't give you a home hardly even a name, and I'll not be living off a wife's charity."

"But there's Leighton Hall. Who will manage the estate?"

"Oh, Lyle can see to that easily enough. He's only kept me on because of our friendship. I couldn't bear to be so close to you and not have you as my own." He looked at me, anguish evident on every inch of his face. "Twill be years, Anne, before I've made enough to set my home to rights, if ever. You're a beautiful woman, and someday you'll find a man who can take care of your properly."

Fright was beginning to take control of me and I turned and clung to him like a desperate child. "I don't care about the money. I don't want it. Let Lyle and Sarah have it all. You can I can manage the estate together and live in the gatehouse. Tears streamed down my face as I pleaded with him. "Please Ian. I can't live without you. Not again. We've come to far to throw our love to the wind. Please. Please." I didn't care that I begged. I had no pride. This was the man I loved. That I had come through eternity for. I couldn't lose him. I couldn't.

I stared, pain welling up and beginning to overflow into anger. How could he ask me to forget him? Me, who hadn't forgotten him for centuries? I wasn't Sarah, a child who could be coddled and forced into action. I was a woman--a woman who, for the first time ever, knew what she wanted.

With fire in my eyes, my voice actually growled when I spoke. "You really haven't learned anything at all from life, have you?"

Now his look turned to anger as well, and he yanked my body close to his. His violence didn't frighten me; I relished it for it shut out that other pain. When his mouth crushed to mine with a hard driving force, I let everything else go, and for a moment our souls seemed to melt into one and we stood, thus locked in that timeless embrace. Why couldn't he see as I did that we were meant to be? That we'd come to this time to be?

I pulled myself back and met head-on the pain and despair in his eyes.

So be it, I said to myself and turning, I ran from him. Wanting only to put as much distance between the two of us as possible, I gave no thought to direction, but almost instinctively I went toward Maddie's hut.

I ran and ran, across the moors blossoming into spring, through the forest, its leaves just beginning to peer out with sleepy eyes, and on and on to the Valley. Sharp rocks and stones cut into my thin slippers like glass, but undeterred, I climbed the jagged hill until at last I stood, a weeping frustrated form, before my friend's abode. It waited as always, snug and safe in its sheltered nest, and I moved toward the gate and threw it back, running heedlessly toward the door. "Maddie!" I called, rushing inside, "Maddie!"

And then when there was no answer, tears burst forth.

"Maddie, why? Must I lose him too? You said it be better. You promised!"

I knew I sounded a bit like the petulant Sarah and I thought I heard the gentle flutter of Maddie's laughter, but all I saw was the empty room, devoid not only of presence, but of her warmth as well. I moved to the grate and proceeded with trembling hands to lay a fire as the chill of winter still clung to the air. After a few moments, a roaring blaze greeted me and I held out my hands to warm them in its heat. The bed in the corner beckoned and I went to it and sat, pulling the colorful comforter close, needing the scent and caress of her belongings.

A sound at the door drew my attention and looking up, I saw that Ian had followed me here. "Get out!" I screamed at him, "You don't belong here! Get out!" All the while my tears fell carelessly into the cloth pressed against my breast.

191

Ignoring my tirade, his gaze left me and began to study the room in which he stood. His thoughts were almost audible as he wondered about this place. He took in the daintily curtained windows, the neat table with its now-wilted bouquet, the brightly burning fire, and at last, his eyes came to rest where mine always did, on the painting above the fireplace. But then amazingly, he moved toward it like one in a trance, and I saw moisture beginning to gather at the corners of his lashes. With a slow movement, he gently traced a finger along the face of my young friend.

"Where is she?" he said in a whisper.

I stared at him in astonishment, unable to believe he hadn't guessed.

"It's Maddie," I spoke at last, not knowing what more to say.

There was no need to speak further for his face paled even more and he moved from the mantle like a dead man, then sank into the chair by Maddie's table. Covering his face with those long strong hands, I heard, rather than saw, his racking sobs. I moved to him in concern and knelt by the chair.

"What is it, love? Something about Maddie? Tell me," and I touched his knee tenderly.

At length he uncovered his face and looked at me. "My grandmother," he said quietly, pain evident in his voice. "The woman in the picture is my grandmother." What seemed like an eternity of silence passed between us as my mind tried to comprehend what he'd just said. How could Maddie, my Maddie, be his grandmother? It couldn't be.

And yet, I remembered her words on our last evening had seemed familiar. The truth whirled back and struck me. Ian's grandmother had told him almost the same thing when he was a child that he'd told me that day under the birch trees at Leighton Hall. But the name was different, something about the name was different...

"Ian," I proceeded very gently, "what was your grandmother's name? Her *full* name?"

He brushed a hand across his cheeks. "Elizabeth Hardgrove Madden McCrae," he responded, pride evident in his voice. "That was Gran's full name."

Now it was my turn to look shocked. So she *was* his grandmother. Maddie had never told me her last name. I'd always assumed it was Madden, but it appeared that was her maiden name instead. Rising, I crossed the room, stopping before the mantle; I wanted to look closer at the picture, to find some resemblance that I'd heretofore missed between these two people I loved most in the world. I reached up to take the portrait down, and as I did, something fluttered to the floor. Bending down, I found it was an envelope, and more surprising, addressed to Ian. If I needed further proof that Maddie was indeed his grandmother, now I had it.

"Ian, look," I said, walking back to the table where he sat head still lowered in sorrow.

He raised his eyes and saw the envelope in my hand. "It's a letter, Ian. To you. It must be from Maddie."

Hesitantly, he took it from me and stared at it for a time. "The last letter I held had bad news," he said, I knew he spoke of the one he'd brought me from Lyle.

"She would have only good words for you," I said at last. "That was the way she was. She preferred not to tell the bad."

After another moment, he broke the seal and studied the yellow sheaf of paper inside. He scanned it once, then twice, and yet again, then looked at me with a glow of happiness in his eyes that, has stayed with me always. He passed the letter to me, and I read the parting words of my dearest friend:

My darling,

I know you must think me cruel for leaving you when I did, but your father, although he was my son, was different from you and I. He didn't love the castle, and would have gambled away you inheritance, had I not gone as I did and put the funds away for you. If you will contact the Honorable Jon. R. Frye in London, he will be prepared to explain the details of your trust. I think you will see that I have left you well provided for at last.

Be good to RoseAnne, love her gently and wisely, and may your souls find respite in your present life.

Always,
Gran EHMM

Misty eye touched misty eye when they met at last over long that yellowed piece of paper. Finally, it was Ian who broke the spell of silence. "We can be married," he said slowly, as if afraid to speak the words for fear they once again would be snatched away. "But how did she know?"

"Don't you know, Ian?" I said quietly, "Maddie knew everything. She knew our past and our present and our future. She would have wanted more than anything for you and I to have the life we deserved to have. That we'd been denied once before."

His look was vague, but I think he too, was remembering our talk that day beneath the birches, and was starting to accept that our lives were more than what they seemed.

"Now we can do that," he said at last, "because of her."

"For her..." I answered and no more than a second passed before I was in his arms, and for the first time that day, I saw sunlight in the depths of his shadows. Its brightness flowed from him into me and as we stood, locked unto one another, suddenly the room was filled with the warm glow of Maddie.

"Wait," I said, and taking my dearest friend's colorful coverlet, pulled Ian out the door. "Come with me."

The flowering buds of Maddie's garden were just beginning to peep through a sea of green and I spread the quilt across a soft spot in the midst of that ocean.

He smiled, and in another instant we lay side by side and he was removing my garments slowly, one by one, with infinite loving care. I did not shrink; I had no fear of pain, for I knew Ian would be a tender lover and I would always be safe in the harbor of his embrace. My present thoughts left me then and for an endless time we were, once again, nothing more than drifting souls, flowing in and out of one another.

Our life together truly began that day, in the garden beside the cottage of the one we both loved so well. The same one who had made our lives together possible. I have never doubted that as we lay there then, 'sharing our bodies, our love, indeed our very essence, Maddie was there with us, not only sanctioning the act, but blessing our future and glowing with the brilliant joy of our forever.

Epilogue

Shadows grow long across our garden as at last I lay my pen to rest. The years have come and gone like flowers since that precious day when Ian and I first claimed the love so long denied, and I have ceased to count them, except to thank the heavens for allowing us this bliss. As I look back I wonder I was even a part of that extraordinary time, for my life now seems so normal, indeed so very ordinary I could easily believe none of the things I have written ever happened at all.

I have questioned those events many times--why didn't I press my friend Maddie for more information; how did she know as much as she did; and even, yes, did I really know her at all? Were it not for the fact that she truly was Ian's grandmother, I might today believe she was a mere figment of my imagination, an invisible friend come to comfort an unhappy lonely girl.

As for the lives I believe we lived in centuries past, Ian and I do not discuss this. Perhaps we accepted it as fact in our hearts so long ago that it no longer matters; all that is important now are the moments we spend together in this life. Soon the sands of mortality will run out for us once more and who knows when our paths will intersect again?

Our happiest days have been spent here at Castle Crae--we've had to work hard to rebuild Ian's home but the effort has paid off in contentment for us both. Sarah and Lyle eventually found each other as Ian and I often hoped they would, and I believe their love has been as satisfying and fulfilling as the love they dreamed of with each of us. Their home rings with the laughter of children, some of whom are grown by now. The oldest, my nephew Roderick, is helping Lyle to make the estate a profitable farm.

Several years passed before Ian and I had a child of our own--long enough for us to suffer the thought that we might never have children; and for myself, that I might never be free of my dreaded sin and this was to be my eternal punishment. Our daughter too is grown and married, but she visits during summers and brings along the greatest treasure we have found--our granddaughter, Elizabeth, whom we have taken to calling Maddie. She is so like my dear old friend, I marvel each moment I am with her at the resemblance-- the sunflower eyes, soft white skin, golden warmth exuding from her. Even her laughter teases gently at the threads of memories that have long slumbered within the depths of my heart. She is with us now and partly I have written this story for her, so that she will know her grandmother's weaknesses as well as her strengths, and may learn from my many mistakes. In a moment I will go to the garden and Ian will meet me there; we will sit beneath the pines and breathe in the fresh crisp scent of autumn. Maddie will run and kiss me and I will hold her close, inhaling the remembered fragrance, smiling joyfully at Ian over her shoulder. After she scampers away once more we will sit in silence, watching as the sun begins to set, and our fingers will slowly entwine, and turning toward one another, we will become lost once more in the season of our love.

About the Author

Cathy Richard Dodson not only works as freelance writer and editor but, along with her husband, owns and operates a Victorian bed & breakfast in mid-Missouri. Dodson has also published several novels, a novella, *Miss Cornett's Courtship,* and a book of walking mediations, *Walking Wonders: Stepping Your Way to a More Creative Life.*

For more information, or to contact the author, visit her web site at www.crdodson.com.